THE INFERNO COLLECTION

THE INFERNO COLLECTION

JACQUELINE SEEWALD

FIVE STAR

An imprint of Thomson Gale, a part of The Thomson Corporation

THOMSON

GALE™

Detroit • New York • San Francisco • New Haven, Conn. • Waterville, Maine • London

LIBRARY OF CONGRESS CATALOGING-IN-PUBLICATION DATA

Seewald, Jacqueline.
  The inferno collection / Jacqueline Seewald. — 1st ed.
    p. cm.
  ISBN-13: 978-1-59414-576-6 (alk. paper)
  ISBN-10: 1-59414-576-8 (alk. paper)
  1. Librarians—Fiction. 2. Clairvoyants—Fiction. I. Title.
PS3619.E358I54 2007
813'.6—dc22   2007000441

First Edition. First Printing: June 2007.

Published in 2007 in conjunction with Tekno Books.

Printed in the United States of America on permanent paper
10 9 8 7 6 5 4 3 2 1

This novel is dedicated to my husband, Monte, who supports me in every way possible.

This book is also dedicated to my wonderful children, and to reference librarians everywhere. They are truly the world's greatest information detectives.

Special thanks to Alice Duncan who edited this book with good-natured thoroughness.

"Abandon all hope, ye who enter here!"

—Dante
The Inferno

CHAPTER ONE

"May I help you?" Kim Reynolds said the words automatically to the next person who approached the information services desk as she replaced the *World Almanac* under the ready reference counter.

"I certainly hope you can help me."

The soft voice was familiar, and Kim quickly looked up to see an attractive young woman gravely watching her.

"Lorette, how have you been?"

"All right." The words did not seem to go with the nervous way Lorette chewed her lower lip.

"Need help with a paper?"

"Always, but there's something else. When will you be going for lunch?"

"Someone's coming back in a few minutes. I could take my break then."

Lorette agreed to wait. She moved around restlessly, glancing at a book now and again but never actually perusing it.

Kim knew instinctively that something was wrong with Lorette. It was obvious some dark cloud hung over her friend. Kim didn't even need to tap into what her grandmother had referred to as *the awareness,* a family trait, which seemed to reoccur in females on the maternal side of her family every second generation.

Outside the university library, it was a vivid October afternoon. A gaggle of students sat on the benches and grassy lawns consuming sundry food and beverages. It was a comforting sight, and one that Kim had seen so often it gave her the illusion of permanence.

"We could buy some junk food from one of the lunch trucks along College Ave.," she suggested.

"I'm not very hungry." Lorette walked over to a stone bench that gracefully abutted a stone wall. "Maybe we can just sit here for a while." But as soon as she had spoken, a handholding boy and girl seated themselves at one end of the bench, and Lorette beckoned her to continue walking again.

They decided to walk to the commons and visit the Rathskeller. The "rat" had been their favorite place to go and relax when they were both in the graduate English program sharing courses together.

Kim took a deep breath of the fresh autumn air. There wouldn't be many wonderful days like this before the cold weather grasped them in icy tentacles. She was determined to enjoy the bright azure sky and multicolored leaves that looked like impressionist splotches of paint on canvas. Too much of her time was spent indoors, incarcerated like a felon. At this moment, she felt wonderfully alive.

"I need to talk to you privately."

"I got that idea."

There was definitely something bothering Lorette. Kim sensed it, even though they weren't as close as they'd once been.

As they walked, Lorette kept furtively glancing around, occasionally checking out the people behind them on the busy street. It almost seemed as if she were frightened and thought someone was watching or following her. Kim wondered what sort of emotional stress her friend was under; Lorette was definitely not behaving like herself. Usually she appeared calm, cool and controlled, although Kim conceded that could merely be a façade.

They made their selections in the Rathskeller, down in the bowels of the student activity building, then seated themselves in the dining room, which was dark and fairly empty at this hour. One couple sat off in a corner: an older man with a salt-and-pepper beard dressed in a Harris tweed jacket and wrinkled gray slacks who looked like a psych professor, and a young girl who stared at him adoringly, as if his words were those of the Messiah. Kim rolled her eyes.

"I used to be like her," Lorette said, picking at a salad without enthusiasm. "I was so naïve."

"How's your dissertation going?"

Lorette bit down on her lower lip. "I'll be happy when I finish. It's not going the way I would like."

"You have a standing offer. I'll be glad to help you with the research."

Lorette looked up and smiled for the first time, but the smile did not extend to her eyes. "Yes, you've always been a real friend, someone I can trust . . . maybe the only one."

Kim studied Lorette thoughtfully. Some time ago she'd read that women dress for other women. She did not believe that to be true of her friend, who appeared to dress to be noticed by men. Today was no exception. Lorette was arrayed in a brown leather miniskirt and lacy, textured hosiery that made the most of her long, shapely legs. A silk, V-neck beige blouse was complemented by a slim-fitting velvet jacket of rich chocolate. Lorette had a way of combining elegance and sophistication with sensuality. Her soft, shiny black hair gently brushing her shoulders framed a heart-shaped face with eyes the color of spring wisteria; Lorette could have easily been confused for a model or an actress. Kim was aware of her own plain appearance in comparison.

"I miss you in the program. I wish you hadn't dropped English."

"More like it dropped me," Kim admitted with a wry smile. "I'm a good academic librarian. I seem to be more suited to that."

"Actually, you have the cleverest insights into literature. I don't think you were treated fairly. They don't seem to respect original thinking."

Kim understood Lorette was talking as much about her own situation as Kim's.

"So what are you teaching this semester?"

"Same old Expository Writing 101. But I was promised lit courses for spring semester." The lavender eyes glowed momentarily.

"That's wonderful," Kim said, biting with zest into a ripe cherry tomato. She thought she meant it, hoping there wasn't any jealousy behind the words. She'd always loved the teaching part and missed it to some extent. But opting out of the program after finishing her Master's in English was not a mistake. She did like her job. And her awareness, a kind of seventh sense, made it possible for her to locate what other people needed quickly and accurately. That was about the only benefit of her odd sensibility. Mostly, it had made her feel different and isolated her from others. So she ignored that peculiar insight, pretending it didn't exist.

"I do get tired of being paid the wages of a medieval serf. Hopefully, I'll complete my dissertation sometime next year, get my degree and be able to teach full-time."

One of the things they shared in common was that they'd both received teaching assistantships. Kim had been a scholarship student all the way. She didn't think that was true of Lorette, but she never asked. Their friendship rarely crossed the lines of privacy. Kim did not ask personal questions of Lorette, and her friend reciprocated. It was one of the reasons they got along so well. They were also older than most of the other grad students. Lorette was twenty-six and Kim twenty-nine. They'd both spent time in the real world before entering the lofty tower of academe. Kim had taught English at the high school level, while Lorette had worked in business.

"So you've finished all your classes?"

"Not quite. This semester is the last. But I haven't been able to concentrate very well on my work. The thing is, I have this problem."

Lorette was finally getting to the point of their meeting, and Kim could not help but feel curious.

"Hello! Imagine seeing you down here where only trolls come to dine." Don Bernard tossed Kim an engaging smile.

Lorette, who had been stirring her coffee, started slightly, spilling the beverage on the table.

"Sorry, didn't mean to startle you." Don sounded uncomfortable, a rarity for the suave, sophisticated Dr. Bernard.

"I'm a bit on edge," Lorette said, frowning into his face.

Kim was fond of Don Bernard. She'd come to know him during the last year as a colleague rather than a teacher.

"I didn't mean to intrude." He smiled again directly at Kim. "I'll look for you at the library later."

He was a very attractive male with his fair hair and light-colored eyes. He left them and joined another professor.

"No airs about that man. He's so nice."

Lorette did not respond, but the look on her face told Kim that she disagreed with the assessment. Kim decided not to probe. Some things were better not to know about.

"Kim, can you come over to my apartment later today? I'd like to talk where we won't be disturbed or overheard." Lorette got ready to leave, claiming that she was due in Dr. Barnes's office to discuss a proposed paper. "He says he can get my work published, but he's so full of hot air, I think I'm just going to blow him off." Then she left. Kim noticed Lorette had barely touched her lunch. Kim's instinct told her Lorette's problem was very serious, and that she might be involved in something very dangerous.

Kim drove to Lorette's apartment on her way home from work. The La Reine Gardens development in which she and Lorette lived was attractive. The brick buildings, set around large courtyards, were lushly landscaped, the lawns elegantly manicured. Kim drove past trees that were a blur of red, green, orange and brown in their luxurious foliage.

She parked in front of Lorette's building, rang the doorbell, and was greeted by a tall, gray-haired woman who looked as if she'd been quite striking when she was young. The gray hair was the color of steel with the slightest hint of blue tint, a color reminiscent of delicate robin's eggs.

"So you're Lorette's friend," she said. "Won't you come in? Like you, I'm visiting this afternoon."

The apartment, an efficiency, had only one real room with a tiny kitchen space and a small bathroom, very similar to Kim's own. But the furnishings suggested grace and elegance, mirroring Lorette's personality.

A moment later, Lorette came toward her dressed in lime-green slacks and matching silk blouse that suited her slim figure. Her dark hair fell softly around her thin face like a raven's feathered wings.

"I'm glad your friend's come to visit. Lord knows, I don't seem to have the ability to calm you down. Or maybe it's my visits that upset you."

"Mother, please!" Lorette's face paled.

"It's all the pressure you're under, isn't it? All those papers they make you write and grade."

Lorette didn't reply.

"Your daughter's doing extremely well in the program. She's suited to the academic life, Mrs. Campbell."

"My mother's *not* Mrs. Campbell."

"Just call me Miranda." A smile slipped through thinned lips.

"It's nice meeting you," Kim responded in a warm manner.

"You'll stay for dinner, won't you? I brought enough for three—or even four, considering the way Lorette eats."

Miranda was right about the way Lorette ate. Just as she had at lunch, she left her food virtually untouched at dinner. Of course, Lorette had never been much of an eater. Kim remembered very well during the Eighteenth Century novel course they'd elected to take together that Lorette had identified with Richardson's Clarissa, a heroine who closely resembled a modern anorexic, wasting away in an effort to effect some control over wretched circumstances.

"You are getting a little too thin," Kim told her friend.

"As the Duchess of Windsor said, 'You can never be too rich or too thin.'"

"I most certainly disagree," Miranda said.

They ate in relative silence, each woman locked into her own thoughts. Afterward, Kim offered to help with the dishes, but Miranda wouldn't hear of it.

"Mother likes doing those things. She's a total perfectionist about housework." Lorette eyed her mother impassively.

"Lorette knows me. I like to put her place to rights when I'm here. So why don't the two of you take a walk while I clean up?"

There wasn't any arguing with Miranda; she had a take-charge sort of personality. Kim also realized that Lorette wanted to talk away from her mother. Curiously, Miranda appeared to understand and not really mind.

"Let's walk through the woods where it's peaceful."

It was twilight, and a feeling of gloom prevailed among the trees.

"I like it here. It reminds me of home. Mother still lives in our old house. When I first left home, that was what I missed the most, just the brooding forest with few people about." Lorette's eyes brightened momentarily. "I suppose you know the Puritans considered the woods evil. My mother thinks that's stupid superstition, but then again, she does sell real estate and considers forests as valuable property for development."

"I can understand the early settlers fearing the forests. Woodlands were full of frightening native people, unfamiliar flora and fauna. Don't we all fear the unknown?" Kim knew she certainly did.

"My father used to tell me stories about Colonial times when I was little. He was a great storyteller; that's where I first got my love of literature." Lorette was talking rapidly, her manner edgy.

"You were fortunate to have a father like that," Kim said.

"Not so fortunate. He died when I was eight. A few years later, my mother remarried. Then everything changed."

Shriveled leaves stirred restlessly in the wind like an army of brown-shirted soldiers on the march. The brown leaves crunched under Kim's sneakers. A sudden chilling breeze in the autumn air made her feel very cold inside.

"Do you believe that the forces of evil are created by supernatural powers, that they are a constant threat to mankind?" Lorette's eyes were unnaturally bright.

Kim was pensive. "I believe people often create the things they fear."

"Mother thinks it's all foolishness too. However, Dr. Forbes makes a convincing argument. He's been discussing the power of evil in our class on occult literature."

As they walked along the woodland trail, Kim wondered what

was really on Lorette's mind. Her friend's moods were not always easy to fathom. "What did you want to talk with me about?" It was probably best to be direct.

A lock of dark hair fell across Lorette's forehead, and she shoved at it nervously with her long, slender fingers. "I wanted to ask if you know anything about an inferno collection at the humanities library."

The question surprised Kim. She tried to recall exactly what she'd read on the subject. Usually, an inferno collection consisted of materials deemed salacious or inappropriate for children. In public libraries during the Victorian era, they had been kept locked away in a separate place and could only be retrieved by asking the reference librarian for access. The philosophy behind this policy was based on the premise that librarians were the gatekeepers. However, Kim saw the notion of an inferno collection as being thoroughly antiquated.

"You really think there's an inferno collection at the humanities library?"

"I don't think it. I know it."

Lorette's certitude perplexed Kim. "Scholars have total intellectual freedom. I don't see why any such censorship could or would exist at a university library."

"Maybe there are those who wouldn't approve of the nature of a particular collection." Lorette seemed agitated. Kim observed a slight twitch in her right eye.

"What sort of a collection are we talking about?"

"If it doesn't exist, then there's no point talking about it, is there?"

She was finding this conversation with Lorette perplexing. "If I happen to hear anything about an inferno collection, I'll let you know. I haven't worked at the humanities library all that long, so I don't know everything, but I can find out."

"Do that, but be careful who you ask."

The warning in Lorette's voice gave Kim pause. "Why should I have to be careful?"

"It might be safer. Some people might not like you asking."

"What are you implying?" Kim didn't bother stating that Lorette was weirding her out.

Lorette licked her lips as if they were terribly dry. "Do that for me, please." She was shivering.

"Let me reassure you. It's not likely there's any kind of inferno collection at the university libraries. I doubt they exist in public libraries anymore either. Could someone be playing a stupid practical joke, telling you spooky stories? In a few weeks it'll be Halloween."

Lorette continued walking, barely listening, looking pre-occupied. "Last week I found this note in my mailbox at school." Lorette slipped a folded piece of white paper from her slacks pocket and handed it to Kim, who observed the neatly printed words. Because of the gathering darkness, she had to bring the note up close to make out the words.

" 'For he who lives more lives than one/More deaths than one must die.' Sounds vaguely familiar."

"It's Wilde. I checked."

Kim shook her head. "I'm not certain I know what it means."

"I think someone might want to kill me." Lorette's words hung oppressively in the still, gloomy air.

"The note doesn't have to mean anything of the sort." Lorette's offhand comment had shocked her.

"No, I agree it doesn't. And I wouldn't think anything of it either, except for the matter of the accident a few days ago."

Kim looked up. "What accident?"

CHAPTER TWO

Lorette shrugged uneasily. "I was driving home from school and my brakes failed. I wasn't driving very fast, so everything was okay, but it was still frightening."

"What did the mechanic say?"

"I didn't ask." Lorette refolded the note and placed it back in her pocket.

"Why not?"

"I just couldn't." She began to walk briskly again.

"Lorette! How could you not ask?"

Long dark lashes blinked nervously. "It's probably nothing. I'm behaving stupidly. As you said, I've created what I fear."

"Not necessarily." Kim studied her friend thoughtfully. "Has anyone actually threatened you? Angry students? Jealous boyfriend? Anything like that?"

Lorette shook her head. "Forget I said anything or showed you the note."

"Maybe it's nothing, but if you're afraid, there could be something to this."

"I did tell Jim. He thought I was being foolish, too."

"I never said I thought that."

"Jim wants me to move in with him. Mother wouldn't approve, of course, but I'm hardly a child. What do you think?"

Kim tried to recall who Jim was.

"What I think doesn't really matter. It's how you feel about Jim."

"He's not the first man I've slept with. But I've been burned once too often in the past. I have this talent for selecting guys who ultimately hurt me. When it comes to men, I seem to have a sign pinned on me that says victim."

"Do you think Jim might want to hurt you?"

Lorette looked at Kim pensively, her eyes the color of ripe blueberries. "Jim? No, I very much doubt it. He's so good-natured and there's this strong physical attraction between us. But then sometimes I think it could be an act, just a nice-guy pose. Oh, listen to me, I've become quite a cynic."

"I've always considered you very sensitive and perceptive about people." Kim looked up at the gibbous moon that cast an eerie glow over them.

"I've lived long enough to know how devious people can be. At the university, they're all out for themselves. Screw the next guy. Outside of you, and possibly Jim, there are very few decent, honest people I can trust."

The sight of a snake sliding across a fallen log increased Lorette's pace. "You know what I'm talking about, don't you? That's why I always kept quiet in class. There are those who would rip me to shreds for the sport of it."

Kim had on occasion voiced her thoughts and ideas in grad school and found herself the recipient of some snide remark or other, so she knew Lorette was not merely paranoid. But she had accepted the criticism philosophically. When she stuck her neck out, she had to expect others to try and chop it off. It was human nature. Backbiting was common in the English grad program. The game was always who could impress the professor most.

"Jim's not like that?" Kim questioned.

"No, he's modest and self-effacing, but with a brilliant, creative mind. He's also the only real man in the program. The others are a bunch of effete, intellectual snobs. Who would think a Montana cowboy would have a sensibility for literature? Kim, he writes such moving poetry."

"So let's assume that Jim has nothing to do with threatening you. Who might?"

"No one." Lorette spoke quickly, frowned deeply, biting down on her lower lip. Kim thought Lorette had the kind of look on her face that a person displayed when arriving at the dentist's office and deciding the toothache wasn't so bad after all.

"Just for the sake of supposition, is there anyone who might be jealous of you or hold a grudge?"

Lorette shook her head, eyes lowered. Kim felt frustrated. She had a distinct feeling that Lorette was holding something back, not telling her the whole truth. Why bring up the matter if she wasn't really willing to talk about it openly? So annoying! But that was the way their friendship had always been. There were things in their pasts that neither wished to discuss with anyone.

"Just check around about inferno collections—but do it discreetly—please."

"You really think there's some danger involved, don't you?"

Lorette's eyes met her own directly. "I think there could be."

"You won't tell me more about it? Like how the threat is connected?"

"It's best I don't. In case I'm wrong. Regardless, I don't want any trouble for you."

"But you think there's a connection between it and the possible threat against you?"

Lorette narrowed her eyes and nodded her head.

"I'll do what you ask. We better go back. It's gotten awfully dark."

"Come back to the apartment. Mother likes you. I can tell. And she doesn't like many people—not even me very much of the time."

Kim was tired and would rather have gone home; still, she didn't want to appear rude. They walked back the way they had come. Lorette's mother was waiting for them.

"I fixed an apple cobbler for dessert. I warmed it up in the oven. Thought it might be nice with a dollop of ice cream."

"Mother's trying to fatten me up."

"I have no ulterior motives." The voice was as expressionless as the face. Mother and daughter masked their emotions very well indeed when they chose.

"Don't you have ulterior motives?" Lorette stared at her mother until the older woman looked away.

"Let's sit down."

Kim complimented the dessert, which wasn't hard to do because it tasted delicious. They had almost finished when the phone rang. Kim tried not to overhear the conversation, but the apartment was too small.

"I'm sorry, Dr. Packingham," she overheard Lorette say. "I couldn't possibly. No, I have company. Yes, I'll see you in class." She hung up abruptly and Kim could tell that her friend was distressed.

"What is it?"

"I'm having some problems with one of my professors."

"Dr. Packingham?"

Lorette nodded.

"What sorts of problems?"

Lorette took a teaspoon of ice cream, then pushed the dessert away. "He tells me I need to rewrite this paper I did for him, that it needs work."

"Why, you write beautifully," her mother said.

"I don't think it's really the paper that's at the root of the problem, is it?" Kim asked.

Lorette lowered her gaze. "He says it is. He says that if I work with him on it, he's certain I'll get an A in the course."

"Well, that does sound good," her mother said.

"But you think there's more to it?" Kim was sure the uneasiness she sensed in Lorette indicated a more serious concern.

"He's coming on to me, hitting on me in his own smooth way. He's been pushing pretty hard for me to go to his place for a private meeting. I don't want that."

Kim tried to place Professor Packingham but found she couldn't. "I don't seem to recall him."

"There's no reason you would. He's new at the university, on exchange from England for the semester. His credentials are impeccable. He's had two books of criticism published on medieval literature. I'm grateful to study with him, if only he weren't such a . . ."

"Lecher?"

Lorette smiled as if grateful for Kim's comprehension.

"Can't you just be pleasant to the man and let it go at that?" Miranda inquired, her forehead wrinkling.

"I don't think he's looking for friendship, Mother. I've tried saying no politely. He knows I'm seeing Jim. He's seen us together in class and out, but he won't stop bothering me. The thing is, I'm afraid he'll give me a bad grade if I don't go along with him."

"You could report him for sexual harassment," Kim said. "It would be the right thing to do. He shouldn't be allowed to get away with it."

Lorette shook her head. "To get along in this world, a woman needs friends in high places, not enemies. I seem to have made enough of those already without even trying. Anyway, you know what happens to whistle-blowers."

"I don't want to see you getting yourself worked up, honey, not like that other time."

"And whose fault was that, Mother?" Lorette rose from the table. "I'll be in the bathroom for a while," she said. Lorette looked close to tears, as the door shut behind her.

"I guess it's time for me to leave," Kim said.

"Her problems are all my fault," Miranda said. Tears glistened in her eyes.

"I don't see how that could be."

"Lorette had trouble in school. I sent her away to board when she was fourteen. I thought she'd be better off. My second marriage had taken a bad turn. My husband didn't want Lorette at home. He was very possessive of me and jealous of our relationship. I wanted to give the marriage a chance, so I sent her away. It was a good school, or so I thought. But those bored, rich girls had no morals. They introduced her to pills and liquor. By the time she went to college, Lorette was badly addicted. She cut most of her classes. I didn't know anything until the college notified me. She overdosed and ended up in a hospital ward. Lorette climbed back from the bottom. It was a hard struggle, but she's no quitter. I'm very proud of my daughter. I don't want her to have to suffer anymore."

"Neither do I. But life is full of problems. We have to hang tough in order to survive."

"Except that Lorette is so sensitive and vulnerable."

"Try not to worry. I'm going now. Please tell Lorette I'll help her in any way I can."

"Thank you," Miranda said in a quiet voice.

Kim drove back to her own apartment lost in thought. Lorette had never told her about her addiction; of course, that was not surprising. Lorette did not confide in other people, even her friends. Kim wasn't very different herself, so how could she fault Lorette?

Once back in her own little apartment, Kim fixed herself a cup of chamomile tea and thought about what Lorette had told her. Why would anyone want to kill Lorette? She was, of course, an unusually attractive woman who might excite sexual jealousy and hostility, but that hardly seemed enough of a motive. Then again, how much did she really know about Lorette? Hadn't Lorette said she didn't trust people in general? Had that begun when she perceived her mother's rejection and abandonment in adolescence? Kim was certain that was the case.

Her friend was definitely frightened of something or someone, and Kim firmly believed that Lorette must have good reasons.

Kim was having a difficult day. It seemed whatever she did, she could not please Wendell Firbin, her immediate supervisor. His position as Associate Director of Information Services meant he was constantly evaluating the performance of the academic librarians who served at the reference desk.

"Ms. Reynolds, I also see a candy wrapper on the floor near the reference desk. We never leave anything of that sort around. This is a university library with certain standards."

Kim sighed deeply; it wasn't easy enduring Wendell's prissy bitchiness. He was often petty and irritating. He had a tendency to micromanage and occasionally tried to startle her by sneaking up and looking over her shoulder unexpectedly. Fortunately, her seventh sense usually warned her when he was around.

She had to be fair-minded, and the fact remained that Wendell was a fine librarian. He knew almost every volume in the vast reference collection by heart. She'd been a full-time reference librarian for only a half year. So, although she often wished she could murder him, she also respected his knowledge and abilities, and treated him with the respect due a fine teacher.

She was showing a student how to do a periodical search when Don Bernard entered her line of vision. He came over and stood beside her, smiling and listening as she finished her explanation. Then he led her toward an empty corner by the encyclopedias.

"Did you want something special?"

He gave her a warm smile, his hazel eyes flecked with specks of green. "You're pretty special, Ms. Reynolds, and I certainly want you."

He'd never spoken that way to her before. She felt heat rise to her face. "Don, you're a lady-killer." Why had she said that?

"Don't give me more credit than I deserve. I haven't murdered a woman in at least a month." He gave her a teasing smile. "When I saw you at lunch yesterday, it reminded me that I haven't talked with you for a while. I thought we could have lunch together."

"I'd like that."

"Are you free at noon?"

"I can be."

"Good, there's a wonderful Hungarian place near the train station. Several colleagues have recommended it. I thought we might share the adventure together."

"Sounds good. I'll look forward to it."

She watched him leave. Their friendship had been ongoing for some time. But Don had never asked her out on a date or expressed any romantic interest in her. They were just two people who shared academic interests and held stimulating intellectual conversations. They were both malcontents to some extent, seeing the weaknesses in academia and wanting to change the system for the better. Something of an idealist, Don was the most interesting and witty person she knew. But she was just as happy that their relationship had remained one of friendship. She did not want complications in her life.

Independent and self-supporting were terms she could apply to herself. It would be nice to be as immutable and insensitive as a rock. A rocky island. Was that her? It could be. Hadn't she successfully reinvented herself? She could be what she chose to be, whatever was needed. She had deconstructed her life and reconstructed it to suit her. Now there was no pain, no shame, no past to leave her shaking with bad dreams—if only that were entirely true.

"Can you help me find a book?" Kim looked up, jolted out of her woolgathering.

"Certainly, what are you looking for?"

"It's a criminology text." The man handed her a folded piece of paper.

Their hands touched and she felt an odd charge of energy. She looked at him carefully. He was a strange mixture of disarming and imposing. He had steady gray eyes, wavy black hair and a straight, well-formed nose, but his jaw was square and his features chiseled. He was tall, very tall, and powerfully built. He wore a casual sweater over a denim shirt and worn jeans that hugged his hard body. Definitely a studly hunk. He also had an amazing smile. She blinked and without saying a word, began searching the online catalog for his book.

"We don't have it," she said. "But we can order it for you. Do you think we ought to buy it rather than borrow it from another library?"

He shrugged. "I'll ask my professor and let you know."

"Why don't you fill out this form, and we'll borrow it for you in the meantime." She handed him the appropriate paper and a pen but was careful not to let her hand touch his this time.

"Thanks, you're very efficient."

When he turned to leave, Kim noticed a bulge pushing out his sweater at the base of his back. And she recognized it for what it was. It sent a chill right through her.

She glanced down at the name on the form: Michael Gardner. She wanted nothing to do with the man, nothing to do with any man who carried a weapon, legally or otherwise.

Kim's lunch date was pleasant enough at first. Don Bernard seemed to know just how to put her at ease. He joked about students, the administration, his colleagues. He was the only person who could make her laugh easily. Don ordered goulash for them. She preferred not to eat meat, and especially not veal, but made an exception this time. As Don promised, the meal was delicious, the vegetables fresh and savory. She ate in pensive contemplation, her mind drifting back to the conversation she'd had with Lorette the previous evening.

"Is something troubling you? You seem quieter than usual today."

"Do I? I suppose I've been a bit preoccupied."

"Anything to do with Lorette Campbell?"

"You know Lorette, don't you?"

He answered slowly, as if choosing his words with care. "Of course, I know her. She's a very promising grad student."

"That's good to hear. I suppose you know that we're friends—or should I say friendly?"

"Is she having a problem?" His tone of voice was guarded.

"Lorette thinks someone might be out to harm her."

Don's broad forehead crinkled thoughtfully. "You mean physically hurt her?"

"That's exactly what I mean."

His eyes met hers. "I can't really believe that's possible. I'm certain she's wrong."

"Several things have happened. They may or may not be significant. But she's uneasy."

"Do you want me to talk to her about it?"

She remembered Lorette's reaction to Don. "No, I don't think so." She sensed there had been something between Don and Lorette, something that had not ended well.

He smiled that wonderful smile of his, betraying a dimple in his cheek. Then he took her hand and held it. "We should be more than just friends."

She found herself withdrawing her hand from his. It wasn't

anything she thought about; the action was almost a reflex. Don immediately picked up on it. He was too intelligent to do otherwise.

"At first I thought it was just me, but it's not, is it?"

She found herself flushing. "I have to get back," she said. What could she tell him after all? That she avoided close relationships, that she didn't trust many other people, especially if they were male? No, she could not allow the intimacy of such a confession. Self-protection was the best strategy, no matter how charming Don could be. No need to divulge her feelings or the reasons behind them. Her secrets were her own.

Don pulled his Buick up in front of the main entrance to the humanities library and Kim unfastened her seat belt and prepared to depart.

"Let me get the door for you," he said.

"Please don't bother."

"All right. I'll be around to see you soon," he said.

She should have felt happy and flattered by Don Bernard's behavior, instead she was surprised and just a tad suspicious.

CHAPTER THREE

Wendell Firbin was at the reference desk when Kim returned from lunch. It seemed she was destined to work with him this afternoon as well. She would have preferred to be on the desk with one of the other women, but working with her supervisor was, she supposed, to be looked on as a further learning experience. With that in mind, she decided to bring up the question Lorette had put to her the other day.

"Wendell, is there an inferno collection in this library?"

At first he looked surprised, then upset. He seemed to quickly compose himself. His charcoal brows lifted as if he considered the question totally absurd. "Not that I'm aware. What made you ask such a question?"

"A patron inquired. I found I couldn't answer her."

"Which patron?"

She shrugged uneasily. "I have no idea."

"Can you describe the woman?"

She found his tone of voice to be unusually sharp. "What difference does that make?"

"None. I would just like to know if it was a library student doing a paper for a course. It seems to me that you should have asked. How can you help a patron if you don't ascertain the intent?" Now he was accusatory as well as patronizing, looking down his long, aquiline nose at her.

How stupid! When would she learn her lesson regarding Wendell? He could smell out any sort of lie like a bloodhound. Any form of mendacity was grounds for verbal abuse on his part, which he relished with uncommon zeal. He was forever finding fault. But she was of the firm conviction that he did know something, and that Lorette was right. There was an inferno collection somewhere in the humanities library.

She was grateful when a student came to her and asked a question that took her away from the desk and Wendell's watchful eye. Students usually came first to her because she looked friendlier than the others. In fact, she really did like helping them find what they needed. She took great satisfaction in being useful, in putting her talents to a good cause.

The afternoon passed quickly, with Kim spending minimal time around her supervisor. But several times she caught Wendell looking at her with a speculative glint, as if he were trying to decide something about her. Kim felt distinctly uneasy. The only thing she disliked about her work was being under Wendell's vigilant eye.

Wendell was lean as a rake and always dressed impeccably in a neat suit, shirt and tie. He was the epitome of professionalism. There was no doubt in her mind that he would be advanced to Executive Director shortly. If there was any form of passion in the man, it was his burning ambition to get ahead in his chosen field. She shuddered when she noticed him watching her again, a dark, almost sinister expression on his face. Asking him about inferno collections had really been a big blunder.

Kim walked quickly, aware of the sudden chill in the air. Winter would arrive early this year. T. S. Eliot had been wrong: April was not the cruelest month; it had to be October. There was something painfully sad about seeing all those beautiful leaves dying, falling from their respective trees in a final agonizing blaze of colorful glory, like fighter bombers shot down in flames. She observed the ancient buildings covered with ivy that crawled parasitically along their sides, unnaturally uniting with the sepia brick walls. She wondered in a bemused way what the walls would say if allowed to speak. Had they listened to the learning within? Could they discourse on Aristotle's *Rhetoric* or perhaps speculate on whether or not Wolfe ever did go home again?

She was in a strange mood. It was her lunch hour, but she wasn't really hungry. She decided to take a walk around Kinley Hall and see what was going on in the English classrooms these days.

Dr. Barnes was droning on. He always did run over. She was glad that he was no longer one of her professors. But Lorette had mentioned that Barnes was in contact with her. Kim stayed at the rear of the room, observing students swaying restlessly, some glancing surreptitiously at their wristwatches.

Richard Barnes was a tall, imposing figure, dressed in an austere black suit, immaculate white shirt and blue silk tie. His straight black hair was balding on the top and graying at the temples. He had a certain distinguished air, and his voice was deeply resonant. As everyone knew, he was a former minister who held degrees in divinity and philosophy as well as literature. A slight tremor was in evidence in his richly cultivated voice. For someone who spoke so well, it seemed a shame that he always muddled literature, philosophy and religion together as if each were part and parcel of the other; yet no matter what he spoke about, he always turned it back to damnation.

"An incident occurred this morning, something which I believe has a crucially direct bearing on the point of today's reading and discussion. As I entered the building to come to this classroom, I opened the outer door and held it open for a student to pass through. The young woman hurried by without even so much as a thank you. Can you imagine?" His eyes bulged like those of a bullfrog. "I simply do not understand what is happening to the values of today's youth. I decided to bring the matter to your attention because this class does, after all, represent the current generation of young people. And what better time to discuss values than in conjunction with our study of the Bible as literature, since the Bible is the source of ethics and morality."

He looked from one person to the next. "How many of you have given thought to your philosophy of life? We all have one, you know. In this age of shocking moral decadence and degeneration, how many young people are taking drugs that will ultimately destroy them, body and soul? As you must know, sexual intercourse is flagrant among single, young people. The newspapers tell us that AIDS and venereal diseases have reached epidemic proportions. And the extent of sexual deviation and perversion is staggering. Many parents are too busy playing spouse-swapping games themselves to become concerned about the activities of their progeny. Our society is a veritable Sodom and Gomorrah. I believe that the judgment of God is upon us, when we will be held accountable for our sins. Our entire civilization is doomed to hellfire and damnation."

Kim groaned; she could see him in the role of Jonathan Edwards, spearheading the great reawakening of Calvinism, reducing grown men to whimpering like dogs. A pity he had not lived in an earlier time when Bible-thumping was *de rigueur.*

A dubious hand was raised in the third row and the professor-minister nodded.

"Do you actually believe that there is such a place as hell?" The student sported a lion's mane of tawny hair and beard.

"Such a place as hell?" Dr. Barnes's voice repeated the words with scornful emphasis, as if the heresy were obvious and shocking. "No, there is no hell if we are thinking of physical place. However, I do believe that hell is a state of being that the damned will enter into after death."

"You can't mean to imply that most of our society is doomed to damnation."

The comment made Dr. Barnes angry and his face reddened, reminding Kim of a waxed apple. He finally dismissed the class and the students left quickly. He closed his briefcase with an air of finality and lifted it from the dark wood podium. Kim could have easily told him that she knew him for the hypocrite he was, but she held her tongue. He walked past her, showing no sign of recognition.

At that moment, Lionel Forbes, the renowned scholar in the field of writing theory, entered the classroom and floated toward the podium. There was an ethereal quality about him that made Kim shiver. He was white-haired and small, but agile as a trout. His slender, diminutive body was fixed at direct center. Electric blue eyes charged nervously from one student's face to another as they filed into the classroom. His hair, as pure and perfectly white as fresh snow, was set off by a striking pink complexion. He made her think of the white mice used in laboratory experiments. This was an undergrad course, but Lorette was in one of his graduate classes. With that in mind, Kim decided to remain inconspicuously at the back of the room for a bit longer.

The professor made eye contact with his audience. A silence descended over the assembled group that stared at him in a kind of awe akin to dread. He smiled to himself, as if enjoying some private joke.

"I would like to discuss some of the work you produced for our last meeting."

An overweight young man leaned over to whisper something in the ear of the girl sitting beside him.

"Don't slobber over her, you worthless blob of protoplasm! I am the most fascinating object in this room. Your eyes must perpetually be riveted to mine. Do you understand?" Forbes spoke with fanged ferocity.

The student was too mesmerized with fear to respond. That seemed to amuse the professor; his blue eyes twinkled like January sunlight reflecting on a frozen lake. He continued to speak without pausing.

"Acceptance is the kiss of death. I want you all to remember that and start to think critically about your own work as well as what you read. We are the chosen few, the elect. We're all going to hell in a hand basket together. But what a ride we shall have." The professor looked from one student to the other. Then his gaze fixed on Kim and he smiled, showing an expanse of shark-like teeth. His glistening eyes had a strangely diabolical glow about them.

Kim shuddered with distaste. After that, the professor launched into a detailed discussion about what the student papers specifically lacked. Kim left quickly.

Outside, the day had turned even colder; the wind cut across her cheek like a switchblade. Thick, dark clouds hung ominously overhead. She felt as if the total malice of the universe had turned against her and she shivered, cold inside and out.

"I got a call that my book was in. You're certainly efficient." It was *him*, Michael Gardner. She hadn't forgotten his name, couldn't forget it.

He was looking at her in a way that suggested he knew her intimately. The look felt like a caress. A frisson of awareness rippled between them. Her blood heated and she turned away, awkward and embarrassed. It was as if he had the ability to reach into her very soul.

"We don't hold books here at Reference. You have to ask at the circulation desk." She hoped her voice sounded calm and professional; she certainly didn't feel in charge at the moment.

"Right, I'll do that."

★   ★   ★   ★   ★

Michael Gardner studied her intently. Of course, he'd known the book wasn't behind the reference desk. That was just an excuse to talk to her again. They shared a psychic awareness. He'd sensed it immediately. But his innate sensitivity told him that she repressed hers, just as she clearly repressed her sexuality.

He scrutinized her with his typical thoroughness, studying the chestnut hair highlighted with auburn brilliance and pulled back severely, forced into a tight bun that negated her liveliness. No make-up, dowdy gray suit to hide what was clearly a slim but womanly figure. A disguise if ever he'd seen one. But she couldn't hide the flush in her cheeks or those moist, kissable lips. He sensed a passionate nature in hiding. Now why was that?

Mysteries always intrigued him. This librarian was an exciting puzzle. He was aware of a need to reach out and touch her. He wanted to fully explore her essence. He wanted to lie naked with her, to have sex with her. It could be wild and wonderful. He would get her to open to him and she would ignite in his arms. He wondered what would happen if he told her that? But he recognized that she wasn't ready for such revelations; not yet. She was eyeing him nervously, like a skittish animal ready to bolt.

"Excuse me," she said. "I have other duties to which I must attend." Her backbone was stiff as a poker.

His gaze followed her as she walked away from him. They were most certainly going to make contact. It was something he knew in his bones. He didn't know the details. It wasn't a question of how or when, but a matter of destiny. He could have told her, but she would discover it for herself.

For just a moment she turned back and stared at him. Then

she hurriedly quickened her pace. He clearly frightened her; the question was why. He wondered what she was hiding.

CHAPTER FOUR

Kim pulled her Toyota onto the highway only to discover that traffic was very heavy—but then, it always was around this time of the day. She stopped off at a supermarket to pick up some basic staples and then contended with the traffic once again. She was very glad to be going home; small as her studio apartment was, it was hers, her sanctuary, far from the madding crowd's ignoble strife.

Soon she was passing the small, man-made lake in the heart of the complex. On impulse, she stopped for a moment to watch the ducks and geese that populated the lake. It made her feel peaceful inside to see them. How nice it must be to live entirely by instinct alone, no worries, no cares, no fears. There was a family of Canada geese she'd been watching since the spring. At first, the goslings had been tiny balls of fluffy gray feathers. There were six of them who swam two abreast, the father and mother protectively swimming nearby, one at the front, the other at the rear. She envied those small, innocent creatures. How wonderful to have a safe, secure childhood, to be cared for in a normal, natural way. Each day, the goslings had grown a little larger and a little stronger, until now they looked just like their parents. She supposed they would soon fly away.

Kim sighed deeply as she pulled up in front of her apartment. It was as neat, sterile and empty as when she'd left it. The sounds of silence greeted her entry. She ought to get a cat or a goldfish, she supposed, but she fought against the stereotypical old-maid image. She put away her groceries, sat down on the cream-colored couch that opened into a bed and kicked off her shoes. She didn't really mind being alone. People needed time to themselves, just to think, to relax. She closed her eyes and visualized the geese and ducks gliding on the water. A moment later, she was jarred by the ringing of the telephone. She was even more disturbed by the caller.

"Karen, honey, how are you?"

"It's Kim."

"Yes, Kim. Well, I'm not comfortable calling you that."

"I'm not Karen anymore. I haven't been for a long time."

The voice at the other end was low-pitched and husky for a woman, just as it had always been.

"That's right. Karen would have called me once in a while."

The accusation was an accurate dagger to the heart.

"I've been very busy lately." The lie sounded exactly like what it was. She regretted it the moment it passed her lips.

"I really miss Karen."

"Did you call about something in particular?" To her own ears, her voice sounded unnaturally shrill. She felt like a recalcitrant child and didn't much appreciate the guilt associated with the image.

"Matter of fact, I did. Cousin Mary's been asking me for some time to come live with her in Florida. She's all alone now too. We always did get along well. I've decided to rent our house with an option to buy. If it works out, I'll be selling the old place. I thought you'd want to know. Maybe you'd like to stop by and take a look in your room. There are things here that are yours."

Kim hesitated, not wanting to commit herself.

"Well, you can suit yourself, of course. I won't beg you. If you hate seeing me that much, that's your right."

She could hear the hurt. God, she hadn't meant to cause

that! "Ma, it's not what you think. It never was."

"I wish you'd explain. I don't understand."

"I believe we talked about it," Kim said carefully.

"Maybe not enough."

No, they hadn't really talked all those years ago, so what was there to say now? Still, she ought to make the effort. Then at least her conscience would be clear.

"You're much stronger than I am. You handled it differently. I couldn't face the shame, the humiliation."

"It wasn't your shame," Ma said in a quiet voice.

"I felt as though it were. Look, I'll come by."

"When?"

"As soon as I can."

"Don't wait too long. I'm giving the furniture to the needy, taking what I can, and most everything else I'll have hauled away."

"I want to go through the things in the attic."

"As you choose."

The strain of the conversation had grown too much for her; with a lump in her throat, Kim quickly said goodbye. She wouldn't think about Ma or any of the rest of it right now. The sense of sorrow could too easily be conjured if she allowed her mind to associate freely without constraint. Depression could suffocate her like a soft pillow.

No, she wasn't Karen, not anymore; she was Kim. She wouldn't let Ma make her feel sorry about her decision. Yesterday was dead. Kim was a person free of the past, whole and self-sufficient. The ghosts no longer remained, except in her nightmares. Kim Reynolds was who she was now and who she would remain, a new person with a new name and a new identity. There were things Ma hadn't wanted to tell her, hadn't wanted her to know, and she'd accepted that. Why dredge everything up now?

Kim felt no real appetite. After heating up a can of chicken noodle soup, she took only a half bowl and promptly put the rest away. Although she had walked on campus at lunchtime, she was too edgy to remain in the apartment. A walk around the lake soothed away some of her ambivalent feelings.

The television proved to be the perfect sedative. She tuned in on a series of inane comedies, lay down on the couch and dozed. The sound of the telephone ringing pulled her back to consciousness. Her mouth felt dry; she had no immediate way of knowing how long she'd slept. Glancing over at the clock, she saw only two hours had passed. She lifted the receiver on the third ring.

It turned out to be Lorette. "I'm glad I caught you. I hope I'm not disturbing you. You sound sleepy."

"No, it's all right."

"Something happened today. I wasn't going to bother you about it, but it's been troubling me. I'm not sure what to do."

"What happened?"

There was a pause, a heartbeat. "I got another threatening note."

"In your mailbox at school?"

"Yes." Lorette's voice was higher pitched than usual, like a violin strung too tightly.

"What did this one say?"

"Does it matter?"

"It might." Somehow Kim was sure it did.

"I don't even want to look at it again. It crawls in my hand like a snake."

"Read it to me. Maybe I can help in some way."

"All right." Lorette paused, and then her voice sounded clear and somber. "The deaths ye died I have watched beside/And the lives ye led were mine."

"Obviously a quotation. You want me to check Bartlett's?"

"I already have. It's Kipling. I don't think that's the significant part though, do you?"

"No," Kim agreed.

"I've thought about it quite a bit already, you see. I believe this person is saying he or she wishes to watch me die and that the death will be slow and painful, as if I died many times. And my death will belong to this person because he or she intends to murder me." Lorette sounded as if she were on the edge of nervous collapse.

"You could be interpreting the note too broadly."

"No, this person expects that my mind will move in just that direction."

Kim admired the fact that, even in a situation like this, Lorette was able to be keenly analytical. "It seems this individual is attempting to psyche you out."

"And succeeding admirably."

"You can't permit it." Kim spoke in a gentle but firm voice.

"I'm frightened."

"I know. Do you want me to come over?"

"No, Jim is coming by. I'll make certain he stays with me. I can't be alone tonight."

"If for any reason he doesn't show up, you can always come over here, or call me and I'll come to you. And there's also your mother. You're not alone." Kim hoped she sounded reassuring.

"I'd never call Miranda. There are things you don't know, things I don't tell other people. Let's just say, contrary to appearances, Miranda has not been the most nurturing of mothers." In spite of an effort to sound unemotional, there was a trace of bitterness in Lorette's voice.

"Look, tomorrow is Saturday. If you and Jim don't have any special plans, you might drop by my place in the evening and we can talk. In fact, come for dinner and bring the two notes. Maybe we can compare them."

"I threw the first one away."

Kim found that troubling, but was careful not to say so. "Well, we can look at the second one together."

"I don't want to impose on you."

"You won't be imposing. I never have company. It'll be nice to break my solitary pattern of isolation for a change."

"Promise you won't fuss with dinner."

"It'll just be something informal," she said. "I'm not known for my culinary skills."

"I'd rather not talk about this problem in front of Jim."

"We'll figure out something. Fix yourself a cup of chamomile tea in the meantime."

The conversation ended with Lorette sounding calmer and in control again. Kim had done her best to put her friend's mind at ease, but in her own mind, she was uncomfortable with the situation. She sensed Lorette was not telling her everything. Her awareness, her odd sensibility, was kicking in again. Kim was certain there was real danger in this situation. The problem really ought to be turned over to the police.

She considered the matter more thoroughly while she brushed her teeth. Death threats should not be taken lightly. But the police would probably pay little attention to Lorette's notes because no actual crime had been committed. Besides, Kim had very little faith in them. The police couldn't be trusted; hadn't she found that out for herself? As for a private investigator, such services were expensive. She doubted Lorette had much money, nor was she likely to ask her mother for any.

That night, Kim slept restlessly, in the morning rising to vague remembrances of bad dreams, lurid nightmares. It seemed she could not escape her ghosts. Carl was in those dreams, like some demon from hell. She had to remind herself that those were Karen's dreams, not the dreams of Kim, who could and would brush them aside like the wispy cobwebs they now were.

Later in the morning she drove to a supermarket. As she selected a firm head of lettuce and two ripe tomatoes for the salad she planned, Kim thought about Lorette and her problem. If she were going to talk to Lorette privately, Jim would have to be occupied in some manner. There was nothing wrong with Jim being included in their discussion, but Lorette did not want him to be. Kim didn't understand that kind of reasoning; wouldn't it be better for Jim to know what was going on so that he could help? Still, Lorette would do as she wished. Kim sighed in frustration. She would like to be more helpful. Moving on down the aisle, she wondered at her need—almost a compulsion—to assist other people with their problems. Was it an expiation for sins? Maybe helping others was her way of proving to herself that she was worth something after all.

As she stood waiting in the express line, a misnomer if ever there was one, she considered that it might be better if there were another person for dinner, one Jim could talk with, someone who would even things out. Threesomes were always awkward. But whom to ask? She thought of Don Bernard, then immediately talked herself out of calling him. He was such a suave, attractive man; he must have dozens of lady friends. He would be busy on a Saturday night. She would just make a fool of herself. Her indecision was agonizing. By the time it was her turn to place her purchases on the checkout counter, she had vacillated back and forth countless times.

In the end, she phoned him. He picked up on the fourth ring when she was just about ready to put the receiver down. His deep, well-modulated voice sounded a little breathless. She identified herself and he sounded genuinely glad that she phoned him.

"I hope I'm not disturbing you."

"Not at all. I just came in from playing tennis. I'm about to hit the shower and then collapse for a time."

She cleared her throat nervously. "The thing is, I'm planning to have a friend over tonight. She's bringing her boyfriend, and so I thought, maybe a friend of mine might like to join us." Did she sound like a nervous, pimply adolescent, or was that her imagination?

"It just so happens I'm between mad, passionate affairs this week and was looking for a friend to spend the evening with."

She let out a deep breath; Don's teasing manner always did cause her to relax. "Well, dinner will be at seven—nothing fancy. I'm not much of a cook. Would you like to drop by around six—that is, if it's convenient."

"Six it is. Thank you, Kim. This has been a pleasant surprise. I never expected to receive a phone call from you."

"I suppose I do come off as pretty old-fashioned."

"No, you just like to keep your distance. You're reserved. Maybe I can show you all men aren't ogres. You devout feminists are mighty cautious creatures."

When their conversation ended, she considered what he said. He thought her a dedicated feminist? She'd never spouted chapter and verse. She lived the way she did as an act of self-preservation. But then Don couldn't know that. No one did. It wasn't something she talked about.

She took the rest of the afternoon to clean up the apartment and do a little maintenance on herself as well. Rarely did she bother with make-up, but for some reason, she felt she ought to spend some time on her appearance for this evening. She used eyebrow pencil, a touch of eyeliner, mascara and blush, but no lipstick, which she thought made her look clownish.

She didn't own jeans and wished now that she had bought a pair, but her navy blue slacks looked casual with a western-yoked shirt. For tonight, she wanted to appear less than the serious, austere academic.

Lorette and Jim arrived a few minutes before six o'clock. Lorette looked beautiful and chic as usual. She wore a white silk pantsuit that clung provocatively in all the right places and contrasted dramatically with her flowing ebony hair. Only a woman as tall and slim as Lorette could look quite so elegant and regal in such an outfit. Jim, ever the cowboy, was dressed in jeans, denim shirt, cowboy hat and boots. They were a study in contrasts; he appeared ready to ride out on the range, she to pose for the cover of *Vogue*.

Jim glanced around her apartment. "Same layout as Lorette's place," he said.

Lorette handed her a square white bakery box tied with multicolored string. "For dessert. Jim picked it out. Black Forest cake."

"Worth the calories." Kim took the cake and moved some things around to make a space for it, aware how small and cramped the refrigerator was.

The doorbell rang and she called out to come in. Don Bernard entered, sophisticated and handsome in an eggshell-colored Irish cable-knit sweater and matching flannel slacks. There was a look of surprised recognition as he caught sight of Lorette and Jim. He didn't seem at all pleased. For a moment there was an awkwardness in the room. Kim felt the tension acutely. She swallowed guiltily. She'd been aware there was friction between Lorette and Don Bernard and still she'd decided to invite him, to ignore the hostility. Why had she arranged this? It was uncharacteristically selfish on her part. She felt a distinct stab of guilt. The truth was, she'd wanted to see Don Bernard, looked for an excuse to be with him socially.

A neon sign registering the word *mistake* in bold red letters lit up in her mind's eye. She was painfully aware at this moment of how tiny her apartment actually was. It was a miniature, too small to comfortably accommodate four adults, especially when the tension in the air was as thick as split-pea soup. Why hadn't she realized that before?

"Well, it's nice to see familiar faces," Don said, his composure returning. He turned a warm smile on Kim and held out a gift-boxed object. "I thought you might like to serve this after dinner. It's an interesting liqueur."

Kim thanked him and put his gift on the kitchen counter without so much as looking at him. Quickly, she brought out cheese and crackers.

"I have beer, white wine and soft drinks," she told them.

"Beer," Jim said.

Don opted for the white wine. She and Lorette each drank a glass of ginger ale. Don glanced over at Lorette. Their eyes met and he quickly looked away. Kim wondered about that, because the look was clearly hostile. It seemed out of character for Don to feel enmity toward anyone. His personality was generally easygoing and amiable.

Don began conversing with Jim. Kim was glad to discover that they were acquainted.

"What made you go back to school?"

"I sometimes ask myself why I'm still at the university," Jim said with a wry smile. "Truth is, I never imagined myself leaving the ranch. It always seemed to me that I was born and bred to work livestock. But I used to write poetry. It was all about ranching—at least on the surface it was. My English teacher back in high school took an interest in me. Said he thought my poems were really good. To prove it, he sent some around to these small literary magazines. Anyway, some of them got published. His confidence in me made me want to continue my education. 'Course I couldn't go off to college right away. Couldn't afford it. But I worked my way through college slow and easy. Then I got my Master's back in Montana. My advisor thought it would do well for me to get my Ph.D. in the East. So here I am. The university was generous in its offer to me. I got this fellowship. I'm older than most of these kids, but I got my sights set on becoming a professor of American literature."

"I take it you don't plan to stay in the East permanently."

Jim shook his head, a lock of hair falling across his forehead. "Not a chance. Out West when you look up at the sky at night, you feel as though you're looking straight into the face of heaven, 'cause a million stars are showering their light on you. A body can breathe out there. You'd really like it," he added, turning to Lorette and taking her hand. Lorette did not reply; her pale, slender fingers were swallowed up by his large, callused hand.

"So then you're happy at the university?" Don said.

"Sure, I've been given a chance to better my life. I'd still be baby-sitting beeves if I weren't being educated. I'll never be rich, but I do like reading, learning and teaching a whole lot."

"Worthy sentiments," Don said and raised his wine glass in salute. "May you always feel that way. I would like to read some of your poetry one day."

"My pleasure."

"Why don't you ask me what I think about the way the university prepares students to teach in academe?" Lorette said. Her voice had a hollow sound.

A look passed between Lorette and Don Bernard that Kim found disturbing.

"By all means, tell us," Don said, as if she had challenged him on some level.

"I read an article in which the Association of American Colleges was quoted. Do you know what it said? If the professional preparation of doctors was as minimal as that of college teachers, the United States would have more funeral directors than lawyers."

"And just what would you change?" Don asked with a tight smile, which Kim knew was false.

"To start with, in the graduate English program, why not offer some writing courses instead of limiting us solely to literature?"

"Ah, yes," Don said, "of course that could prove beneficial. However, every course you take demands considerable writing."

"Precisely why we should have a course or two on the graduate level which emphasizes the needed skills."

"Not necessary," Don said.

"Too practical, Dr. Bernard? You and your colleagues look down on anything not connected to literary criticism, don't you? Ironic, isn't it? You revere famous writers and study their work, yet you ignore the writing process as if it's merely a basic course for freshmen." Lorette's tone was bitter, accusatory.

Kim began to squirm in her chair, thinking that her dinner party was fast turning into a disaster.

"I agree with you entirely, Ms. Campbell. Intellectual snobs are not to be trusted. They have the wrong slant on things because they're always looking down their noses." With that, Don smiled and took the edge out of the argument.

Quickly, seeing her chance, Kim stood up. "We may be a bit crowded, but dinner is about to be served. It was going to be lamb chops, but I did remember that Jim was a cattle person."

Jim smiled, craggy lines forming at the corners of his mouth and eyes. He had the tanned face and sun-bleached hair of a man who preferred to spend as many hours as possible out-of-doors.

"I truly am a beef man. Fact is, I can't remember ever swallowing any lamb. My grandpa used to tell stories about how it was in the days of the range wars with sheepherders. That old man would have starved before he touched mutton."

"Then you'll be happy to know we've got salad and a large

pizza with everything."

"Sounds perfect," Don said.

"There's only one little problem. I have to pick up the pizza. Lorette, you can come with me. We'll leave the men to finish their drinks and discourse on world problems."

So saying, she led Lorette out to her car. "That was so we could have our talk privately. I thought you'd prefer it. Although I do think Jim should know about the threats."

"It's not a good idea."

"You can show me the note when we get to the pizza place."

Lorette looked around as if she expected someone were watching, then nodded her head and followed. Lorette was rather subdued as they drove along. Kim thought she seemed distant and troubled. When they drove into the parking lot of Vito's, Kim asked to see the note.

"I didn't bring it." Lorette lowered her eyes, training them on the floor of the car.

Kim was perplexed. "I don't understand. I thought you wanted me to look at it."

Lorette met her gaze. "I had other things on my mind. I forgot it."

It was clear to Kim that her friend was not being entirely truthful; she was puzzled by this bit of mendacity.

"I will help you if I can, if you let me."

"I think I ought to just toss this note away as I did the first one."

"You can't be serious! Tell me about the note. Was it typed or handwritten?"

"Typed."

"What kind of typing? Manual machine, electric or computer printed?"

"How can you tell the difference?"

"Manual strokes are usually uneven in some respects. Electric strokes are smoother. And the computers might use dot matrix, bubble jet or laser print. What did you notice?"

Her expressive eyes glanced up. "You think there wasn't any note, don't you?"

"I didn't say that or even think it." Kim decided to drop the subject.

"Did you find out anything about the inferno collection?" Lorette ripped at a fingernail distractedly.

"I asked my boss, and he looked at me strangely."

With surprise, she saw a look of fear come over Lorette's features.

"You shouldn't have asked anyone in authority. If they knew, they'd cover it up."

"Cover what up?" Kim was growing impatient.

"There's no point talking about it. Forget I asked. Don't bother with it."

"Wendell was displeased, but I didn't sense any conspiracy," Kim said.

"I don't want you getting in trouble with your boss. He makes me uneasy. I don't trust him."

"Neither do I, but he does know everything that goes on at the library. He's very professional, even if he is a creep."

Lorette pursed her lips. "Just be careful what you say to him."

"Are you going to confide in me? Tell me something about this inferno collection you want me to find. What's supposed to be in it? Do you know?"

Lorette turned away from her. "Drop the whole thing. Forget I asked about it, will you?"

Kim found Lorette's behavior infuriating. Maybe she should stop making any attempt to involve herself. If Lorette did not trust her enough to confide in her fully, there really was no point in continuing. She picked up the pizza and drove back to the apartment without further discussion.

Don and Jim were discussing Shakespeare when they returned to the apartment and she was glad they at least seemed to be getting along well. Her mind was preoccupied as she got the salad from the refrigerator.

The two men did most of the talking through dinner, mostly to each other. Lorette ate little and said less. Kim wasn't feeling very sociable herself.

"I'd like the two of you to be the first to know that I proposed to Lorette today. I asked her to marry me right and proper." Jim looked very pleased with himself.

Lorette appeared unhappy, and Kim could not help but wonder if that was the distraction that had caused her to forget to bring the threatening note.

"Congratulations," Don Bernard said, his voice cool.

"I wish you hadn't said anything just yet," Lorette said, her eyes lowered.

"I was fairly bursting with the news, darlin'. Besides, Kim is your friend. No need for us to keep it a secret, is there?"

Lorette did not answer. Kim went out to the kitchen and saw to the coffee. Lorette joined her.

"Are you going to accept?"

Lorette trained her gaze on the red-checkered linoleum. "I don't know yet. Living together is one thing. Marriage is something quite different."

They didn't speak about it again, and soon after everyone had been served their cake and coffee, Lorette complained of feeling exhausted. Jim would have gladly lingered, but Lorette told him that her head was pounding and they quickly left with a brief apology.

After the other two had gone, Don opened the liqueur he'd brought and poured them both a small measure in juice glasses.

"Sorry about not having wine glasses," she told him. "I rarely drink or have company."

"That's all right. Come sit down on the couch with me and relax a little. You seemed tense tonight."

"I'm not used to playing hostess. I guess it shows."

He gave her that charming smile of his, showing his dimpled cheek to advantage. "This peach brandy will help. I also give an excellent massage."

"I think the brandy will do for right now," she said and took a sip, letting the heat of it burn from her throat to her stomach.

"She's going to turn him down," Don said.

"Why do you say that?"

"I don't think she's capable of committing herself."

"I hope you're wrong. Jim seems terribly nice."

Don drank some more of the liqueur slowly and thoughtfully. "He does have his head on straight which is more than I can say for a lot of other people."

"Meaning Lorette?"

When he didn't answer, she continued. "Why don't you like her? You gave me the initial impression that you thought highly of her."

"I do as a student. She's very bright and an excellent writer."

"But?"

He shrugged. "A gentleman never tells."

She felt suddenly awkward. "Sorry, I did have a sense that you and she had a personal relationship."

"Over and done with nearly a year ago and not at all memorable. I'd rather talk about you than Lorette. I was pleased but also surprised when you asked me over here tonight."

"We are friends."

His arms moved to her shoulders. "You are a very attractive woman, although you do your best to hide it. I can't think of anyone I'd rather get to know better. But I've always felt that you wanted to keep our relationship entirely platonic. I can respect that, however . . ." He stopped speaking, leaned forward and kissed her on the lips.

It was not an unpleasant sensation. He tasted of alcohol, coffee, and cake. His kiss deepened and the mixed flavors gave an exotic quality to the evocation. She sighed, allowing herself the luxury of enjoying this intimacy. His mouth opened to hers and his hands began to move ever so gently over her body. Then suddenly, old thoughts and feelings took hold of her, and she pushed him away and got up from the sofa.

" 'Had we but world enough and time, this coyness, lady, were no crime.' "

She shook her head. "I'm sorry; I can't."

"Can't allow yourself to feel more than friendship for me?"

"For any man."

"Why not?"

She shook her head. "It's not something I can discuss."

He looked at her with concern. "Can't or won't? All right, we'll leave things as they are for now. I value you too much to press you."

He was out the door in a matter of minutes, leaving behind the wonderful male scent of his after-shave. She picked up his glass, took a sip from it, put it down again on the end table, and willed herself not to cry.

"Damn you, Carl! Stop haunting me!"

CHAPTER FIVE

On Sunday morning, Kim woke up feeling miserable, both physically and emotionally. Her throat ached, but even worse was the knowledge that her tentative efforts to host a casual dinner party had been a fiasco. She hadn't even gotten to examine Lorette's threatening letter, and she'd probably ruined her friendship with Don Bernard by inviting him over and sending mixed signals. In short, everything she'd done was wrong. She felt woefully inadequate.

No, she was not going to continue to think this way! It wouldn't change anything and she would just hurt herself. She was thinking with Karen's mind again. Kim Reynolds did not think negative thoughts. Kim Reynolds looked for solutions, for ways to set matters right. No loser mentality. *Our fate is in ourselves, not in our stars.* There would be no more self-pity, no defeatist attitude.

She closed her eyes against the light; under her coffined lids, patterns of red and green dots formed against the darkness. She willed herself to relax and rest but could not. Slipping from the sofa bed, she retrieved her robe and walked into the kitchen area. When upset, she found it best to keep active. She busied herself boiling water for instant coffee and cutting an orange into quarters.

Sunday morning—coffee and oranges in a sunny chair— *Death, the mother of beauty.* For some unaccountable reason, that line of poetry caused a chill to slither down her back. She drank

57

her instant coffee thoughtfully.

Kim knew she ought to call, ought to make arrangements to see Ma. But she picked up a romantic suspense novel instead and buried herself in it for more than an hour, fully aware that it was cowardly and foolish to avoid the inevitable. Eventually, she made the phone call. The phone rang several times before it was picked up. She found herself hoping that it would not be answered, then hated herself for thinking that way. The conversation was brief and strained. It was agreed that she would come by in the afternoon.

The drive to the beach brought back many memories. The old house was very much as she remembered it, weedy lawn with sandy places, the house badly in need of a paint job. It had been over a year since she'd been back, although they lived not more than a half hour apart.

Ma looked older, her hair grayer, lines etched in her forehead. "How's my girl?" she asked.

The question made Kim ache inside. "Fine," she said.

"I'm looking forward to Florida. It's lonely here."

She wondered for a moment if Ma meant to make her feel guilty but decided that wasn't like her. Once Ma had friends, but they'd turned away. That was so often the way when bad things happened.

"I went to the cemetery yesterday, just to make sure his grave was tended. I wish you'd come sometime."

"I hate cemeteries." She didn't say that she hated *him*, although that was the truth.

"You see the ghosts?"

"Sometimes I see them. Sometimes I just hear them."

Ma sighed. "Just like your grandma. I'm sorry you've been cursed with her awareness."

"It's not a bad thing when I can use it to help other people. Trouble is, I can't always depend on it. Sometimes, it's there with me. Lots of times it's not. I never really know. It's just not reliable."

At least, she could talk openly about it with Ma. She was cautious not to discuss it with other people. How do you explain that you have a form of psychic ability, a kind of intuition? They'd think she was mad, eccentric at the very least, a few slices short of a loaf.

There was an awkward moment of silence.

"Guess we don't have very much to say to each other anymore, do we? What a shame that is." Ma looked so sad, Kim wanted to comfort her.

Instead she said: "I'd like to look at the old things."

"Sure. I've kept your room exactly the way it was when you left for good. Always thought you might come back someday."

Memories rushed through Kim's mind. The full scholarship she'd earned had allowed her to live away as an undergraduate. It had freed her. Summers, she managed to work for the college. But holidays had been difficult. She recalled the day she'd started her first teaching job and could afford to leave home for good. She could remember the immense sense of relief that had permeated every part of her being. The ghosts wouldn't haunt her anymore.

Ma allowed her to go to the room by herself, which she appreciated. She looked around and saw that everything had indeed been kept neat and clean, just the way it once was when she resided there. Even some of the old clothes were in the closet, the ones she'd left behind. But as she looked through the dresser drawers and the closet, she realized that these things belonged to Karen. They had no part in her present life.

However, there was something that she wanted, but she wasn't sure that Ma would let her have it. She decided to ask anyway. Ma was in the living room dusting the old family pictures when Kim came into the room.

"I don't want anything from my old room."

"Not even the high school yearbook?"

"No, not even that. But there are a few things in the attic."

Ma's expression immediately changed; she looked closed and wary. "What would you want up there? There's only dust and things from a time you weren't even born."

Ma had never liked her being there. It seemed some things never changed.

"I just want to look around a little."

"There's loose floorboards. It could be dangerous."

"I'm a grown woman, Ma. I'll be careful."

"What are you looking for? Maybe I can find it."

"I'm not sure. I just want to have a look before you throw it all away."

Ma was right about it being dusty in the attic. It was the one place Ma rarely cared to clean. Sometimes as a child, Kim would sneak up to the attic to play. She'd go through the old trunk of clothes, ancient things that had belonged to her grandparents. It was fun trying on the clothes and pretending she lived in those long-ago times.

When she was fifteen, she found out about Jen. Once in a while people, mostly relatives, mentioned Jen. Kim never thought much about her. Who thinks to ask about someone who's been dead so many years? Besides, Ma always looked so sad and unhappy when people mentioned her.

But one day when she was playing in the attic, she'd found an old book. It turned out to be a diary. She'd begun reading it out of curiosity. The diary, it turned out, had belonged to Jen, Ma's younger sister, the one who'd died so long ago. The interesting thing about it was that Jen had started writing it when she was only fourteen. Jen stopped writing it at fifteen, the same age that Kim had been when she discovered it. She left it in the attic and read it slowly, a little at a time, until she'd finished it. By then, Jen was very real to her.

She began asking questions and getting unsatisfactory answers. Ma didn't like her asking, that was certain. Now all she wanted was to find the diary and take it with her. She wanted to read it all over again, to make Jen come alive once more. She went through the old trunk where the diary used to be, but it was not there. She looked through old books and an unpainted desk, but still there was nothing.

Downstairs, she confronted Ma. "I was looking for Jen's diary."

"You could have asked in the first place if that was all you wanted from here." There was an accusatory note in her mother's voice.

"May I have it?" Kim kept her own tone of voice calm and even.

"If I find it."

"Ma, you always know where everything is."

"Carl might have thrown it out." They looked at each other, exchanging understandings.

She had no desire to talk about him, not now, not ever again. Someday she might have to, but not today.

"If you find it, would you please call me? I really want to have it."

"Why does it matter?" Ma asked, her eyes searching.

"I don't know, it just does."

"Sad memories are best tucked away and forgotten like old clothes that don't fit anymore."

"I've tried. I changed my life as best I could."

Ma took her hand. "No, you closed me out, and you closed away who you were and what you felt. That wasn't right, Karen. I'll look for Jen's book. I promise to call you if I find it. I guess it's only right that you should have it. You are a lot like she was in many ways." Ma moved toward her, but Kim didn't want to be embraced, so she quickly said goodbye and departed. If she had been in that house another moment, she would have broken down and cried.

On Tuesday morning, Lorette visited Kim at the library. Kim was surprised to see her so early in the morning.

"I came to visit you before heading to class. I went to my mailbox yesterday and had an unpleasant surprise."

"Another of those nasty notes?"

Lorette bit down on her lower lip. "In a manner of speaking. But a different kind of threat this time." She handed the note to Kim. "This is from the Director of Graduate English Studies."

"Simpson-Watkins?"

"The very same." Lorette's eyes looked puffy, as if she had been crying recently.

"Did you see him?"

"I did indeed. He said that he thinks it might be best if I finished my degree at another university."

Kim was shocked. "Did he offer some explanation for making the suggestion?"

"He claimed that there were questions regarding my background. I asked him to explain, but he was reluctant. When I pursued the matter, he finally opened up enough to say that certain accusations had been made against me, serious ones. Then he reiterated that it would be best if I withdrew from the university as soon as possible. I'm afraid I really lost my temper. I told him about the threatening notes and the accident. I said I was determined to find out who my accusers and enemies were. But he wouldn't say another word."

"I can't believe anyone would do this to you."

"Neither can I. I'm furious! It's totally absurd." Her eyes burned with rage. "You know how I feel about having a meaningful career. I would do just about anything to become a professor. I'm thinking about taking legal action. I need that information about the inferno collection if you can get it. I know it's here somewhere. Certain people are covering it up. Please try to find out about it, Kim, just be careful. I don't want anyone threatening to harm you too."

"All right, I'll see what I can find out."

"Teaching's given me the greatest rush imaginable. When I connect with a class, when they get enthusiastic about what I'm teaching, it's a greater high than drugs, alcohol, or even sex. I finally know what I want to do with my life. I can't and won't give that up. I'm going to fight what they're trying to do to me!"

Kim touched Lorette's arm. "I understand. I'll help you in any way I can."

"Thanks. That means a lot to me. I've got to get to class. I'll call you soon."

Kim observed her supervisor at a distance watching them, his expression anything but friendly as Lorette swung out through the electronic doors. No doubt Kim would hear a lecture later about not engaging in personal conversations on university time. She let out a deep sigh and got back to the business of filling an interlibrary loan request.

CHAPTER SIX

On Thursday evening, the telephone rang around eleven o'clock. Kim was already asleep, having dozed off in front of the television set. She reached for the phone next to the sofa bed. Her hand was a little unsteady and the phone rang again before she could pick it up.

"Hello," she said in an uncertain voice still groggy with sleep.

"Kim, it's Lorette. Sorry if I woke you. I seem to be making a habit of it. I could call back tomorrow or maybe stop by the library."

"No, that's okay. You can stop by and we can have lunch tomorrow, but what did you want to talk about?"

"Just to tell you that I found something out. I might even be able to get this thing settled before I see you. I blundered miserably. Ironic, isn't it? I, who tried so hard to court favor."

"You found out who's behind the nastiness."

"I'll tell you all I know tomorrow. I can't talk too much now. I just had this fanciful notion. Wouldn't it be wonderful if I were like Sir Gawain and could receive a magic token that would protect and keep me safe from all harm?"

To Kim, Lorette's words seemed cryptic. "Where are you?"

"I'm at my mother's place. That's one reason I don't want to talk much at the moment. She might overhear. I don't want her involved."

Kim found it significant that Lorette wasn't at her own apartment or with Jim. She would have liked to ask more questions, but it seemed inappropriate.

"We'll talk tomorrow then."

"Right. I'll be at the library around noon and if I can't make it at that time for some reason, I'll let you know."

The conversation ended as abruptly as it had begun. Kim tossed and turned for hours afterward, unable to rest peacefully, filled with a sense of foreboding.

On Friday morning, Kim woke up at seven. Looking at a box of oatmeal, but unable to bring herself to cook it no matter how healthy it might be, she rummaged in the cupboard and found a half empty package of cold cereal. As tired as she felt, Kim doubted that even the breakfast of champions would totally rejuvenate her. She glanced in the refrigerator for orange juice or oranges, and finding neither, made do with some tomato juice which, having been there for a while, had seen better days and thickened. She whimsically toasted the air with the beverage.

"Bottoms up. Drink it before it clots." She imagined herself the Queen of the Damned and managed half a glass before spilling the rest down the kitchen sink drain. By the time she'd gotten herself together, it was after eight. She hurried out the door. If there was one thing certain, she never wanted to be late for work. Wendell revered punctuality the way cavemen worshipped fire. But as Robert Burns so aptly put it, the best laid plans of mice and men gang aft agley. A highway accident backed traffic up for miles. She got to the parking deck at 9:30 a.m., one-half hour late for work.

There was no point telling Wendell about the accident. He himself was punctilious, too much the perfect machine ever to be late. He was the first person to arrive in the morning. Long before anyone else came, he was at his desk, working his computer programs, sipping a cup of coffee or reading the *Times*. As she breathlessly walked behind the reference desk, Wendell was there looking meaningfully at his watch. She felt her face color.

"You will, of course, make up the extra half-hour today."

This was definitely not the time to ask his permission to leave for lunch at noon instead of whatever time he deemed appropriate. She would just play it by ear and hope Lorette was able to wait for her if it proved necessary.

As it turned out, Lorette never came. Wendell informed her that she could go to lunch at one, and Lorette still hadn't arrived by then. Kim was concerned because it wasn't like Lorette to forget an engagement. One of her friend's good traits was reliability. The rest of the day, she had a nagging feeling that something was very wrong. Her awareness kicked in big-time.

But work kept her busy and diverted her thoughts from Lorette and her problems. Students came and went all afternoon in need of help with research papers. And then there were the phone calls. One man claimed he was calling from Zurich, Switzerland, and needed to find out if they had a certain treatise.

Rita Mosler turned up her needle nose at this bit of information. "They'll tell you anything to get you to hurry up and get them the information they want. He's probably calling from Kinley Hall around the corner." Rita was an old-timer and somewhat jaded by the job. People rarely went to Rita for help when they could ask Kim. Rita was too sharp-tongued. Her caustic manner frightened students almost as much as her bony, arthritic fingers that resembled bent twigs. Her customary expression was that of someone who'd swallowed a lemon whole.

Later, Rita received a phone call from the Mad Movie Fan, as she referred to him. "Take it for me," she said. "I can't stand to talk to that idiot again. If I do, I'll give him a piece of my mind."

Kim got on the line. It was an old man's shaky voice. He asked her to look up information for him and she did so as he held on. He wanted the original cast list, director and producer of *A Streetcar Named Desire.*

"It didn't seem like too much to ask," Kim said after she'd finished with him. "He's likely a shut-in or something."

"He's a pest. Calls everyday with some silly question. I'd like to wring the old geezer's neck."

"The man is probably just lonely," Kim said. There were times when she would have liked to phone somebody and just talk for no particular reason herself. She understood about feeling isolated.

The workday ended a great deal better than it began. For one thing, Wendell seemed preoccupied most of the morning and left for the day early. She knew he had some teaching responsibilities at the school of library science and was grateful for it. She'd been braced for some sort of subtle punishment and was relieved that it had been averted.

That evening, she phoned Lorette's apartment as soon as she got home from work. There was no answer. She called again later. Still no answer. She would have phoned Jim, but did not know his address or phone number. Anxious, Kim decided to drive over to Lorette's apartment around nine o'clock to see why she wasn't answering her phone. She couldn't shake the sense that her friend was in serious danger, even if that seemed illogical.

Kim rang the doorbell several times but no one answered. She could see light emanating from the interior. Trying the door, she found it was not locked. Taking a deep breath, she walked into the apartment and called out Lorette's name as she moved. The kitchenette light was on, and it partially illuminated the living room area. As her eyes adjusted to the limited light, she saw that Lorette was on the couch, slumped over. At first, Kim thought her friend was sleeping, but when she went to touch her, Lorette felt oddly cold. She called Lorette's name again, but there was no answer. She tried to lift her friend's head up. This proved difficult because Lorette's neck seemed stiff; Kim saw her eyes were open, staring at her sightlessly, the corneas clouded. And then she knew. Oh God, she knew!

Her hand trembled as she used the telephone to call 911. She simply stood there and stared blankly as if in a trance until the paramedics arrived. She could not believe that Lorette was dead. It brought back awful memories, terrible memories of another time and place.

"Lorette, what were you going to tell me?" she asked.

But the dead did not always speak, and this was one of those times. The silence was deafening.

Police and ambulance arrived together. They asked her questions that she somehow managed to answer, although later she could not remember what she said. When they put Lorette's body on the stretcher and covered her, Kim let out a cry of astonishment and disbelief. The sound came out of her involuntarily, as if someone had punched a hard blow to her stomach, knocking the wind out of her. She could barely catch her breath.

A young policeman in uniform took hold of her. "Ma'am, are you all right?"

"No, I'm not. She was my friend."

He had a small notebook that he began writing in, and started by asking her name and address.

"How long did you know the deceased?"

Lorette, *the deceased.* The words held no reality for her. "I knew her for several years. She is, I mean was, a graduate student."

They surrounded her now, four men in blue uniforms. The policeman who'd been speaking continued to ask her questions. She tried to answer slowly, to organize her scattered thoughts, reluctant to say very much. The questions they were asking, did they believe she had something to do with Lorette's death? All she could think of was how badly she wanted to get away from here and go back to her own apartment. She had an awful feeling that she'd somehow let her friend down, that there was something she could have done to help her but hadn't. She tried to shake it.

Kim slept very little that night and was grateful she did not have to go to work the next day. The schedule called for one Saturday or Sunday per week. She would work Sunday, but not today. She felt paralyzed with depression. She didn't get dressed, but merely lay on the sofa bed lost in thought.

At ten that morning, the telephone rang. The voice at the other end asked for her and then identified himself as a Lieutenant Gardner of the Wilson Township Police. He wanted to talk to her, he said, and asked if he could drop by the apartment in an hour if it was convenient. The voice, resonant and deep, sounded sympathetic and familiar.

Acquiescing to his request, she wondered what he could possibly want to ask her. *I'll make the bed. I'll get dressed. I'll cook myself an egg. But I just want to stay curled up in a fetal position and not talk to anyone.* Even as she thought it, she knew it was sick. *Life goes on.*

Kim recognized the policeman who came to her door, wondered why she hadn't realized who he was before. He was just as tall and well built, with the same calm, steady gray eyes. But he was no longer casually dressed as he had been at the library. His conservative gray suit matched his eyes, making him look more like an accountant than a law enforcement officer. His manner was friendly and not the least bit intimidating. But Kim wasn't fooled. She studied his rugged, masculine features. This was a formidable, dangerous man, even if he chose not to emphasize those qualities.

Michael Gardner took out his shield and showed it to her.

69

"May I come in and talk with you? I've been assigned to check into the death of Lorette Campbell. I understand you found her body and identified yourself as a friend of the deceased."

Kim could only manage to nod her head. For a moment, his eyes met hers. Then he was staring at her, connecting on a metaphysical level. She resented the intrusion into her psyche, into her soul, and met his gaze with defiance. Something passed between them, a jolt of kinetic energy. She recognized it for what it was. Why should there be this potent attraction between them? She quickly looked away, confused and frightened, denying the chemistry—and that something more.

He followed her into the living area and sat down on a straight-back chair, removing a small notebook and clicking a pen.

"I want to go over what you told the uniformed officers last night." Much to her relief, his tone was polite and professional. "I have some questions for you."

She furrowed her brow. "I told them everything I knew. Why do I have to go over it again? It was awful." *Careful what you say to him. You can't trust a policeman.*

He gave her a kind look. "I don't know if you're aware of this, but your friend didn't die of natural causes."

She did not respond, waiting for him to say more. He studied her thoughtfully, no doubt observing her lack of surprise, and then he continued.

"What was your overall impression of Ms. Campbell's health?"

The question bewildered her. What was he driving at?

"She was a little on the thin side and sometimes seemed nervous, but basically she was in excellent health."

"Did she take drugs in your presence?"

"No, never." So that was it; they'd somehow found out about Lorette's past history. That hadn't taken very long.

"You never saw her ingest illegal substances of any kind?"

"I said not." He was beginning to annoy her. "Maybe Lorette had some problems a long time ago, but she overcame them. She didn't drink, smoke or take drugs at any time since I've known her, and that's been several years."

"I wasn't referring to her past. She took a substance that brought on her death. Ms. Reynolds, we found cocaine in her purse and in a hypodermic needle that had been injected into the vein in her arm. The ME has done a preliminary postmortem exam and has ruled her death heart failure brought on by an overdose of the drug. He estimates she injected a full gram of coke. That's a very heavy dose. What do you think about that?"

Kim began pacing the room. "I'd have to say someone murdered her." Her eyes met his with directness. "She would never have become involved with drugs or alcohol again."

"You're a loyal friend, but there's a big difference between fact and opinion."

She shook her head with conviction. "No. I knew her, and I'm positive."

He looked at her askance, clearly pitying her naïveté. "Are you a detective or a psychologist?"

"Neither, but I deal with people every day on my job, too, and I get to understand how they feel and think."

"How close was your friendship?"

"There were limits to it. We were both very private people. However, she was frightened lately. Things had been happening to her. She asked for my help. Really, I think she just wanted someone she felt she could trust to confide in."

"I think you'd better tell me what was going on." His strong, square jaw implied character and tenacity. He reminded her of a pit bull.

And so she told him everything: about the threatening letters, the auto accident, the harassment at school. It was a relief to unburden herself to a professional this way. But when he asked for names, she felt awkward. She didn't want to tell him about Jim or even mention Professor Packingham, so she shook her head and pretended ignorance. Lieutenant Gardner didn't press her; he looked at her as if he knew exactly what she was thinking and how she felt. It was just a police trick, she decided. He couldn't possibly guess at or understand her reluctance. She wasn't certain she fully understood it herself.

"You see any copies of those threatening letters?"

"Not the second one," she admitted. "Lorette threw away the first one, but I think the second was still in her apartment. She was going to show it to me but never got around to it. Yesterday, she was supposed to have lunch with me. She said she'd learned something important in connection with the trouble she was having. I was also supposed to check into the whereabouts of an inferno collection that she believed was kept at the university." Kim explained about her job at the university.

"Inferno collection? What's that?" The gray eyes had sharpened to the color of steel.

"They're special collections that aren't open to the general public."

"Secret stuff?"

"Not necessarily. Inferno collections really belong to another era. Banned books. Victorian sensibilities. An inferno collection has to do with manuscripts that would be considered morally unacceptable. You can see how that normally wouldn't exist at a university where free thinking and intellectual awareness are the status quo."

"Yeah, I suppose." The policeman scratched his ear pensively. "But then why was Ms. Campbell asking you about it?"

"I can't say. No one seems to have heard of any such thing. We have special collections, but they're all open to our patrons."

"You think your friend knew something that got her into

trouble? Something about this inferno collection?"

"I don't know. It's possible. I could ask around more."

"Let me do that," he told her. "It's my job. You don't want to see me unemployed, do you? I got a family to support."

Kim stiffened. Of course, he would have a family, a wife and children. He was around thirty-five, maybe a few years older. Why wouldn't she expect him to have a family?

"You sure you can't tell me more about who her friends were?" Back to that again. He was a shrewd interrogator.

"She didn't have a lot of friends."

"Well, I'll be talking to her family and her teachers. Maybe they have some ideas. Meantime, I'll keep the investigation open. If you find anything out or you remember anything that you think would help, just call, I know you've got my number, and ask for Mike Gardner. I'll get back to you."

She was relieved when he left. Talking to a police detective was a frightening experience and had been terribly stressful. Still, she supposed he wasn't as bad as some of them. But there had been that tension between them, that frisson of awareness.

I want to talk to Ma, she thought, knowing it was a mistake before she dialed the familiar number. But she needed to hear that reassuring voice once again, even if it brought back painful memories.

"How you doing, honey?"

Somehow, she had to talk about it, about finding Lorette, about being questioned by the police. The story poured from her like wine escaping a shattered bottle. Ma listened quietly, speaking only when Kim had finally finished.

"What a terrible thing to happen. That poor girl! I realize it wasn't easy for you talking to the police, but you have to remember, they're just doing their jobs. Mostly, they help people."

Ma did have a way of making her feel better. She remembered

how it had been when she was little. Even though Ma worked hard at the supermarket, there had never been a time when she didn't care about "my little girl."

"You're very generous. I wish I could feel the same way, but I don't trust them. I haven't forgotten the way they treated us afterwards."

"Yes, dear, but it was understandable under the circumstances."

"No, it wasn't. We didn't do anything. They acted like it was our fault."

"Really, they didn't. You were very upset, very sensitive."

But she hadn't forgotten what the one with the beer-belly and the red face had said to Ma: "You must have known or suspected. You might have prevented it from happening."

"Ma, did you find Jen's diary?"

There was a hesitation on the other end. "It would be better if you forgot about it."

"I want to read it through."

"Your Uncle Joe called. Said it's beautiful in Idaho this time of year. Wanted me to send his regards and those of Aunt Sarah."

"That's nice to hear." She knew Ma was changing the subject. There was nothing very subtle about her. All the same, she wanted to know about Jen. Ma could have told her the details of Jen's death, but that was one of the secrets they never discussed. A house full of secrets. A house of pain and anguish, a house where people lived in denial. That was how she had grown up. She was weary of lies, deceptions and half-truths. Since Ma wouldn't tell her, she would have to discover other ways to find out.

It was the same with Lorette. There was a need for connection. Lorette had wanted her friendship and her help, but she wouldn't tell her the whole truth. Now Lorette was dead. Should she try to probe further? If someone had murdered Lorette as she suspected, what would stop that individual from trying to kill her if she became too nosy? But she wanted, needed, to know more. She could always call that hot hunk of a policeman, tell him everything she knew. No, only as a last resort would she do that.

CHAPTER SEVEN

Since she had to be at work by nine a.m. on Monday, Kim decided to go over to Kinley Hall early and walk around. There were several people she wanted to talk with about Lorette. She wasn't certain what she was going to say, but she couldn't just forget about what had happened. Someone had threatened Lorette; someone had killed her. Maybe she could find out the reason. Maybe she just needed to find a way to lessen her own feelings of grief and guilt.

Kinley hadn't changed very much since the days when she was taking the courses that led to her Master's Degree in English. She had thought to talk to one or two of the secretaries, but had forgotten they didn't start until nine o'clock. Consulting her watch, she realized it was now 8:30. She walked through the nearly deserted building toward the graduate student lounge, striding along the central corridor with its old classrooms on either side of the hall. The lounge was in the furthest corner at the rear of the corridor right near the entrance/exit that led out to the parking lot. At this hour, it was rather empty. One or two grad students who taught freshman writing courses stopped by to check their mailboxes, but no one actually occupied the lounge.

The room itself was spartan, with four or five beat-up chairs and a table that would later hold a hot water urn. An array of instant coffee, tea bags, Coffee-Mate and white foam cups adorned the table in permanent, unappealing, institutional splendor, as worthy of a prison as a university.

She looked in the mailbox marked "Campbell, L." and found that it was empty except for a Xerox announcing some organizational mixer. There were no answers here. She would come back another time and maybe talk with some of the students. Unfortunately, it was too early to catch Dr. Simpson-Watkins. She very much wanted to ask him who had tried to boot Lorette out of the school by sullying her reputation.

Consulting the schedule of classes, she found that Dr. Forbes would be teaching upstairs shortly. She knew Lorette considered him an outstanding teacher and had been pleased to get a class with him this semester. Kim had never taken a course with him, but was aware of his reputation. Supposedly, he was an expert in the art of classical rhetoric as well as the study of occult literature. When she'd briefly observed his technique as a lecturer, she'd seen for herself that he mesmerized his classes. He also frightened his students. She'd sensed something dark about the man. She decided to stick around for a while.

The only person in Dr. Forbes's classroom at that hour was a custodian. She watched him clean wastepaper baskets and straighten chairs. He was a small man, no more than five-foot four at most, but he was broad and well muscled with a round Slavic-looking face. Embroidered on his shirt was the name Frank.

"Is there any problem if I stay here a while?"

"No, except the class won't start for at least another hour."

"That long?"

"Dr. Forbes, he doesn't start to teach right away. Sometimes he talks to students before he begins. He also likes to talk to me."

"It sounds like you know him pretty well."

The custodian smiled. "I do. He doesn't like everyone, you know. He's very particular. He likes the way I clean. I'm thorough. He even hired me to clean his house for him."

"You must be very good at your job."

"He says he especially likes me 'cause I'm not taller than him." The custodian spoke unguardedly with a kind of naive pride, almost the way a child would. She wondered if he were mildly retarded. A heavily tattooed arm reached over for some papers carelessly tossed on the floor.

"Dr. Forbes has a thing about height?"

The custodian smiled at her and leaned forward as if he were sharing a secret with her. "He's a real important man, you know. But he likes men who are smaller than him and women who are much taller—calls them his giraffes." He gave her a wink.

"I can see you take pride in your work," she said. "You probably know some of the students. Would you remember a tall, black-haired woman, a student in Dr. Forbes's class? She was well dressed and attractive, like a model. Lorette Campbell by name. Maybe Dr. Forbes mentioned her to you?"

Frank's small, flat eyes showed no recognition. "I wouldn't know. There are so many students here every day."

"A very beautiful woman?"

"They're all beautiful to me."

She nodded and left. There was no point waiting around. She would just have to come back another time.

During her lunch break, Kim phoned Lorette's mother. She wasn't sure what to say to the woman, but she knew the call was necessary. Miranda's voice was soft and solemn, different from when they had met in person.

"A police officer told me," she said. "I still can't believe it."

Kim expressed her condolences. They spoke only briefly. Miranda told her the day and time of Lorette's funeral, and Kim wrote down the information carefully. Miranda also asked if she would say a few words at the funeral.

Two days later, she drove south for the service at a funeral chapel not far from where Miranda lived. She wondered if she should have come. Funerals were for the living not the dead. Lorette was gone; this gesture was not really for her. Who then? Perhaps herself. It was as if a part of her were being buried. Yet she and Lorette had never been what other people would call truly close. Still, there was a part of Lorette that was very much the same as herself, a likeness between them. It was fitting that she be here today.

She was kept company by Jim Davis. He looked as if he were ill. His eyes were bloodshot, his clothing disheveled. There was no need to ask how he was taking Lorette's death. During the service, she took his hand. He gave her a small, grateful smile. A clergyman spoke briefly in the chapel saying the usual things that people did about the dead. It was obvious to Kim that he didn't know Lorette at all. After the empty eulogy, Miranda rose with some effort. She said very little about her daughter, except that she had loved her. Her tall, lean body swayed liked the mast of a sailboat. Then she asked Kim to say a few words.

Ill at ease, Kim came to the podium with sweaty palms. She told these strangers that what Lorette loved most was poetry and she'd chosen to read a poem that seemed appropriate. It was Edna St. Vincent Millay's "Dirge Without Music." She cleared her throat and began in a clear, steady voice. Her voice faltered only as she finished.

Most of the people present were unfamiliar to her, but she went on to the cemetery anyway. The procession to the cemetery, a small chain of cars connected like a spinal cord, crept along under the brain-matter-gray sky. It had begun to rain, matching the somber mood of the day. It seemed as if the sky's tears were washing away memory, cleansing grief, like a surgeon's scalpel performing a lobotomy.

Jim stood beside her at the cemetery. His pain was palpable.

As the clergyman recited the Lord's Prayer, followed by the Twenty-Third Psalm, those present joined in. Kim heard many voices, those of the living and the dead. She saw a clear, translucent vision of Lorette shedding tears of sorrow above her own grave. Kim wanted desperately to reach out to her.

After it was over, Lorette's coffin was lowered into the ground. Each person shoveled a bit of earth into the open grave, and then they left Lorette with the dead.

Jim turned to Kim as they walked back to their automobiles. "Did she tell you that she decided not to marry me?"

"No, we hadn't discussed it." Kim felt awkward talking about such a personal matter. She had no desire to hear his problems, but she didn't want to be rude to him.

"It wasn't like we really argued or anything. She just said she wasn't ready to marry anybody."

"I think she'd been hurt in the past and that stopped her from trusting people very easily." Kim was aware she was talking as much about herself as about Lorette.

"She trusted you though. She told me that. She said you were the kind of person who would never betray a confidence. Did she talk to you about me?"

There was a kind of urgency to the question; he wasn't just fishing for compliments.

"She only said that she cared about you, nothing else." Kim meant to be kind but didn't know if she succeeded. She studied him thoughtfully. Did she sense relief on his part?

He saw her look of doubt, and ran nervous fingers through his sand-colored hair. "I would never have hurt her."

"Someone did."

He pushed his hands deep into his pockets and dug his booted foot into the grassy earth.

"I loved her."

"I want to find out what happened to her. She deserves that

much. I don't want people to think she killed herself with drugs. I don't believe it's true."

"Neither do I. I'll help you find out the truth." He seemed earnest and caring.

"Good, I need help." That was hard to admit, because she rarely asked other people for anything, preferring to do things in her own way by herself. But this was different. "Lorette told me that she was asked to voluntarily withdraw from the doctoral program. Did she talk to you about it?"

He shook his head. "I knew she was really angry and upset about something, but she didn't see fit to confide in me."

"Do you have any idea who might have known about Lorette's past drug problem? I think whoever killed her had to have known. Since Lorette was such a private person, she wouldn't tell just anyone."

There was a slight hesitation on his part, then a blinking of his eyes. "She did tell me," he said. "But I don't have any idea who else she might have confided in."

Jim didn't appear to know any more than she did. Yet she got the distinct feeling he might be holding something back. Why would he do that, since he claimed to want to find out who killed Lorette as much as she did? After exchanging a few words with Miranda, Kim got into her Toyota and drove back to the highway. She resolved to see the matter through to the best of her abilities. If matters were reversed and it was she who had been murdered, would Lorette have done as much? Probably not, but then friendship needn't be equated or balanced on a scale. This was something Kim felt was important and necessary. Logic dictated that she should leave all investigation to the police. But they clearly didn't think that Lorette had been murdered and she definitely did.

The following day, Kim found herself on the early lunch

schedule and hurried over to Kinley Hall again. It was just 11:30 a.m., and Dr. Ian Simpson-Watkins, Director of Graduate English Studies, sat in his office looking patrician, sporting a reddish beard, a muttonchop affair distinctly Victorian. He wore a brown Harris tweed jacket which added to his distinguished mien.

"Your secretary wasn't out front. I thought perhaps I might take just a moment or two of your time."

"Certainly. I'm always available to students."

"I'm not exactly a student anymore, but I've come to talk to you about one."

"And how may I help you?" Simpson-Watkins looked across his desk at her in a detached and decidedly superior manner. She had the uncomfortable feeling that she was being examined through an X-ray machine, and the professor could see right through her.

"It's about Lorette Campbell."

The professor sat back in his chair. "Yes, her death was most unfortunate."

She moistened her lips. "Shortly before Lorette died, she told me you informed her she was no longer an acceptable student. You wanted her to leave the program voluntarily. Could you tell me why you came to that decision?"

"I do not see the relevance," he said through thinning lips, his manner stern and intimidating.

"Someone gave you information about Lorette's background. It might have been the same individual who was harassing and threatening her. That person was obviously out to destroy Lorette. She didn't know why, or if she did, she was too frightened to tell anyone."

He stood up, rising to his full stature, which was impressive. "That information is confidential. I am unable to discuss it with you." In a gesture of dismissal, his hand shooed her away as if she were a mosquito he would like to squash.

She stood her ground. "Has it occurred to you that this person might be implicated in her death?"

He remained an unyielding figure, folding his hands over his chest. "Utterly absurd! As I understand it, her death was either accident or suicide. No one wished her harm. The poor girl was obviously very troubled."

"Was she? Or are you making yourself an accomplice to a murder?"

"What nonsense." He pursed his lips stubbornly.

"Is it? Whoever told you negative things about Lorette obviously hated or feared her enough to try to destroy her career. Lorette was very angry. Maybe she guessed who that individual was. There could have been a very ugly scene. This other party might have decided to kill her. She'd already received several threatening letters. Did you know about that?"

"Foolish conjecture," Simpson-Watkins said stonily. But he rubbed his hand across his beard in an uneasy gesture.

"Perhaps you won't talk to me, but you might have to discuss the matter with the police."

"If they should ask, but there has been no such request as yet. And you are in no position to request confidential information. Now if you'll excuse me, I'm already late for an appointment. Good day." He looked at his watch meaningfully.

That hadn't gone very well. But investigation was hardly her forte. She'd surprised herself by not becoming tongue-tied, as she'd half-expected. Still, she had no intention of giving up quite so easily.

She next paid a visit to Pat Norris, the graduate English department's secretary who was back at her desk and, as usual, trying to orchestrate three things at once. She was cradling a phone, typing a memo and talking to a student. Kim stood in line, patiently waiting her turn. When she got to speak to Pat, the phone interrupted and Pat was off and running for another five minutes.

"Do you want a cup of coffee?" The secretary indicated the machine she kept near her desk.

Kim replied that she wasn't interested in coffee. She tried not to look at her watch while she waited. Finally, Pat found time to talk to her.

"Okay, let's step outside for a minute. I could use some fresh air and a drag on a cigarette."

Somehow the two actions did not seem synonymous, but Kim decided to refrain from saying so. After all, she needed help; courting hostility was not the best way to get it. They walked out through the front of the building.

"So how have you been? Is there life after leaving grad English?" Pat raised a questioning brow.

"Believe it or not, there is. But I'm still with the university, over at the library."

"That's good to hear." Pat lit up and inhaled deeply on a filtered cigarette. "I'm no good without my cancer stick. It's going to kill me, but I can't seem to break the addiction. So what did you want to see me about?"

"I wondered if you know anything about why your boss would think Lorette Campbell was unworthy to continue in the doctoral program."

Pat anxiously flicked an ash at the ground. A small, slender woman, she fairly burst with nervous energy. "How would I know? He doesn't confide in me."

"When I was a student here, it seemed to me that you knew more of what was going on than anyone else in the place."

"Well, you were wrong." Was it fear that caused her sudden animosity?

"I don't think I'm wrong. Dr. Ian Simpson-Watkins doesn't know enough to wipe his nose if you don't remind him. You know every student's name; he doesn't."

Pat wouldn't look her in the eye.

"You must have noticed something, someone, maybe over-heard part of a conversation."

Pat ground out her cigarette with an air of finality. "I have to get back to work. Good luck with whatever it is you're doing these days."

There was a double entendre there and Kim knew it. She watched Pat walk quickly back into the building and tried to think what to do next. It was pretty obvious she wasn't going to learn anything of consequence this way. She was not a sleuth; that fact had been driven home to her in no uncertain terms. She lacked authority, and she was discouraged. Yet she felt that she somehow owed it to Lorette to continue, to try to ferret out more information.

Kim decided to approach it the way she did a reference question. Weren't they also puzzles? Problems that required searching for answers? This was no different, except maybe for the element of risk. She didn't even want to begin to think about that, except that she couldn't help realizing that something Lorette knew might have gotten her killed. And here she was trying to find out what that was. Dumb and dumber? Kim shuddered involuntarily.

CHAPTER EIGHT

Was it Albert Einstein who said that common sense is not so common? She believed it was good old Albert. Probably her next action was less than sensible, but it seemed the right thing to do. Lorette had said that Dr. Packingham was sexually harassing her. Could he have taken it a step further?

She consulted the graduate course schedule and then arranged to work a split shift, trading hours with another librarian so that she could get to Dr. Packingham's seminar class before it began at the next meeting.

The professor was late and the students were waiting for him, some out in the hallway, others in the meeting room. She recognized Jim Davis pacing up and down the corridor looking like a corralled bull.

Glancing down at her watch, she eventually grew impatient herself. She was standing beside a girl whose hair was notable. The color was one-third brassy blond, one-third tangerine orange, and a final third grass green. It also looked as if she'd last styled it with a chain saw.

"You've done quite a job with your hair," Kim said in a neutral tone of voice.

The girl smiled at her as if she'd been complimented. "I'm expressing my individualism. Like Emerson said, the American scholar should be an innovator not an imitator."

"So you consider yourself a scholar?"

The features, slightly dreamy and disoriented, became

animated. "Of course I am. I'm just misunderstood, like all true intellects. It's nice to talk to someone older who doesn't have a closed mind. I mean, there really is such a generation gap, don't you think?"

Kim felt a tad guilty for considering the student something of an airhead by first appearances, which she realized were often deceiving.

One of the young male students came toward the girl with a cool appraising look. "Hey, Sandy, very trendy. I like all that frizz and frazzle. Hair with three different colors though? You keeping that look?"

"Sure, why not." She threw him a self-satisfied smile. "Now I can have triple the attraction, triple the fun. I'm a trinity." She gave a short laugh.

Jim joined them at that point. He looked anything but cheerful.

Sandy turned to him. "I'm sorry about your girlfriend. She seemed really nice."

"Yeah, she was. Hell's bells, I don't know what I'm doing here today! I'm gonna see if I can still drop this course. I only took it to be with Lorette."

He left abruptly, and Sandy turned to her. "Awfully studly, don't you think?"

Kim didn't respond; she hadn't thought of Jim in that way.

Sandy continued. "It's too bad about his girlfriend."

"Was Dr. Packingham flirting with her?"

Sandy looked surprised, half-moon eyebrows rising. "Well, yeah, maybe. I mean he's definitely a womanizer. You know the type, right? I saw him come on to her at Dr. Forbes's house."

Kim felt a sense of instant intense interest. What had Lorette been doing at Dr. Forbes's house? "I don't know very much about Dr. Forbes. He's something of a mystery man, isn't he?"

"Oh, you've probably heard the stories about him that

circulate on campus."

"When was Lorette at his house?"

Sandy's light blue eyes were slightly out of focus, as though she'd been smoking a joint before class, but she seemed to be making an effort to concentrate. "I guess it was a week—no, two weeks ago. I'm not sure."

"What was Lorette doing at Dr. Forbes's house?"

"Oh, I guess what most people do when they're invited there." Sandy blinked several times.

"Why do I get the impression this isn't leading anywhere?"

Sandy giggled. "It's not a good idea to talk about Dr. Forbes. He doesn't like it. You know what Ambrose Bierce said: speak of the devil and he'll hear you."

"Yes, but you told me yourself that you believe in nonconformity like Emerson."

"That's right. Truth with a capital T, and T for transcendentalist. That's me."

"So you were invited to Dr. Forbes's house?"

Sandy lowered her eyes for the first time. "Well, not exactly. You see, my friend Nick brought me along. He didn't think the old man would mind. But as it turned out, he kind of did and I got kicked out. Dr. Forbes picks and chooses who comes to his special gatherings. Big shot, you know."

"What about Lorette?"

"No, Forbes welcomed her like she was someone he especially wanted there. I remember he called her a giraffe because she was so much taller than him. He was telling her how he had interpreted her handwriting and how well she was suited to his group."

"What sort of group?"

She shook her head. "Nick's pretty tight-lipped about that. If Forbes had let me stay, I might have found out."

"Your friend Nick was invited?"

"Yeah, he's one of the professor's chosen. He makes out like it's a real honor to be accepted. Only a select few ever are. You know the old man's reputation as a literary scholar and critic, don't you?"

"Only by hearsay."

Sandy blew upward through her mouth, her feathered razor-cut bangs floating momentarily like fluffs of windblown dandelions.

"Gosh, I thought everybody in the grad program read his books. He's like a genius. Me, I'd do anything to be part of his coterie."

"Why is that, Sandy?"

Her eyes opened wide and glassy as those of a Barbie doll. Then she leaned toward Kim and spoke in a conspiratorial whisper. "Last time Nick was at one of those gatherings, he came to my place afterwards. It was awfully late and he was really high. They pass around some real quality stuff, you know?"

If Sandy was right, and there was no reason to doubt her veracity, the professor's "chosen" were heavily into drugs. Lorette had been killed with an overdose of cocaine. Kim put little stock in coincidence. This was definitely something she ought to find out about.

Sandy leaned toward her, voice barely above a whisper. "You know what? Nick, he wouldn't like me telling you this. I mean, you seem okay, but Nick doesn't trust everybody. So don't tell anyone else about the drugs. You won't mention it, will you?"

"Only to the police," she said.

Sandy smiled. "I like the way you joke around with a straight face. You know, you'd be real attractive if you wore some stylish clothes and did something with your hair. I could fix it for you."

Kim shuddered involuntarily. "Maybe we can talk again and you can help me. Ask your friend about Dr. Forbes's gatherings. I'm interested in mind-expanding experiences myself."

"You are? Cool. Yeah, I could do that. See, I knew right away that you would understand. You got cow eyes. Lots of soul in cow eyes."

Kim took Sandy's phone number and told her that she would phone her soon.

Then Jim returned. "I can withdraw from the course. It's not too late. I'm not stuck here."

"Oh, that's great," Sandy said, looking less than pleased.

Professor Packingham finally decided to make his entrance. She thought he seemed preoccupied, his pinched features as pale and white as a peeled summer squash. Kim came toward him.

"Would it be possible for me to have a brief word with you before today's class?"

"Hm? Well, yes I suppose. Although you might wish to set up an appointment instead."

"I promise not to take much of your time." She noticed that he and Jim exchanged glaring looks.

"Still around, Mr. Davis? I thought you might be home on the range by this time."

Jim's bulging biceps strained the material of his blue chambray shirt as his fists tensed in anger.

"Are you planning to withdraw from this course perhaps?" The professor looked hopeful.

"You got it. Just one thing, if I ever find out that you had anything to do with Lorette's death, I'll personally kick your sorry butt all the way back to England."

Packingham registered surprise and then indignation. His pale features reddened. "Get out of here!"

Jim turned and abruptly left, his eyes dark as storm clouds.

"I plan on a short class today," he told the group at large as everyone gathered around him in the seminar room. "I'm afraid I haven't been able to do the sort of preparation required. I've had things on my mind the last few days. As to Ms. Campbell's recent demise, it's a bloody shame. I'm certain we all regret the loss of her presence on this earth."

Kim realized that this was not an appropriate time to discuss Lorette's death with the professor. She left quietly, uncertain what she would have asked him if they had spoken. And because of the conversation with Sandy, her mental exploration had taken a different turn.

Maybe Dr. Forbes had something to do with Lorette's death. But besides the fact that Lorette had a class with the well-known scholar and had admired him, there was no reason to believe the association had become personal. Still, from what Sandy told her, Lorette was one of Forbes's chosen—whatever that meant. Why hadn't Lorette told her about that?

When her shift at the library resumed, Kim waited for a free moment to check the on-line computer catalog for a listing of Forbes's writings. It turned out that he was a prolific author. Most of his books were not in the stacks, as she would have expected. His work was in demand. She found articles in the bound periodicals located in the basement and photocopied some of them to peruse at her leisure.

Wendell eyed her askance as she resumed her post at the reference desk. "You've been gone a while," he said. "What were you doing?"

"Some work for a patron," she said, still a little breathless from her quick trip up the stairs. She quickly folded the photocopies so he couldn't read them.

"Which patron?" he asked suspiciously. He was a bulldog following the scent of mendacity.

"One of the English grad students. I promised her several days ago that I'd find certain information for her. In fact, she was the party who asked about inferno collections."

"I thought you told me it was an MLS candidate who was

looking for that information." His eyes narrowed. Clearly, he did not believe her. Wendell never missed anything, it seemed. But then she was a terrible liar, which was one reason she rarely digressed from the truth.

"Actually, we've had two separate requests. Are you sure we don't have information here at the university? Perhaps there's someone else who might know if we have an inferno collection, someone at the library of science or art and music?"

Behind his thick glasses, Wendell's eyes were mere slits. "Ms. Reynolds, I have given you all the information that exists. Now stay at this desk where you belong and help our patrons. There are many librarians who would give a great deal to have your job." That sounded to her very much like a threat.

He stormed off, back stiff as a broomstick, sharp nose held high. She sighed deeply. *Watch what you say to that man. Handle him as you would a cobra.* She wondered if somewhere within her was a desire for self-annihilation. God, she hated to think it. But why had she asked Wendell about the inferno collection again when she knew perfectly well that references to inferno collections irritated him? And she hadn't gotten a bit closer to learning anything; that was the worst part. She did need her position at the library. Being fired would not be the best job recommendation. Sometimes, she didn't understand herself. Obviously, she didn't understand Wendell either.

Kim didn't look at the articles she'd photocopied until arriving home that evening. Because it was past the rush hour, traffic flowed like water. Once she was away from the library, she was able to relax. Driving along listening to music loosened the tightness she'd been feeling in the pit of her stomach.

Sitting down on the couch in her apartment, Kim kicked off her shoes with a sense of relief and immediately reached for the photocopies. Forbes had written some interesting articles for scholarly journals. There was a unique interpretation of *Lord of the Flies* she found intellectually stimulating. Another article examined occult elements in the modern novel.

Her thoughts kept meandering back to Sandy and what she'd said about Professor Forbes. Sandy gave the impression of being a bubble-gum brain, but she was foolish, not stupid. If Sandy thought there was something peculiar about Forbes, it was likely to be the case. Hadn't she sensed it herself? What had he involved Lorette in? If it were some sort of experimenting with drugs, Lorette would never have stood still for it. Kim was sure of that. Perhaps Lorette had threatened to expose his coterie? It could be a motive for murder.

She wanted to talk with Forbes, but not before at least reading some more of what he wrote. She knew very little about the man except that he had the reputation of possessing a rapier tongue; she had no desire for sharp thrusts in her direction. Before she spoke to him, she must be prepared. Knowing his work would afford some form of protection. She could stand up for her beliefs and had done so in the past, but she knew the cost. She wished she had more poise and self-confidence. Nothing, it seemed, ever came easily to her.

An idea occurred and she determined to act on it. She fished in her pocket and found Sandy's phone number and dialed it. The phone rang several times before an answering machine picked up. Kim left her name and number and asked that the girl phone her back when she got in. She was rewarded by a return call a half-hour later. Kim identified herself in case Sandy had forgotten who she was.

"Yeah, I remember you. Lorette's friend. You were smart not to stay for the class. He wasn't very good today. Not prepared. Dead boring. He said a few words about Lorette though."

"Did he?"

"Yeah, he expressed his sorrow and regrets. It seemed genuine, like he really cared about her."

"I believe he said that before I left."

"Oh, yeah, that's right."

"The reason for my call, I was wondering if you could give me your friend Nick's last name and phone number."

There was a silence at the other end.

"Sandy?"

"Why would you want to know?" She was definitely nervous, perhaps a little suspicious.

"I'd like to talk with him about the night Lorette visited Dr. Forbes's house."

"I told you about that. He wouldn't know any more. Hey, are you a cop or something? Undercover narc maybe?"

"Of course not. You did say there was good stuff at those gatherings. I just wanted to find out more about it."

"You don't look the type."

"There is no type. Is Nick your boyfriend?" She wanted to keep the girl talking.

"Sort of—but not exactly. I mean, Nick and I go back a long way. We were both at Berkeley together. He helped edit our underground poetry magazine. He wouldn't like me discussing Dr. Forbes. Thinks he's God, you know?"

"Keep my name and number, and if you have anything you do want to tell me, let me know. You might be helping to find out who killed Lorette."

"She was killed?" Sandy sounded very upset.

"That's right."

Sandy wouldn't talk anymore, and the conversation ended abruptly.

Kim realized it was getting late and she ought to eat, even if she wasn't exactly hungry. She'd forgotten to stop for groceries, her thoughts too filled with how to go about solving the mystery of Lorette's death. She wanted to make a sandwich, but what bread remained looked as if it would yield a bumper crop of penicillin. She rummaged through the cabinet and located a can of Campbell's chicken noodle soup, which only made her think of Lorette again.

The phone began to ring as she poured water from the can into the heating soup. Stirring quickly, she left the pot on a small flame and hurried to pick up the phone on the third ring.

"I'm glad I caught you at home."

She recognized Don Bernard's mellifluous voice immediately and smiled. "I wasn't sure you'd ever want to talk to me again."

"Because you weren't seduced by my incredible charm and sex appeal?" His tone was light and teasing. Apparently, he wasn't angry at her.

"So your ego is not overly fragile. I'm glad to know that."

"I just called to find out how you are. I heard about Lorette, and I assumed you were upset." He sounded warm and caring.

"I am upset. I think someone murdered her."

There was a slight pause, as if the idea shocked him. "Surely not."

"She wouldn't commit suicide."

"No, I agree with you on that. However, it could have been accidental."

"Lorette might have used drugs years ago, but she was strictly off them."

"How can you ever be sure of something like that?"

"You sound like the policeman who questioned me. He doesn't seem to think it was murder either."

"Well, if a professional thinks that way . . ."

"No, I think she was a lot stronger and more resourceful than she appeared to be. Lorette died neither accidentally nor by suicide. I'm positive."

"You're a loyal friend, but much too stubborn."

"I'm convinced. In fact, I've been asking around, seeing what I can find out. I intend to get a line on who killed Lorette."

"I can't believe I'm hearing you correctly. Leave that job to the police." It seemed she couldn't have appalled him more if she confessed to being a murderer herself.

"I'm just asking a few people some questions."

"Don't put yourself in jeopardy."

She wanted to ask him about his relationship with Lorette, but couldn't bring herself to do it. The conversation ended and she went back to pensively stirring her soup. Whatever Lorette had once meant to Don, Kim really didn't want to know the details. Yet she recognized most definitely there had been something between them and it ended badly. Could Don also have wished Lorette harm—or more to the point, done something to hasten her demise? A deep sigh escaped Kim. So much for being a relentless detective in search of truth.

CHAPTER NINE

After eating dinner that evening, Kim had a thought. Although according to Lorette she and her mother had been less than close, Lorette's last phone call was from Miranda's place. Lorette was upset, frightened and worried. At a time like that, surely it was quite possible she would have confided in her mother. Kim checked her work schedule, found that she would be off the next day, and called Miranda. Lorette's mother, formal but courteous, agreed to meet with her late the following afternoon.

Kim slept poorly, her dreams reliving the moment when she'd discovered Lorette's body. In the dreams, Lorette was a lovely statue, her humanity stripped away, a work of art carved out of white marble. Then the statue came to life.

"Help me!" Lorette cried out. "You're the only one who can!"

Kim woke shaken and perspiring. Had it been a dream or a vision? Had Lorette's ghost come to haunt her? It was hours before she could sleep again.

In the morning, Kim did some marketing and cleaned her apartment. These practical activities kept her from feeling emotionally upset. She left to drive south on the early side, tense about talking with Miranda. The highway was not crowded; she enjoyed the sight and scent of pine forest and the occasional glimpse of deer. The directions were good and she had no trouble finding the duplex dwelling.

Miranda appeared to be waiting for her, answering the

doorbell with alacrity. "Come in, won't you?"

She looked unwell, her face pale, eyes puffy and slightly reddened. "You're welcome here, but since Lorette is gone, I don't know what we have to talk about."

Kim conceded a strong element of truth in what Miranda said. "There are certain things about Lorette's death that don't make sense."

Miranda showed her into a neat, uncluttered living room. Kim took a straight-back chair, sitting opposite the older woman.

"Nothing about her death makes any sense. A policeman phoned, the one who called me originally. He believes Lorette's death was accidental."

"I don't. Something was bothering her. She was frightened. Did she happen to talk to you about it?"

The tall, imposing woman straightened in her chair. "My daughter did not often confide in me."

"But she must have said something."

Miranda looked down, her fingers playing absently with the cameo brooch that adorned her snowy blouse. "Lorette and I spent many years apart. I sent her away to boarding school when she was fourteen. She considered it the worst sort of betrayal. I always loved her, but she didn't see it that way. I was a widow with two children. My son was a sophomore in college and was already pretty much on his own when I met Harold. He loved me and wanted to marry me, but he had been a bachelor all his life. Harold was not comfortable around children.

"I think Lorette was a little jealous of our relationship. In any case, she and Harold didn't hit it off. He didn't want her around. The marriage was just beginning, and I thought it was best for all concerned if she went away to school. She never forgave me. She felt I'd chosen him over her. She never trusted me again. As it happened, the marriage did not work out anyway. By the time Lorette was a junior in college, I was divorced. But things were never the same between us."

"What happened to Lorette?"

"That boarding school . . . it was a fine place, or so I thought. Very exclusive. Usually only the children of the wealthy go there. Harold was very generous to pay for it."

"Her drug problem started there?"

Miranda put her face in her hands, lowering her head. "Yes, there were drinking and drug parties among those girls. Who would think wealthy children would be so wild?"

"You can't equate money with morality."

"I suppose not. I found out what was happening when she was put on probation. She wouldn't talk to me. Like a stone wall she was. But she did stop, or at least I thought so, because there weren't any more bad reports from the school. In college, though, it happened all over again. She was away in Boston and I rarely saw her. She even stayed up there during the summers. I think she was under a lot of stress.

"I got a phone call from a hospital. She nearly died then. But they were very good with her, the doctors and nurses. She went into a drug-rehab program. I saw a real improvement after that. For a while, she was emaciated and weak, but she had spirit. She lost a year of school but went back and made it up. She told me that it had started when she went to the boarding school, because she was shy around those fancy girls from their privileged backgrounds and drinking gave her confidence. She promised never to take any drugs or alcohol again. She didn't want to destroy her life. I believed her. Lorette was strong-willed. Once she set her mind to something, she saw it through. Still, she had been under stress again."

"I don't think she changed her mind."

"But the police, wouldn't they know?"

"Not always. They see whatever is most probable, and mostly that's right. But they're not right about Lorette. Like the great bard said, appearances are deceiving."

A mist appeared over Miranda's eyes. "At least she had you, one real friend. She told me how supportive you were."

Kim felt as if she'd been punched in the stomach; she hadn't been that terrific a friend, at least not enough of one to make a difference. "Jim Davis cared about her too."

"That young man who came to the funeral? I think she changed her mind about him."

"Do you know why?"

Miranda shook her head, the iron-gray hair unmoving. "No idea. He seemed very nice. Lorette was odd about men though. She didn't always love wisely. She always tried to excite the admiration of men. Her father meant a great deal to her. She took his death very badly. She was his favorite. She needed that special kind of relationship and looked for it in every man she met. I suppose it won't matter now if I tell you about her. After she graduated from college, Lorette had a very good job with a big company in New York. She left because she got involved with her boss. They had an affair and she got pregnant. He was married, but wouldn't leave his wife. It ended up that she got an abortion. Afterwards, she couldn't stand to work there anymore. She felt very bitter. That was when she made the decision to go back to graduate school. She was very pleased when they offered her the teaching assistantship. Of course, I helped her out financially. I was happy for her. She was very ambitious and really loved college teaching, claimed it gave her a natural high. It would have been the perfect career for her."

"Did you ever discuss current men in her life?"

"No. As I told you, Lorette was short on trust. She did not confide in me. I only knew about her abortion because she was sick afterwards and had to come home for a time."

"I'm certain she appreciated what you tried to do for her."

Miranda smiled ruefully. "You are a very kind person. I appreciate you trying to find out what happened to Lorette. I don't want people referring to her as a drug addict. And like you, I don't believe she was one—at least, I don't want to believe it. I'll help in any way I can to clear her reputation." Miranda's fingers trembled as she moved her cameo first left and then right. "I just thought of something that might prove she didn't commit suicide."

Kim felt a sudden surge of excitement. "What is it?"

"Well, she left some library books here. I know that doesn't sound important on the surface, but what she said might matter."

"Which was?"

"That she'd be back on the weekend. She said she wanted to do some writing there in her old room where she wouldn't be disturbed. She was working on an article for a journal and hoped to get it published."

"Can I see the books? I'll bring them back to the library for you."

Kim followed Miranda into the bedroom that had once belonged to Lorette. There was nothing much to indicate a beautiful, intelligent girl had once lived here. The white, French provincial furniture was far from new, but kept immaculate, probably dating from before Lorette had left for boarding school. On the desk were several books on Satanism and the occult.

"Any idea what she was writing on this subject?"

"I haven't got a clue. I never knew Lorette to have much interest in the occult. She did talk about doing a paper for a colloquium though. She mentioned considering a new subject. I don't know anything about it, really."

Kim placed the three books in the trunk of her car and parted with Miranda on friendly terms. She hadn't really learned anything new or gained insight into what happened to her friend, but there were no regrets for time wasted. Kim now knew more about Lorette's past. That might prove helpful.

It had grown dark as she drove home. There was a sense of peace in watching the twilight, a velvet and lilac sky with a sash of pink satin swirling around it, like an old-fashioned party dress. It saddened her to think that Lorette would never again have the pleasure of seeing such a sight. How much easier it would be if she could still believe in the immortality of the soul, as she did as a child. To think of death as total and final was painful and tragic. She left Lorette's library books locked in the trunk of her car, went into her apartment and fixed herself a salad plate topped with cottage cheese, all the while lost in thought. She found little appetite for her creation.

She didn't sleep well that night either, tossing and turning until well past two in the morning. After that she rested fitfully, her sleep dominated by strange dreams. Lorette was being chased through the forest by a creature half-human, half-monster, something from a bad horror movie. Just as the demon caught up with Lorette, a transformation occurred. Lorette became her, only not Kim Reynolds but Karen Reyner. She woke up sweating, her flannel gown damp. She should have been able to laugh off the absurd nightmare, but she couldn't. That was the end of her sleep for the night.

The telephone rang early, before she was ready to leave for work. The voice at the other end had a hesitant quality.

"Is this Kim Reynolds?"

She indicated that it was.

"Well, this is Sandy."

Kim waited, not sure what to say. There was a pause at the other end.

"I found out something last night. I thought you might want to know."

Kim caught her breath and tried not to sound too interested. "What's that?"

"Well, I can't exactly talk right now."

"Why not?"

"I got something to do, somebody to see." She was infuriatingly vague.

"I could meet you later."

"No, my schedule today is totally unreal."

"Okay, what about tomorrow?"

"Yeah, you could drop by here around noon. I'm free lunchtime."

"Fine, and lunch will be on me."

"No, that's okay. I'm not trying to bum a free meal."

"You're doing me the favor," Kim insisted. She took down Sandy's address and directions.

For a time after the call, she stood wondering what Sandy could possibly have to tell her, then finally gave up and got ready for work. She didn't think of anything but her job for the next few hours. There was a flurry of requests for interlibrary loans and graduate library school students were in doing a reference exercise. Although she was expressly told not to lead them to the answers, the students asked many questions which she endeavored to answer appropriately. It hadn't been so long ago since she'd been in their shoes, and she remembered very well what it felt like.

At lunchtime, she had an hour and decided to take a walk around Kinley Hall. The custodian she'd seen on her previous visit said hello to her as if they were old friends.

"Dr. Forbes is around today," he said. He gave her a smile and a wink. "If you need any more information, just ask me."

Then he progressed down the hall in squeaky shoes whistling off-key.

Dr. Forbes was coming down the corridor. "Frank," he called to the custodian. "I'd like you to clean for me again this weekend. Sunday afternoon all right with you?"

"Sure." Frank gave him the full benefit of his crooked smile.

"How is life treating you?"

"Just fine, Professor."

Forbes's cobalt eyes twinkled brilliantly, like a lake in winter. "I'm glad to hear that you are doing well, Frank. We are brothers, you and I."

"Jeez, I can never tell when you're kidding or not."

She watched the two diminutive men standing together. They were almost of the same height, and she remembered what the custodian had said about Dr. Forbes liking him because he was not taller than the professor.

What sort of interest had Forbes taken in Lorette? Obviously, he'd been intrigued by her, as he was by tall women in general. How would he have reacted if she rejected him? Kim sighed deeply, aware that these idle thoughts were nothing more than pure speculation.

Dr. Barnes was meeting with his Bible as Literature class. She was hungry, but thought the class would be ending soon. Lorette had known Dr. Barnes, too. Maybe Kim could wait until the class ended and have a word with him. She seated herself unobtrusively in the rear of the classroom. The professor's voice filled the room with its power and resonance. It wasn't hard to imagine him in front of a congregation of parishioners. He stood austere and dominating in a black suit, his eyes bright. It was only the way he stared at the young women with shapely legs that undercut his credibility.

"Part of our text for today in the Old Testament relates to Zephaniah. Those of you who have been reading along with the assignments will note that the theme of this section is consistent with that of the Old Testament in general. As you may recall, the word of the Lord is spoken through Zephaniah. And the word is anger, vengeance. Observe: 'I will utterly consume all things/From off the face of the earth, Sayeth the Lord.' Why, my head gets dizzy and begins to swim and my heart thumps and positively skips a beat when I read those stirring words!" His voice gained in momentum and intensity.

A hand shot up; a bearded young man who reminded her vaguely of a tawny lion was grudgingly given the nod.

"I would have to question whether the tone of the Old Testament is predominantly angry and wrathful."

"Well, of course, it is. One has to read very little to see that man's initial disobedience provoked the Almighty's wrath." The professor's outrage sounded pompous and self-righteous to Kim's ears.

Dr. Barnes returned to sermonizing. He ran over the allotted time, his words little more than rhetoric, as if he loved to hear himself talk. He spoke of how the ancient Greeks warned against the sin of too much pride, or *hubris*. Kim could not help but consider his comment ironically apt, since it could be applied to him. He appeared to suffer from diarrhea of the mouth and constipation of the brain. He was frowning deeply as the class concluded and Kim came forward to speak to him.

"Dr. Barnes, may I have a word with you about Lorette Campbell?"

He looked surprised. "Ms. Campbell? Her death is a dreadful loss. But what is there to discuss?"

"She was a friend of mine. She said something to me about seeing you regarding a paper she was writing?"

He did not answer immediately, and studied her as if trying to take her measure. "Of what significance is that now?" he said irritably.

Nervous as he made her feel, she had no intention of allowing him to intimidate her with his temper. "There were some books on satanism in Lorette's possession at the time of her death. Was she doing a paper related to that, and were you helping her with it?"

"That was not the topic under consideration."

"You do teach religion as it relates to literature."

"If she planned on writing about such a topic, she had not as yet discussed it with me. You are most probably aware that Lorette had a gift for critical writing. I did offer to help her write a publishable paper. I wished to nurture her abilities. But we were only in the talking stage so far. She may have found someone else to help her. I couldn't say. She'd become rather distant of late."

Kim noticed that he was perspiring and wondered about it. There was a feeling, a gut feeling, that he was not being totally truthful with her. What would he have to hide or lie about?

"You'll have to excuse me. I'm late for a luncheon appointment." He licked dry lips and was off, leaving her to stare after him and conjecture. She thought about the way he had looked at the legs of those pretty, young things in the front row. Had he been trying to nurture more than Lorette's writing abilities? Just how much might he have resented her rejection?

CHAPTER TEN

Sandy was not at her apartment at noon the next day, but her roommate was. They lived over a flower shop on Tremont Avenue, about a quarter mile from the main campus. Kim introduced herself politely to the roommate and was invited to come inside.

"Do you have any idea when Sandy will be back?"

The girl shook her head, a mop of unruly auburn curls falling into her eyes. "Haven't seen her."

"Since when?"

The roommate was thoughtful. "Well, she wasn't here last night because the rat was squealing and I had to feed it myself."

"The rat?"

She indicated a small cage with what looked like a guinea pig in it.

"His name's Rupert. At least that's what Sandy calls him."

Kim got closer and immediately regretted it. Even a person with impaired sinuses would have been knocked over by the odor. The roommate took a whiff and wrinkled her nose.

"Sandy's got to clean out that cage. Rupert's hers."

Kim attempted to pet the dappled guinea pig but it moved as if to take a nip out of her finger.

"I'd be careful; Rupert has a bad disposition and sharp little teeth."

"You wouldn't have any idea when Sandy plans to return, would you?"

"Nope. I don't mind her business and she doesn't mind mine. That's why we get along so well. I'm Maura, by the way."

"Are you also an English major?"

"No, I'm getting my Master's in Art History. It's a tough field for women, but we're making progress."

"Well, good luck to you."

Maura gave her a small smile, indicating she'd begun to relax a little and let down her guard.

"Would you happen to know Sandy's friend Nick?"

Maura's expression immediately sobered. "I know him. Not a very nice guy is friend Nick. In some ways, he reminds me of ol' Rupert. Why Sandy would hang out with a Neanderthal like Nick beats me. It really sets women back. Would you like to sit down?" She indicated several chairs, but each was littered with clothes, notepads or books. Seeing the mess, Maura politely picked up an armful of clothing from one chair, opened a closet and threw the garments on the floor within. "I call that my shitorium," she explained cheerfully. "Everything I don't know what to do with ends up there. My theory of housekeeping is: those that care don't really matter, and those that matter don't really care."

"Clever," Kim said.

"I like to think so, but the truth is, I heard it somewhere and adopted it. It just seemed to fit—Sandy as well as me. Keeping a spotless homestead will never be one of our top priorities."

"Guess I haven't been freed yet, just a creature of habit and training."

"Screw that. It's never too late to start thinking for yourself and cast off the old shackles of conformity and oppression."

"I'll keep it in mind," Kim said with a wry smile. She glanced down at her watch. "Whenever Sandy comes back, ask her to give me a call."

She left feeling hungry, and was soon passing students buying food from the lunch wagons on College Avenue, which only increased her hunger pangs. Many students with little time for lunch were grabbing chilidogs or tacos and drinking coffee out of white foam cups; others were nervously smoking cigarettes or swilling cola out of cans. It was another brisk, bright autumn day, the kind that made you feel good just to be alive. Kim couldn't forget a similar day just a short time ago when Lorette had first asked for her help. She felt depressed, knowing that she'd let her friend down.

Before buying herself lunch, she decided to persevere and look for Sandy at Kinley Hall. There was always a chance that Sandy had forgotten about their meeting and was somewhere in the building. In her sensible oxfords, Kim strode quickly down the main corridor to the graduate student lounge. It was crowded at this time of the day. Many students who brown-bagged their lunches were sitting or standing, drinking the corrosive coffee that Pat Norris routinely left out in a small urn for them at lunchtime. Sandy was nowhere to be seen. The students all looked so young. And suddenly Kim felt out of place here.

"Hello, Kim."

She turned and there was Jim Davis. He gave her a friendly smile. She could see that he was looking better.

"How are you doing?"

He shrugged. "Surviving. I miss her a lot. Probably will for a long time." His eyes were solemn.

An attractive young woman sashayed up to him. "Hi, Jim, are you free for lunch?" She turned to Kim momentarily, as if some explanation were necessary. "This is my first semester here and I really need advice. You're almost finished with your course-work, aren't you, Jim?" She gave him a deferential look, her doe-like eyes heavily outlined with dark eyeliner.

"I guess I could spare some time to help you," he said in a casual, noncommittal tone of voice.

She took Jim's arm possessively as they left the lounge together, and Kim couldn't help but wonder how long it would take him to forget Lorette. Or had it happened already? But no one was irreplaceable in the scheme of things; that was both the good and the bad about being mortal.

About ready to give up on Sandy, she took a quick look in the student mailboxes, saw that Sandy's was full and walked down the corridor toward the front of the building. Dr. Barnes passed her in the hall. When he saw her, he increased his pace and looked away.

After having a quick lunch of yogurt and a fresh apple at the student union, she remembered Lorette's library books still in the trunk of her car. She walked back to the parking deck, removed the books, and carried them with her to the library. As she placed the books in the return, the final volume caught her eye. The author was Lionel Forbes. She decided to hold on to it. There were still a few minutes before she had to return to work. Kim sat down at her desk in the library office and examined the book more closely.

There were handwritten notes and underlining. Many students wrote in or highlighted passages of books, whether they belonged to the library or were personally bought. Had Lorette made any of these markings?

The telephone on her desk began to ring and she picked it up.

"Hello, Ms. Reynolds." The deep, masculine voice at the other end was very familiar now. "This is Lieutenant Gardner. Do you happen to know a student named Sandra Lorson? Like your friend Lorette Campbell, she was in the English graduate program at the university."

"Yes, I know her. Why?"

"Her body was found in the woods today not far from campus housing."

110

Kim's mouth was suddenly very dry. "Dead?" she said dazedly.

"You got it. Ordinarily, I wouldn't be involved, but this is an odd coincidence, wouldn't you say? There's also a matter of your name and home phone number appearing on a slip of paper in her jacket pocket."

"We were supposed to get together for lunch today."

"She's been dead at least since last night."

"Another accident or suicide, Lieutenant?" she asked archly.

"Doesn't look like either one," he conceded. "Right now, it looks like she died from a skull fracture. Funny how you just happen to be connected with both women."

She didn't like the tone of his voice or the implication of his words. "Are you suggesting that I'm a murderer?"

"Didn't say that, but you have to admit there's some interesting coincidences, if you believe in that kind of thing." Which he obviously did not.

"If you will recall, I'm the person who told you to investigate the circumstances of Lorette's death in the first place."

"So you did, which leads me to think that you know more than you're saying. So I'll be seeing you very soon." He hung up as abruptly as he'd begun the conversation.

She was shaken. How could he possibly imagine that she had anything to do with Sandy or Lorette's death? The phone rang again. She stared at it nervously, as if it were a cobra ready to strike while it rang twice more. Was Lieutenant Gardner calling back? He'd dropped one stone tablet on her; maybe he had another shattering revelation in hand. She forced herself to pick up the receiver again, relying on the same self-discipline with which she managed many tasks she'd rather not do.

It was Don Bernard, she noted with some relief. "I was just starting my office hours and thought of you. Maybe we could have lunch tomorrow."

"That sounds very nice," she said.

"You sound a bit off."

"Oh, I'm just a little shaky. Something happened. I had a phone call from the policeman investigating Lorette's death."

"What did he have to say?"

She told him the little she knew about Sandy's death and how the police were suspicious of her. "So if you happen to know the name of a good criminal lawyer, do write it down for me."

"I can't believe anyone would think you had any connection to murder."

She felt guilty for having unloaded her worries on him.

"From what you're telling me, it seems like whoever killed Lorette—assuming she was, in fact, murdered—also killed the other girl." His mind worked like a grandfather clock, precisely and methodically; she could practically hear the ticking. Somehow, it calmed her nerves. "What do you think this Sandy was going to tell you if you'd been able to meet?"

"Something about Dr. Forbes, I think. She had a friend named Nick who was one of Dr. Forbes's chosen, a disciple or whatever. I believe she might have picked Nick's brain for information."

"Forbes—what did Lorette have to do with him?" He sounded disapproving.

"She was taking his class. She admired him. He even invited her to his home."

"Odd. I always thought Forbes asexual, not really interested in women. He lives alone in that huge, old house of his."

"I believe his interest in Lorette was an intellectual one."

"He is something of a genius by reputation," Don said. "Lorette would certainly feel honored to be included in his group."

"It appears he has an interest in occultism. I also noticed that he has a fascination for horror literature. He wrote an introduction to at least one horror anthology that I know about."

"Sounds like you've been doing some research."

"Just what I could find out here in the library. He's listed for quite a few works in the on-line catalog."

"So you think Forbes might be responsible for harming Lorette or Sandy?"

"I don't know," she admitted. "There are other possibilities. I spoke briefly to Professor Barnes. He supposedly wanted to help Lorette write a paper for publication. He claimed to be very fond of her."

"But?"

"He seemed uneasy, evasive. He's a very angry, hostile man if you get beneath the surface."

"So you think he's hiding something? It could be. Last year, I recall there was some gossip about him. Something of a ladies' man. Supposedly, he's been married two or three times and lost his congregation because there were some serious doubts as to his ethics. Some sort of sex scandal, I believe. Again, that could just be idle chatter, but the source of the information was fairly reliable."

"Dr. Barnes is an ordained minister?"

"So I hear. He didn't come on to you, did he, Kim?"

She found herself smiling. "In case you haven't noticed, I'm not exactly a *Playboy* centerfold."

"You could be if you wanted."

She was glad he couldn't see her face just then, because it had flamed. "What I was getting at is that Lorette had these books on satanism. I wondered if Dr. Barnes might somehow be involved."

"You think he's perverted in his religious practices?"

"I don't know; I'm just speculating, but it is peculiar. All the man thinks about is religion. If he were the person responsible for blackening Lorette's reputation so that they wanted her to leave the program, she might have retaliated by threatening to expose whoever was responsible."

"Blackmail or revenge. Interesting notions. But did she know who was responsible?"

"I'm not certain. I think the last person she talked to before she died was probably Jim Davis. But Lorette didn't seem to want to involve him in her problems."

"Why was that?"

"I can't be sure. I can't believe that he would hurt her though."

"He did seem like a very decent sort of fellow," Don agreed. "Either that or he's a very talented actor. Is there anyone else who might want to harm Lorette?"

"Well, she told me that Professor Packingham was hitting on her. Lorette had managed to keep him at arm's length, but it's possible she might have changed her mind and decided to file charges of sexual harassment against him."

"Lorette used men, not the other way around."

His comment and tone of voice troubled her. He'd passed judgment on Lorette. Obviously, Don Bernard had been intimate with Lorette, and in some ways knew Lorette a great deal better than she did. She also remembered that Don had been clearly hostile to Lorette the evening they'd come to dinner in her apartment. What did Don really have against Lorette? He too was a professor who'd had a sexual relationship with a student. She felt an odd chill enter her bones. Maybe he knew a lot more than he was telling her, pretending to be her friend and confidant, while protecting himself and his fellows, engaging in a conspiracy of silence. How far could she really trust him? His personal interest in her had magnified since he'd found out about her friendship with Lorette. That in itself was suspicious. Maybe she ought to be careful what she said around him. Still, it hurt her to think she couldn't trust Don.

"I've got to get back to work now." She tried to keep the uncertainty out of her voice.

He promised to phone her the next day and the conversation ended abruptly.

No, she did not want to be suspicious of Don. Of all people, not him! But couldn't murderers appear to be charming, caring individuals? How many murderers did she happen to know? How could she judge? God, she wasn't going down that road; such thoughts led to madness. If she let herself, she could imagine almost anything. She'd tamped down her awareness for so long that it didn't seem to be working anymore.

She stared once again at the volume of Dr. Forbes's book. It bore the title *The Demon Lover: A Literary Exploration.* She thumbed through it, observing that it had been read by many students over the years; ketchup stains detracted from its scholarly aura. Pages were dog-eared and yellowed. A poem entitled "The Sick Rose," by William Blake, appeared early in the book with an interpretation, and later the medieval ballad "The Demon Lover" turned up. Comments were written in the margin. The notations did not seem particularly significant.

But Lorette had this book in her possession, indicating that she had an interest in the supernatural. Lorette and Dr. Forbes had shared that, apparently. Still, if the volume held any answers, they were hidden from Kim. She stared at the book blankly. So much for clairvoyance!

First Lorette and now Sandy. Who would commit such monstrous crimes and why? Maybe it was time she spoke with Dr. Forbes.

CHAPTER ELEVEN

Dr. Forbes's office was downstairs at Kinley Hall. In fact, most of the English staff offices were located down there in the bowels of the earth. But his office was considerably larger and more luxurious than the spartan surroundings normally shared by a host of teaching assistants and adjuncts. A pretty, young student was acting as secretary.

Kim tried to look into the inner office since the door was open but quickly discovered that it was vacant, much to her disappointment.

"Can I help you?" The student's cupid mouth puckered as if Kim's presence were some sort of annoying inconvenience.

"When will Dr. Forbes be in?"

There was a narrowing of the eyes, as if the student was sizing her up. "Dr. Forbes is very busy. If you want to see him, you have to make an appointment."

"These are his office hours, aren't they?"

"As I said—" tossing her head of thick hair for emphasis "—you can only see him by appointment."

Kim left feeling more than mild irritation. Passing by the office next door, she saw Nancy Williams sitting at her desk. Professor Williams looked up and gave her a smile. On impulse, Kim walked into the office that was much smaller than that of Dr. Forbes. Here no student secretary danced in attendance. Kim had taken a course in women's studies with Nancy; she remembered the attitude of friendliness and the fact that

Nancy's door was always open to students.

"Dr. Williams, could I have a word with you?"

She received a polite, courteous smile. "Certainly, Ms. Reynolds, what can I do for you?"

"I've been working on a paper, and I thought you might have some ideas about what approach to take."

The professor played with a strand of straight blond hair cut in a Dutch-boy style. "That's what I'm here for. Tell me about it." She indicated a worn wooden chair beside her desk.

Kim observed that Nancy was thinner than she remembered, a petite woman perhaps twelve years her senior. There was a certain air of self-assurance about her, suggestive of having been born to wealth and privilege. Her suit, though conservative, was well cut and looked expensive.

"You lectured to us about some of the post-modernists. Do you believe there's an occult trend in their writing? I remember you talking about it."

"I don't think there's really much to explore there. Have you turned something up? I recall what a hard worker you were when you took my course."

She appreciated the compliment. In her life experience, compliments were rare as rubies and to be savored.

"What about satanic occultism?"

Dr. Williams raised an eyebrow.

"The demon-lover theme, for instance. Is there much follow-up in post-modernism?"

"I'm not versed in that. But Lionel Forbes is a specialist in that area of writing. You really ought to speak with him."

"I've read parts of his book on the subject."

"Have you? He's a brilliant man, isn't he? A truly original thinker—although something of an eccentric."

Had she imagined it or did Nancy sound strained?

"Do keep me informed on your progress. I always like to

keep in touch with former students."

Kim took the stairs back to the main floor, well aware that she hadn't found out a thing. But that was to be expected. If Forbes was not going to be accessible, maybe she could locate the mysterious Nick. What she needed was a student directory. She was on her dinner break and Pat Norris was gone for the day. There were thousands of students at the university, so going through the complete student directory was impractical. Jim Davis would have a current directory for graduate English students, and he had offered his help. That was a sensible way to do things. Research had always been her strength. Maybe sleuthing was suited to a reference librarian after all.

She was back at the library at six-thirty. Before returning to her post, she looked up Jim's number in the student directory and was relieved when he answered the phone. Jim was friendly and cooperative. He looked through the numbers for her. There were two Nicks, and he gave her both numbers.

She thanked him warmly. "Before you hang up, did Lorette ever mention an interest in the occult to you?"

"You mean spooks and Halloween stuff?" He sounded as though he were trying to make a joke of it, as if to imply her question was frivolous.

"Did she ever talk to you about Dr. Forbes or a book he wrote on the demon-lover theme?"

"Like to help you out there but I can't. We never discussed it." Did she imagine it or did he seem tense, uneasy?

"Do you know much about Dr. Forbes?"

"Had him for a course last year. He's okay. Real clever. Does enjoy raking students over the coals though, maybe has a sadistic streak in him, but then that's part of the initiation, isn't it? What's it got to do with Lorette's death?"

"Maybe nothing. I'll let you know."

The first Nick she called wasn't at home. The second Nick

was a first-year student in the program and knew nothing whatever about anyone named Sandy. He sounded genuine. She decided to call back the first number later in the evening.

She was on duty with Rita Mosler and a graduate assistant, which meant most of the work fell to her. Rita spent more time complaining about how hard she worked than actually working. As to graduate students, they were just that, usually able to provide only the most limited assistance to those needing help. This girl was no different and Kim found herself doing as much instructing as assisting. It was a busy evening, with students lining up with questions until well past eleven o'clock. She was entitled to leave at ten, but didn't have the heart.

During the only lull in patronage, she had a thought. Rita had worked in reference for many years; chances were that she would know if there was an inferno collection somewhere on the premises.

Turning to Rita, she asked, "Have you ever heard anything about an inferno collection here?"

Rita's eyes shifted from side to side. She spoke quietly. "It's really not something you should be talking about."

"Why ever not?"

Rita's voice shrilled. "It's just not good to ask."

"But why should there be any secrecy about a collection?"

"Wendell keeps one particular collection under lock and key. I once overheard him talking about it. But then he noticed me and said that I wasn't to discuss it with anyone."

"To whom was he talking?"

Rita shrugged in annoyance. Her expression made Kim think of a constipated chipmunk. "I don't know, just someone who wanted to see it. Think I know everyone that comes into this place?"

Kim had the distinct impression that Rita wasn't being completely truthful. The conversation ended abruptly as a student approached them. Since Rita was unwillingly to talk any further, it made no difference.

Rita left before Kim did that night. When she got her coat, Kim tried her keys to see if she could get into Wendell's office. The secret collection must be kept somewhere within his office locked away. But none of her keys fitted the lock. How could she get into his office to look around?

Rita had to have a key to Wendell's office, because occasionally on the evening shift she needed to go in to check one thing or another. Although Rita had a great deal of seniority, her sour disposition made her one of Wendell's least favorite reference librarians; therefore, she was often consigned to work the evening shift, during which he rarely put in an appearance.

What Kim had to do was borrow Rita's keys the next evening they worked late together. Since Wendell never worked the late shift, she could wait until it was safe to come back to the offices and look around. Yes, that plan should certainly work.

As Kim left the building that night, the sky was overcast. The parking deck was deserted. She walked along quickly, feeling as if she were being followed or watched, and wondering if it were just her imagination working overtime. There were always stories of rapes and muggings on campus at night. After all, they were in a city, and cities were not the safest of places, especially at night. She literally ran up the two flights of stairs to her car, and was totally out of breath when she reached it, her hand trembling on the key. She looked around and saw no one, but she could not shake the feeling of fear. Maybe she was just being paranoid, but then again, maybe she wasn't. At least she'd taken a self-defense course as an undergrad and knew how to protect herself fairly well. Self-reliance was a wonderful thing if you lived an independent life style.

The following day, Kim was scheduled for the late shift once again. To her disappointment, Rita was not working with her. However, her hours were such that she could make another attempt to see Dr. Forbes. She timed her dinner break to coincide with the conclusion of a class. It worked out just as she planned, and she was able to approach him as the last of his students filed out the door.

"Dr. Forbes, I've been trying to see you for some time. Is it possible for us to talk for a few minutes right now?"

He gave her a small, amused smile. "Of course, *carpe diem.* Why wait when you can have me now? But beware. I am like the sun. Do not draw too close, lest like Icarus, your wax wings melt and plunge you to your death." He was playing with her.

"Thank you, I'll keep your warning in mind. I wouldn't want to incinerate."

"Indeed not." His glittering blue eyes surveyed her shrewdly. Without warning, he swept her into his arms, took hold of her, and led her into an exaggerated tango step. Then he released her just as swiftly as he had seized her. Kim nearly lost her balance. She stared at him in amazement. He seemed terribly pleased by her stunned reaction.

"Magnificent, my dear, utterly superb. We must dance together again sometime. Take my Victorian Novel course next semester and I will guarantee it."

"I'm not in the program anymore."

"More's the pity. You must return. You could be one of the elect, one of the chosen few." His mocking tone did not escape her notice.

"Chosen for what?" she said.

He pierced her with the laser-light quality of his blue gaze. "Come and find out. We dance beautifully together, a perfect pair, don't you think? I prefer tall women." His words flowed like maple syrup as his small body rippled lithely away from her. "But you will do quite nicely. Do you find me fascinating, my dear? I am considered a man of wit."

Half-wit was more like it, but she kept that opinion to herself. "I came to talk to you about Lorette Campbell. I'm sure you recall her. She was, after all, rather tall."

The incandescent eyes riveted on her own with frightening intensity and hypnotic power. "That was a tragedy. She was truly meant to be one of the chosen, a gifted young woman. What is your concern in this matter?"

"She was my friend. I mourn her loss."

"And you think that investigating her death will somehow compensate?"

The sardonic edge to his voice made her feel almost foolish. She did not respond immediately.

"Who did you say you were?"

"Kim Reynolds."

"You've never studied with me, have you?"

"No, I was not so honored. Did you know that Lorette was reading your book on the occult at the time of her death?"

"Ah, how interesting. I have been accused of many things in my time—murderous looks, a rapier wit, a switchblade tongue—but never before has it been suggested that my written word kills." He used his hand to brush back his pure white hair, which was neatly combed off his pink face. The gesture made her think of a rat who knows he's snatched the cheese and outsmarted the individual who set the trap.

"I wasn't suggesting that your book had anything to do with causing her death in the physical sense. However, the metaphysical is an entirely different matter."

"Perhaps you would care to elucidate?"

"Lorette seemed intrigued by the demon-lover theme. She might have been planning a paper of her own on the topic. Did she come to you for help?"

"We discussed the matter briefly. She had an idea, but as yet it was rather vague and unformed, no solid thesis worked out. I told her that when she got past the planning stage and had something actually written, I would read it and make suggestions."

"I read some of your book. I found it rather negative and misogynistic."

"Did you now? Did you indeed?" A tolerant smirk appeared on his face.

She disliked being patronized, but kept her tone of voice cautiously cool. "Do you really think women long to be ravished by demonic spirits?"

He gave her a Cheshire-cat smile. "Of course they do—in their fantasies. They romanticize rape, idealize the disreputable male. It's the principle behind every gothic novel from earliest inception to the Brontës, and down to the current vogue of trashy romance novels. There is an attraction to evil inherent in the nature of men and women alike. It excites. It fascinates. Each sex manifests it slightly differently, but to deny it is unrealistic. Evil is the strongest force in the universe. The power of evil rules mankind."

She shuddered. "I'm afraid I cannot agree with you. And I believe that in the world of reality, women prefer kind, decent men to sadists."

"Ms. Reynolds, you are quite naive." He turned his superior smile on her.

Kim found her face flushing both from embarrassment and anger. She determined to change the subject back to Lorette. "What did Lorette's thesis specifically deal with? Would you happen to remember?"

"She was working with several different ideas. There was the connection between the demon-lover mystique, tying it in with an incubus."

"Incubus?" The term was familiar but she couldn't place it.

Jacqueline Seewald

"A demon or devil who sexually assaults women, generally during the night while they sleep. In the Middle Ages, people believed that erotic encounters with demons occurred most often in convents because demons created their physical manifestation from the substance of menstrual matter. The demon always won because it understood the repressed sexual desires of women." He stared at her meaningfully.

Kim sensed that this was more than mere conversation between them. This was a man who exercised power over the will of other people, who would literally control their souls if permitted. A fallen angel, a Lucifer, not so different from the evil genius of a Hitler or a Stalin, only on a smaller scale. She shivered though the room was warm.

"Erotic dreams are as common to men as women," she said in a voice louder than she'd intended.

"Certainly, it is as ancient as the sex urge itself. Freud found psychological explanations, but the fact remains that physical evidence is sometimes left behind."

"You don't actually believe that there is such a thing as a demon lover?"

"Perhaps," he said, "and then again, perhaps not. But I will tell you one thing. Your friend Ms. Campbell believed it—or should I say feared it."

"I find that difficult to believe."

"We'll never know for certain now, will we?" His eyes were quicksand, sucking her down into their depths.

She had the distinct impression that he was playing mind games at her expense. She forced herself to look away, but it was difficult.

"If it is any comfort to you, I think that Ms. Campbell had come to understand something about the nature of universal truth. One does learn such things from examining long-standing literary trends, don't you think, my dear?"

Kim felt as if he were testing her, challenging her intellect and her inner strength. "Is it politically correct to talk of universal truth? Didn't Einstein demonstrate there are no constants except relativity itself?"

"Not so, my dear." His magnetic gaze held her own. "Human nature never changes. Evil is the universal constant in the universe."

"You sound like a Calvinist. You and Dr. Barnes appear to share a common philosophy."

"And you are medieval in your thinking. Everything and everyone neatly pigeonholed and classified." He was sneering at her now. "Dr. Barnes and I, in point of fact, agree on very little, except a shared opinion on the direction that our society is headed."

"Which is?"

"To hell in a hand basket, of course. Ethics and morals are in a state of terminal decay, like a maggot-infested corpse left to rot."

"People were saying the same thing thousands of years ago."

He gave her a deadly look. "We didn't have the same potential for total destruction then. Perhaps human sacrifices are no longer made by cutting out men's hearts as offerings to the gods, but in many ways our barbarism exceeds that of past civilizations. Witness the mass annihilations of the past century, genocide, senseless wars, toxic pollution and the possibility of nuclear holocaust. Never, my dear, never confuse advances in technology with amelioration of the human character. The heart of man is as black and evil as ever."

"I still believe the need for love and hope for redemption are equally strong."

His eyes seemed to probe her soul. "Have you found it to be so in your own experience?"

It was as if he knew her life, could see into her heart. And she found herself unable to answer him.

He moved toward the door, turning one last time to look at her. "The big blast is coming, my dear. It's just a matter of time. Have I shocked you with my outspoken opinions? Well, I won't apologize. Time to take the blinders off and grow up, dear heart." Suddenly he was gone, out the door and away, like a magician disappearing in a puff of smoke.

She felt cold and chilled and very much alone. The eccentric little man had quite managed to intimidate her. She had no doubt that was exactly what he'd intended. Had he done the same thing to Lorette—or worse?

CHAPTER TWELVE

Kim worked behind the reference desk for several hours before the eerie feeling that had settled over her dissipated. Still, she'd begun to think that looking into the circumstances of Lorette's death was becoming more than she could deal with. Two deaths, both unnatural, within a short space of time. She had the terrible feeling that she was at least partly to blame for what happened to Sandy.

As if responding to her thoughts, Lieutenant Gardner showed up later that evening.

"What are you doing here?" she asked when he approached her at the desk.

God, the man was tall! And even wearing a suit, there was no disguising the fact that he was well built. His features weren't so much handsome as strong. He had an unsettling effect on her that she preferred not to consider.

"Since you weren't at home, I figured you were probably at work." His gray eyes were steady.

"Suppose I was off today? You would have wasted your time."

"Oh, I called first. Made sure you were on." His smile was friendly, as if they shared an old acquaintanceship.

She recognized the smile for what it was, an attempt to throw her off-guard. She knew enough to be wary. Past experience had taught her policemen were not to be trusted. "So do you still think I'm the reincarnation of Lucretia Borgia?"

He gave a short laugh. "You've got me wrong."

"Do I? Maybe Lizzie Borden then?"

"There are just a few questions I'd like to ask you."

"Should I hire a lawyer?"

"If you want, but you don't need one—at least not yet."

Why did he have to be so attractive? It was distracting and she needed all her wits about her to spar with him. "As you can see, I'm busy working now."

He looked around. "Doesn't seem too busy to me."

"It will be."

"Can you take a few minutes off? It's important." He gave her a warm, gentle smile.

He wasn't fooling her; she knew what he was doing. "All right. I can take a fifteen-minute break. I just have to tell the other librarian on duty."

She took a walk with him down College Avenue and around the Commons, letting him lead the way, letting him talk.

"It's been confirmed that Sandy Lorson was killed by several blows to the head from a blunt instrument. The first blow was in itself only strong enough to render her unconscious. But the perp obviously was determined to finish the job. There was no rape or robbery, so that rules out any of the more typical motives connected with murder. She also showed no signs of putting up a struggle. It looks as if whoever killed her was someone she knew and likely trusted. Someone she might have a meeting with, for instance." He gave her a speculative look.

She froze in her tracks. "And you think I had some motive for killing her?"

"Did I say that?" He was friendly and ingratiating again.

She'd had enough of men playing mind games with her for one day. "I'll tell you exactly why I was going to meet Sandy. It had to do with something she told me about Lorette." Kim went on to explain Sandy's story about meeting Lorette at Dr.

Forbes's house. "I spoke with Dr. Forbes today. He was interested in Lorette as a student. She was writing a paper on the supernatural for him. The subject fascinates him. These gatherings of select students at his home seem to have something to do with his interest in the occult."

"So you think that this professor had some reason to kill both women?"

"I can't be certain, but it seems that way to me. I intend to find this friend Nick that Sandy talked about. He might tell me more about it."

"You trying to do my job?" His tone was accusatory.

"If you want to locate Nick and ask him some questions, that's fine with me. I'm just trying to help."

"And to suggest that other people might have killed your friend?"

"When you thought it was an accident or suicide, I told you I didn't believe it. I'm just as concerned as you are that Lorette's killer is brought to justice—more so."

He gave her another irritating smile. "Glad to hear it. And if you are as innocent as you say, maybe you should stop asking questions. Two women are dead already. That's enough, don't you think?" His eyes met hers.

"I'm touched by your concern for my welfare, Lieutenant."

"Yeah, like hell you are. Oh, by the way, Ms. Reynolds, there is a little mystery you might clear up for me. It seems Kim Reynolds didn't exist before seven years ago. How come?"

She shifted uneasily, looking ahead of her. "Very simple, really. I legally changed my name."

"What was wrong with the old one?"

"I decided to reinvent myself."

He cocked a questioning brow. "Karen Reyner isn't such a bad name."

So he knew; why had he bothered to ask her about it then?

"If you know about that, then you must know why I changed my name."

"You sound hostile."

She looked at him. "Maybe that's the way I feel."

"I guess you've got a right." He had a sympathetic look on his face, as if he cared and wanted to listen to whatever she might want to say. *Don't fall for that!*

"My mother thinks it was wrong of me. She thinks I was ashamed of him."

"Of Carl Reyner, you mean?"

She inclined her head slightly. He knew everything, just as she suspected. "I don't like to talk about it."

"Yeah, I understand. You smoke? You want a cigarette?"

She shook her head. "We breathe enough air pollution around here as it is. I hope you don't smoke."

"I'm trying to stop," he responded sheepishly. "You sound like my daughter, Evie. She's after me about it all the time."

"Well, it's a bad habit. You're lucky to have such a caring daughter."

He gave her another warm smile. She tried to ignore how handsome he was. He seemed so nice, she could almost forget that he was a policeman.

"You must have been a good schoolteacher. You got the look."

"I don't know about that. But I always wanted to do something meaningful with my life. It's made me fairly restless and dissatisfied."

"How come you're not married?"

The way he switched gears nearly threw her. "I've never managed to have that kind of loving relationship with a man," she said.

"Your old man turn you off men?" He was blunt and insightful.

"What makes you ask that?" She could have done without his

probing. There was a fluttering in her stomach.

"Cop's intuition," he responded with an easy shrug. "You get like that when you deal with people day after day."

"I don't like people asking questions about my personal life. I kind of like being left alone." She managed to keep her voice even.

"Just think of me as someone who wants to help you."

"Now why should I do that?"

His eyes were a guileless, dove gray. "Your old man hurt you, didn't he? Made you think the worst of people?"

"I suppose he did, but in a sense, he did me a big favor. I know how to protect myself." She didn't know why she was opening up to him, except there was something about the man that made him easy to talk with.

"Did your old man abuse you?"

She shook her head, not quite meeting his direct gaze. "Not in the way you mean. But his words could be cruel. Ma said he was sick from the time he came back from serving in the army. He just wasn't himself. He was overseas for several tours. But he chose to be there. He was seriously wounded and awarded a Purple Heart and a Bronze Star."

"He must have been a brave man."

"I guess. I just remember him being very mean to me and especially to Ma. She had a big heart. She always forgave him, but I couldn't."

"Why was that?"

"I don't know," she said evasively. Some things were too painful to talk about.

"Were you ashamed of him?"

"Of what he did? It was horrible."

"Yeah, it was nasty."

"The police acted like we were criminals, Ma and me. So many questions. As if they thought we knew what he was going to do that day, like we helped him plan it."

"He never talked about it?"

"Not to me, and I'm sure not to Ma either."

"I know it must have been hard for you and your mother."

"It was. Ma's forgiven him and moved on with her life. I've been devoting my life to helping other people solve their problems—those that can be answered from books anyway."

"The Mother Teresa of the library stacks?" His teasing was surprisingly gentle.

"Not exactly. I'm no saint and I don't pretend to be one. I don't have a martyr complex."

"Don't forget," he said, "solving your own problems comes first."

"I don't have any. Like Thoreau, I keep my life very simple."

He took her arm, pulling her back from the street. She felt a strange surge of energy where he touched her, almost like an electrical shock. It was totally unexpected, and she stared at him open-mouthed like a fish caught on a hook.

"You didn't see that car coming toward you, did you?"

"What?" She realized that he was right; they were crossing a busy intersection and she'd hardly paid any attention to the traffic, too engrossed in their conversation.

"Thanks, guess I was distracted."

"Can't thank me since I was doing the distracting." The smile looked genuine this time. When he smiled that way, he didn't look as tough or rugged, not nearly as intimidating.

"Which just proves if you're going to psychoanalyze people, you better use a couch and an office."

"The kind of people I work with would probably steal the couch the minute I turned my back." He had a way of not taking life too seriously, which made her almost relax her guard—but not quite.

"It's time I got back to work."

"Call anytime if you need me," he said. "And remember what I said about not asking too many questions."

"But you still think maybe I killed Lorette and Sandy, don't you?"

"Well, not really. I just wanted to see what I could shake loose if I approached you that way. We can pretty well establish time of death by the disposition of the body. At the time you called for assistance, Ms. Campbell had already been dead approximately six to eight hours. I checked you out and discovered you were right here working at the time. So you're off the hook." He grinned broadly.

"Thanks for letting me sweat!" Damn him!

"Don't mention it. Mind fucks are my specialty."

That was probably not the only kind of fucking he was good at. Now where had that stray thought come from? They walked the rest of the way back to the main library entrance in silence.

She wasn't opposed to taking Lieutenant Gardner's advice about not asking any more questions; she just couldn't do it. She had to continue. A momentum had been building. Maybe it had become a form of obsession; she didn't really know.

Gardner didn't care about finding out who killed Lorette, not the way she did. It was time to talk to this Nick person. Before she could get busy again, Kim phoned the first number that Jim had given her. This time there was an answer. It wasn't easy talking to a complete stranger; by nature she was reserved, reticent, but she forced herself to do it.

"Is this Nick Margrove?"

He indicated that it was.

"Sandy asked me to contact you." Where had that lie come from?

"What about?" He sounded wary.

She explained who she was and then carefully told him about her conversation with Sandy. "She offered to help me find out what happened to my friend. I believe you knew Lorette Camp-bell?"

"Saw her around campus. I heard she took an overdose of cocaine and died. So what's there to find out?"

"Why it happened."

"She was a user. It doesn't get any simpler." His voice crackled with belligerence.

"Then what happened to Sandy?"

"Some nut attacked her. Happens all the time. Sandy was an airhead, a freak, an easy target; anyone could sneak up on her."

"I believe there's a connection between the two deaths. I'd like your help."

"There's nothing I can do." His tone was surly. "Look, I'm busy. I got a deadline on a paper; it's due in the morning."

"Could you talk with me tomorrow then? Just for a few minutes. I could meet you at the graduate student lounge in Kinley. Would that be convenient?"

"I guess." People were more eager to visit the dentist.

"What time?"

"After my morning class. Twelve-thirty. But I'm not hanging around if you're not there."

"I will be there."

No hardship was involved, since Wendell had scheduled her for the late shift all week. It was the worst schedule, of course, but she did not complain. First, outside of the graduate assistants, she was the newest librarian on staff, and second, she did not have a husband to answer to or children to care for as many of the women did.

She was not only on time to meet Nick Margrove the next day, but actually about fifteen minutes early. There were a number of students in the lounge drinking coffee and gobbling down their lunches between classes. Here and there she overheard snatches of conversation.

Two young men were talking. One was thin and slightly hunched, wearing rimless eyeglasses; the other was of average height and build, but with a complexion marred by acne.

"Sorry to hear about Sandy," the one with the glasses said. "I know you and her were close."

The one with moon craters on the surface of his face looked around nervously. "I don't want to talk about her."

"Sure, Nick, whatever you say."

Kim approached Nick Margrove, studying him thoughtfully. Instinct told her to be careful around him. She politely introduced herself. He looked her up and down in an insulting manner.

"Sandy told me that you're from California."

"So?" His eyes were narrow slits.

Already this was not going well. "I understand you have a talent for writing."

He shrugged; the compliment obviously pleased him.

"Sandy thought you were one of Dr. Forbes's chosen group of students. You were invited to his house, I believe. Apparently, so was Lorette. The question is, what were you chosen for?"

He licked his lips. He had a thick bush of kinky, ginger hair that he ran his hands through nervously.

"I don't have time to talk with you. I have to get going."

"Fine, I'll just walk along with you."

He took off at a quick pace, but she kept up with him. There were benefits to wearing sturdy shoes.

"If you're not forthcoming about this, I'm going to give your name to the police. They'll probably want to question you."

He seemed upset; his hand suddenly snaked around her wrist. "What do you want to know?"

She freed her hand indignantly. He'd hurt her, but she wasn't going to fuss about it. "Do you have any idea who murdered Sandy?"

"Of course not." He sniffed in a supercilious manner as if she'd spoken like an idiot.

"Did you kill her?"

His eyes flashed angrily. "I would never hurt her, and I have no idea who did."

"All right, but you do know what goes on at Dr. Forbes's house, don't you?"

When he didn't reply, she continued. "What went on at the house the evening Lorette was there?"

"Just the usual." He sounded as if cotton were stuffed in his nose and rubbed at it irritably.

"What was the usual?" She was trying not to sound exasperated.

"You'll have to ask Dr. Forbes." His eyes were so narrow that she could barely see the pupils. He sniffed at her with his clogged, runny nose again.

"You ought to take care of your cold—if it's a cold." With that, she left him in front of the building and took off down the square.

She was too annoyed to go directly to work. Besides, it was much too early. Nothing had been accomplished. So frustrating! Nick Margrove wasn't going to tell her anything. She thought he might be a cocaine addict, and Lorette had been killed with an overdose of that very drug. So there was a possible connection. However, suspicions were one thing and clear-cut evidence was quite another.

There was a gnawing in her stomach. Breakfast had consisted only of a quick bowl of Total corn flakes. She took a walk to the McDonald's near the university bookstore. It was a cheerful place where she could sit quietly and think. She ordered a cup of coffee and a grilled chicken sandwich and then sat down to eat. Maybe she should do what she'd told Nick. It wasn't an idle threat; why not inform Lieutenant Gardner about him? Nick's attitude with a police officer would not be so snotty.

She finished her sandwich, chewing meditatively, and then walked over to the university bookstore. It was a nice place to browse around. She did so in a leisurely manner. Libraries and bookstores were her favorite places; she could lose herself for hours in either one. Lost souls could be located on bookshelves, maybe even her own.

Too soon it was time to walk back to campus and begin her workday. She decided to phone Lieutenant Gardner the next day. It wasn't like her to procrastinate, but seeking out the police for any reason was alien to her nature. Deep down, she felt only trouble could come of it. Still, there was nothing ordinary about Gardner. She knew that instinctively.

Rita Mosler was working with her again. Before Rita left for the evening, Kim told her that she'd left her own office keys in her car. She asked to borrow those belonging to Rita, who was annoyed but gave them to her anyway. Kim waited until Rita was busy with a patron. She hurried to Wendell's office and opened it, then went back to the reference desk. She returned Rita's keys promptly and thanked her. After Rita went home for the night, Kim left a graduate assistant alone at the desk for a little while and rushed back to Wendell's office.

The search was difficult because she wasn't precisely certain what she was looking for. The desk itself was locked, but what she was looking for wouldn't be in a desk. It was a collection of books or manuscripts and, therefore, had to be in some sort of cabinet. She studied the room carefully. Everything seemed quite ordinary, except for the incredible degree of neatness. Then she saw it. In a recessed corner stood a small, mirrored cabinet, ornate, like something from another age and time. On a hook above it, a large antique key sat as if waiting for her to place it in the lock. She turned the lock on the first drawer and opened it, quickly looking inside. Kim saw at once that the manuscripts were very old and fragile, delicate to the touch. She was just about to examine them more thoroughly when a noise sounded outside the office door. Her heart was palpitating as she hurriedly closed the cabinet and relocked it, placing the great key back exactly where she found it.

"Kim, are you in there?"

"Yes," she answered, setting the door to lock and then closing it behind her. Why did her voice sound so breathless?

Mary Parkins eyed her with curiosity and suspicion. "What are you doing back here?"

That wasn't any business of a graduate assistant, but Mary was always pushy and nosy. She also had a jealous nature. Kim didn't like the girl and thought Mary had the same reaction to her.

"Do you need me?" She found herself still short of breath.

"I thought we were never supposed to leave the floor while we were on duty."

"I needed to locate something." She tried to keep the irritation out of her voice.

"In Mr. Firbin's office?"

"You're a student, Mary. My duties are more complex than yours."

"I'm still learning, but I do just as good a job as you, although I don't get much pay for it."

She ignored Mary's surly comment. "Let's get back. Now what's the problem?"

"I couldn't locate a set of government documents this student was looking for."

"We'll do it together."

As she finished her final hour of the evening, several times she noticed Mary turning a malevolent look on her. She left feeling upset that Mary knew about her being in Wendell Firbin's office. An excuse had to be created that Wendell would believe in case Mary mentioned it to him. It was very likely that she would.

The solitary walk to the parking deck further discombobulated her. Was she imagining footsteps behind her? She'd spent so much of her life ignoring her special sensitivity, pretending that it didn't exist, but in some ways, she realized, it could be a form of self-preservation. She did not want to turn and look to see if she were really being followed. She began to run, taking the stairs to the third level as quickly as she could. Near the top of the stairs, a hand caught her around the throat. She felt something cold, sharp and metallic against her neck and let out a scream. She had the presence of mind to reach into her handbag. Her fingers gripped the can of pepper spray she'd bought just for such an occasion. She sprayed it in a quick movement behind her, not certain if she'd caught her assailant in the face or not.

A surprised curse told her she'd been successful. Her hand loosened on the weapon, and she ran as if the devil were chasing her. Kim turned only once, thinking she caught sight of a bush of ginger hair escaping down the stairs into the darkness below. She was choking and gasping for air when she reached her car, her hands shaking almost too much to open the driver's side lock.

But no one was there anymore. She was alone now and could hear only the sound of her own frightened breathing. She put her hand to her throat and it came away with blood. There was no use trying to control the shaking; it wouldn't stop. A scarf in her jacket pocket served as a good bandage. As she drove the car from the parking deck, tears welled up in her eyes.

Stop that! He only scratched you. It's nothing. You're all right. You did what was needed, no point falling apart now. He only meant to

139

scare you. She ground down on her back teeth, but her trembling did not cease.

CHAPTER THIRTEEN

The following morning, Kim phoned Wilson Township police headquarters and asked for Lieutenant Gardner. She came directly to the point when he got on the line.

"A student named Nick Margrove took Sandy to Dr. Forbes's house. Sandy was the one who told me that Lorette was invited there. Nick appears to be a regular in Dr. Forbes's group. Oh, and I think it's likely that Nick snorts cocaine."

"I'll have a talk with him."

Should she tell him about the previous night, her suspicions regarding the attack on the parking deck and her belief Nick Margrove had initiated it? Finally, she decided that he ought to know.

He listened without interrupting. "Get someone to walk you to your car in the evening from now on. I can arrange for it if you want." His tone was serious.

"No, I don't think I'll be bothered anymore. I fought off my attacker. He won't be after me again." She did not tell him about using the pepper spray, although its use was perfectly legal. The simpler she kept things, the better.

"I'm not as certain about your safety as you seem to be. I think you better stop asking people questions from now on. I suggested it to you before, now I've got to insist on it. Two women have been killed. You don't need to be the hat trick." His authoritative tone annoyed her.

"I'm part of the university. There are things I'm knowledgeable about that a policeman wouldn't understand."

"Now look, I asked you nice, but you don't seem to comprehend. Stay out of this from now on." He definitely sounded angry.

She wasn't going to argue with him; it would accomplish nothing. "I'm glad you're finally seeing the connection between the two murders. You do think both Lorette and Sandy were murdered, don't you?"

"Yeah, and that's all the more reason for you to keep a respectful distance. I'll talk to your Dr. Forbes if it proves necessary."

"Oh, it's necessary all right. Both Lorette and Sandy were at his house, and now they're dead."

"They also shared a course in Medieval Romance. Why couldn't that be the crucial connection?"

"You do have a point," she conceded.

"Besides the one on top of my head?"

He was joking with her again, acting as if they were friends, but she wasn't fooled, nor was she about to relinquish her own argument.

"Regardless, Nick Margrove behaved very suspiciously and I really think he attacked me."

"Fine, like I said, I'll look into it. You just keep your nose out of police business. You're a civilian and I'm saying it for your own protection."

She didn't answer him. She supposed that his were the best of intentions, and what could she say anyway? Yet an hour after talking to him, she was already reasoning that a phone call to Dr. Forbes would not be out of order. Why should she let herself be intimidated by anyone, good intentions or not? Karen Reyner would have cowered but not Kim Reynolds.

Dr. Forbes's secretary announced that he would not be at the university that day. She could try his home number, if she had it. No, his secretary was instructed not to give such information out. That went on Kim's list of things to discover when she returned to the library the following day. She also wanted Dr. Forbes's home address. She would give a lot just to look around his house. Whimsically, she imagined herself in the Roaring Twenties walking up to the door of a speakeasy and demanding to be let in. "Joe sent me," she'd say. What was behind the green door?

A thought occurred to her. Frank would know, wouldn't he? He cleaned the house. Maybe if she offered him some money, he'd give her the necessary info. Most likely he could use a few dollars extra. Trouble was, a few was all she had to spare.

Her phone rang, jarring her out of her speculation.

"I don't mean to rush you, but you didn't take anything with you last time, and I'm planning to leave for Florida next week."

"Ma? Those things are part of my past. I'm living in the present—except you did say I could have Jen's diary."

There was a deep sigh on the other end of the line. "You can come by for it anytime. It's waiting for you."

She decided to see Ma that day, maybe give her some help packing and figuring out what to do with the old things they didn't want.

"I'm free today. Why don't I come around noon?"

Ma was waiting for her, just as before. She looked every one of her fifty-odd years. There were lines etched in her face, and her hair was graying noticeably. She was weary from a lifetime of hard work and disappointment. Kim wondered guiltily how much she'd added to Ma's burdens.

"You'll stay and have lunch with me, won't you?" Ma asked hopefully.

"Why don't I take you out?"

"A waste of good money. I know you don't earn that much.

Of course, you should, doing the valuable job you do, but life isn't always fair, is it? I've got tuna salad all made up and I baked a cheesecake from this low-calorie recipe. It substitutes egg white and cottage cheese for the high-fat stuff. I have to watch it these days. Gall bladder's acting up Doc says."

"Sounds like a terrific meal, but you shouldn't go to so much trouble for me."

"You're my girl," she said with a smile. Her brown eyes were warm as toast.

Kim felt a painful lump form in her throat. "I was thinking that you could hold a garage sale to get rid of some of this stuff. You could advertise in the local paper. Your trash might be someone else's treasure."

"That's a wonderful idea."

They sat down to lunch together. Ma asked about her job and her friends. Kim didn't talk much about Lorette and avoided mentioning the death of Sandy. She let Ma do most of the talking. When they finished the cheesecake, which turned out to be different but tasty, Ma brought up a difficult subject for both of them.

"Some magazine writer phoned me a few days ago. He had questions about Carl. Said he was writing an article and he wanted to include Carl in it."

Kim's stomach muscles contracted. "I thought we were through with that. Now they want to dredge it all up again. What did this man want to know?"

"He says there's a lot of people like Carl who go crazy and start shooting people. You know, like those postal workers. In fact, he called it going postal."

"But Carl did it in a veteran's hospital."

"Because they weren't doing anything for men like him. He was trying to make a point. He was dying and no one seemed to care."

"Ma, you sound as though you condone what he did."

Ma started collecting the dishes from the table and stacking them in the sink.

"He was a good man, Karen. If you'd known him before he went over there, you'd understand. He gave everything for his country and his country forgot about him, wrote him off like an embarrassment. He didn't want his life to mean nothing. He thought about it long and hard. He killed those people because they were hospital administrators who didn't care. Of course, he was wrong to do it, but he wanted publicity. He wanted to be heard. Violence is what the world is interested in. So he took those hostages to draw attention to the problem."

"He didn't have to kill them!"

"He didn't have to kill himself either, but he thought he had a reason, a cause."

Ma was expecting something from her that she couldn't give. "I'll never understand or accept it. Those people he killed, two administrators and a secretary, they weren't making policy. He killed innocent people. You've also conveniently forgotten his temper and how he treated you. I think you should have divorced him long before he went postal."

There were tears in Ma's eyes. Kim put her arms around her mother. "Don't cry. I didn't mean to upset you."

"No, we should talk about it. We never have been able."

"It's not easy to talk about a thing like that. It's not easy to talk about him. I don't think we'll ever agree. That doesn't mean I don't care about you, though."

She didn't stay much longer; she just couldn't. There were too many memories here, too much pain. Before she left, Ma handed her the small diary.

"I don't know why you want to read it, but you might as well keep it."

145

"I read it when I was fifteen. That was when I first understood about her."

"When you finish reading it, if you want to talk about Jen, let me know."

"I think I would."

Ma hugged her tightly. "I love you," she said in a quiet, almost desperate voice. "Always remember that."

Kim found herself unable to reply and left quickly.

The following morning, she went to the graduate English lounge shortly before the meeting of Dr. Barnes' Bible Literature class. She moved around unobtrusively, watching and listening—exactly for what, she wasn't certain. She recognized the girl who'd been so interested in Jim Davis. The pretty young student went to the metal coffee urn, placed her Styrofoam cup under the spigot and yawned dramatically.

"Honestly," she said turning to the heavyset male student who stood beside her, "there isn't enough coffee in the entire world to keep me awake during one of Dr. Barnes' sermons."

"Definitely not New Critical," the young man agreed, slurping down some of his coffee. "I mean, anyone worth anything is New Critical, don't you think?"

Kim found his artificiality grating. A third student joined the other two, a dime-thin blonde in a long, flowing patterned skirt and fuzzy green sweater.

"New Critical is passé. It's like Art Deco, a prehistoric dinosaur that's bit the dust. Just because professors favor close reading does not mean it's the only approach. What about deconstruction? Now that's meaningful."

The discussion continued until it was time for them to go to class. Then the moaning and groaning commenced again. Kim caught snatches of other conversations.

"Don't take Danford, whatever you do," one young man

cautioned another. "He's doddering and senile. Skips from discussing *Paradise Lost* to describing how he plants rose bushes, then starts to yawn at his own lecture."

It all seemed so superficial, petty, and phony. All these young people were locked in the ivory tower of academia, hiding in their study of books, far from the world of everyday reality. Had she once been like that?

She walked down the corridor looking for Frank and finally found him on the second floor, cleaning up a broken juice bottle near the women's bathroom. She could tell by the look he gave her that he recognized her. She withdrew twenty dollars from her wallet and held it out to him.

"For what?" he asked suspiciously.

"To give me some information about Dr. Forbes's house."

"Like what?"

"You tell me. What's unusual about the house? Where do his students meet with him? Do you know what goes on at his gatherings?"

Frank had small, dull eyes, yet there was a shrewd quality about them. "My time is valuable," he said. "Make it another twenty and I'll go somewhere private to talk."

"All right," she agreed and followed him down the corridor to a deserted classroom.

He closed the door behind them. His breath reeked of alcohol. "You just want an excuse to flirt with ol' Frank, don't you?" He gave her a leering smile and moved his body close to hers. He stank of stale sweat.

She shoved him away, practically retching. "Forget it. Sober up and maybe we'll talk again."

"Oh, I could tell you plenty, cutie," he called after her.

She left the room without looking back, aware that her twenty dollars had not succeeded in buying any information. No one seemed to take her seriously. Too bad she'd never acquired an intimidating persona; it would make this much easier. She supposed that Lieutenant Gardner was right about leaving investigative work to professionals. She certainly wasn't getting very far with it. There was no doubt that when he spoke, people paid attention.

At the library, she sat down at her desk and tried to think what she should do. Devoid of inspiration, she checked her mailbox and found a brown paper bag stuffed in it. Within the bag, there was a doll, a crude effigy with a fringe of brown yarn for hair, obviously meant to represent her. A steel needle pierced through the chest. Her first angry reaction was to throw it in the trash, but then she realized it had to be shown to Lieutenant Gardner. She placed the offensive object back in its paper bag and tossed it in the bottom drawer of her desk. She felt chilled with a sudden premonition of evil.

It was time to find Dr. Forbes' home number, to talk to the man again. Who needed Frank anyway? Dr. Forbes' number was listed in the faculty directory, and he answered on the second ring, almost as if he were waiting for her call, although she knew that thought was ridiculous—or was it?

He appeared to recognize her voice before she identified herself. "Ms. Reynolds, was there a special reason you decided to honor me with a phone call?"

"I have the strangest feeling you already know."

"You give me too much credit." His mocking voice was like a singsong melody played on a flute.

If he was responsible for the voodoo doll being placed in her mailbox, she certainly didn't intend to give him the satisfaction of bringing it up directly. Then again, if he had nothing to do with it, there wasn't much point either. She remembered back to her days as a teacher and could not recall a single incident of mischief in which a student confessed unless he was caught in the act.

"I've been informed you have an interest in my home. Is that correct?"

So Frank the custodian had phoned the professor. She wished now that she had snatched her twenty dollars back from the lecher.

"I understand Lorette was invited to one of your gatherings."

"Indeed she was. Perhaps you would like to be a guest at one of my gatherings too. You seem so very fascinated."

"Possibly. What is the criteria for selection? Academic superiority? Or is it something else?"

"Let's just say I look for a certain level of inquisitiveness. I think, Ms. Reynolds, you have an amazingly inquiring mind."

She thought that his euphemism was a bit much. Another person would have come right out with it and told her she was too nosy. Professor Forbes definitely had a subtle way about him when he chose.

"I'm flattered you would consider inviting me."

"Oh, it's more than that. I intend to help you find out what happened to your friend. So let's say that you come over here tonight."

"Tonight?" He was throwing out a challenge to her, and she was on her guard. "I'm at work."

"Come when you finish." He gave her his address and directions. He just assumed that she would come. "I shall look forward to seeing you again. I believe we have much to discuss." He sounded very pleased, like a cat purring after imbibing a saucer of cream.

She held the phone in her hand thoughtfully for a few seconds after he'd hung up, staring at nothing in particular. An uneasy feeling gripped her. Only a few times in her life had she felt this way, once before she'd fractured her leg and a second time before Carl went on his rampage of carnal destruction. She was not clairvoyant, but she did have a distinct sense of wrongness.

However, scared as she was, she would go to Dr. Forbes' house. There were answers there. This was some sort of test for her. She felt herself a failure at so many things in life, like a dog futilely chasing its own tail. It was time to take hold, to take root, like a tree, and find her way in the world.

Nevertheless, she was on edge the rest of the day. She tried to lose herself in her work, but it didn't seem to help. The agitated feeling in her stomach, as if butterflies were flapping their wings and screaming in warning, prevented her from being able to eat any dinner later on.

Finally, before she left the library, Kim picked up the phone and made the call she'd been contemplating all evening. Talking to him might help. But Lieutenant Gardner wasn't in. Rather foolish to think that he would be just sitting around waiting for her to phone. Even policemen didn't work twenty-four hours a day. He'd worked his shift and gone home to his family. She left her name and phone number with a policewoman.

"It might be important for him to know that I'm going to see Professor Forbes tonight at his home. You'll make certain the lieutenant receives that message as soon as possible?" She was reassured by the disembodied voice that asserted she would. Kim left Dr. Forbes' address, just in case.

There was no repeat of the incident of the other night. No one following, no footsteps; still she hurried to her car, her heart palpitating. In her automobile, she whirled through the darkness like a child on a calliope, feeling that this entire experience was slightly surreal. But she reminded herself that this was, in fact, quite real. She was not in an amusement park riding through the funhouse. Several times, she wondered why she was doing such a foolish thing. She ought to turn right around and go home. It was late and she was exhausted. However, who else could discover the answer to the question she was seeking? Forbes had promised her insights if she came tonight. It was probably stupidity on her part, but she needed to know.

Dr. Forbes' house was not far from the campus. The alumni association had purchased the dwelling as an incentive to keep him at the university. Because he was a world-renowned scholar, Columbia had tried desperately to lure him away. The house had turned the tide in favor of the university, and Forbes had remained.

The domicile was a large old Victorian, set back from the tree-lined avenue with no near neighbors. Tall hedges surrounded the structure, creating an aura of supreme privacy.

She parked up the street from the house. It looked almost deserted and the upstairs was dark, but there was a light on the front porch indicating she was expected. Still, she had the sickening thought that perhaps no one else had been invited, that this was not one of the professor's student-gathering evenings after all. She couldn't possibly be early. Her thoughts focused momentarily on that effigy with the sharp metal pin through its chest. With a final queasy sensation in the abyss of her stomach, Kim walked up the winding path to the porch steps. There was an eerie creak as she ascended. There was also a tinkling sound she recognized as wind chimes; they were oddly desolate and reminded her of how alone and vulnerable she actually was.

Dr. Forbes answered the doorbell almost immediately and showed her into his foyer.

"May I take your coat?" he asked. His eyes glittered like sapphires behind dark-framed lenses.

"No, I'll keep it with me," she said. "I feel rather cold."

He smiled as if he understood her perfectly. He was dressed casually, not in a suit as she remembered him before, but a black mock turtleneck sweater and black slacks. "Step into my parlor," he said. "Won't you sit down, my dear?" He indicated a large, old-fashioned loveseat.

Her eyes made a quick sweep of the room. The dark mahogany furnishings were large and Victorian in style. There were bookcases everywhere filled with finely bound volumes. They did share a love of books, she realized. An antique Persian rug of the finest quality in part covered the parquet floor. A large fireplace with an elegant marble mantel dominated the room.

"I am pleased that you decided to visit with me," he said. "You are gifted. I sensed that immediately, but you've denied your talents. I believe you are meant to be one of us."

"One of what, precisely?"

"All in good time, my dear. You must be patient. You will know everything when you are ready for it."

The intensity of his gaze was unnerving her. "Is anyone else coming tonight?"

"We are not entirely alone, if that makes you feel any easier. Now tell me why you were so eager to see my house."

"I wanted to know what Lorette was doing here."

"And so you shall in due time." He smiled at her, the sort of smile that implied she was some inferior being invited solely for his indulgent amusement. "But you are in too dreadful a hurry. Why don't I get us both some refreshment first?"

"No, thank you."

"I don't poison people," he said, smiling his superior smile once again.

"Of course not."

"But that is what you were thinking. The Borgias were fascinating, weren't they? Their guests were never bored."

"Could we just talk about Lorette and why you invited her here?"

"Of course. In fact, I shall lead you on a personally conducted tour of my house. But first, I must insist on bringing out some wine." He left before she could protest.

For a brief moment, she felt a sense of relief at being alone and having the opportunity to look around a bit by herself. The great variety of books again caught her interest. She observed there were a vast number on the subject of the occult; however, by and large, the professor's tastes seemed eclectic.

After five minutes had passed, she sensed that something wasn't right. Where had he gone? She decided to look for him. The parlor led out to the main foyer, which she followed to a formal dining room, from there walking into the kitchen. There was no sign of the professor in any of the rooms. She nervously called out his name but got no reply.

What to do next? She was tempted to simply walk out of the house and forget the whole thing, but she reminded herself she had come for answers. He was the one person who could give them to her. She decided to look around a bit more. Wine was often kept in cellars; maybe he'd gone down for a bottle. She went back to the kitchen where she'd seen several doors; one appeared to lead to a basement, another led outside. Quickly, she looked in the pantry first before going any further. It was stocked with an array of gourmet foods but no sign of the professor. She opened the door to the basement that had stood ajar and found herself at the top of a staircase. It was dark and the atmosphere was close. A strange odor assailed her nostrils, wafting upward from down below. She tried to accustom her eyes to the lack of light, looking for a switch. Groping around, she finally found one. A ghostly light transfixed her surroundings. From the steps she could see the basement very well. It was quite large, apparently extending the length of the house.

She was very surprised by what her view afforded. The walls of the cellar were black with scarlet tapestries hanging along them. They also effectively blocked off any windows, as if a protection from curious eyes. Light glared down from a fixture in the ceiling shaped like an enormous eye. At the front, or focal point, of the room was some sort of an altar outfitted with an inverted cross. Black candles were set on either side of it. She took a step backward when she realized what she was seeing. This was no ordinary chapel. It must be here to celebrate some sort of Black Mass. The professor had obviously carried his interest in the occult past the stage of mere passive reading. He was involved in some cult of devil worship. The trembling had begun again and would not stop. So this was what Lorette had discovered, what she obviously wanted no part of. Kim turned to go up the stairs.

"Thinking of leaving so quickly? We haven't even had our wine as yet." Forbes seemed to appear from out of nowhere.

She was hardly able to speak. "I was looking for you."

"Ah, well you have found me. Tell me, now that you have seen where our gatherings are held, do you think you would wish to be part of our group?"

She swallowed hard. This was neither the time nor place to denounce him. "I'll have to consider it."

He grasped her hand. "You're very cold. Are you frightened, my dear? I assure you that there is no reason to feel fear." The hypnotic power of his gaze was upon her.

"Did Lorette die because of this?"

"No, she did not." His eyes were directly set on hers. "She did prove a bit squeamish and unstable, which I confess surprised me mightily. I had thought she would fit in perfectly with our little group, our band of brothers, but she did not wish it."

The smell of incense assailed her nostrils. "What was she squeamish about?"

He gave her an enigmatic smile. "Our symbolic sacrifice. Merely a cat, I assure you, but poor Lorette was not as strong in her mind as she would have had others believe. I truly think

the girl was ill. It's clear to me that she either committed suicide in the grip of deep depression or that her death was an accident."

"You can say that after I've seen this?"

"My dear, what have you seen, after all?" His satin-smooth voice did little to put her at ease.

"Quite enough. I believe I want to leave now."

"My dear, you truly disappoint me. I had hopes for you. There was something about you. I sensed your need to belong with us. Don't be afraid to give yourself over to me. You fear freedom just as most people do. Give yourself over to me and you never need to be afraid again." His voice was smooth, seductive.

"Who are you? What are you?"

"Can't you guess?"

Oh, she could indeed! "I'm not ready to sell my soul at any price."

"Who said any such thing? That is just a foolish literary device. When one devotes one's existence to Satan, one is rewarded with power. There is no greater power in the universe than evil. It controls the minds and bodies of so many, both spiritually and physically."

"You're insane," she said.

"Am I?" He moved into a circle with symbols in lines of red and began chanting words in Latin. "I call for the power of Lucifer!" He raised his hands and looked upward.

All of a sudden a shaft of light transfigured him. He became incandescent. Kim turned away, blinking, temporarily blinded.

"See what I have become," he demanded.

When she looked again, he was no longer human.

"I am the temporal incarnation of Satan. Can you, a mere mortal, feel my power?"

Kim was unable to speak. She turned her back on him,

figuratively and literally, taking a final look at his sinister chapel. She would phone the police as soon as she got out of this place of evil. Lieutenant Gardner should be told about what went on here.

She heard a sound behind her as if someone else were coming hurriedly down the stairs. Before she could turn around, there was an impact. Pain shot through her head.

CHAPTER FOURTEEN

Kim's head ached. It ached so violently that she couldn't think. She tried to focus her eyes. Where was she? *Try to concentrate!* Dr. Forbes' house. The cellar. Darkness. She felt rather than saw steps. Fear ripped at her throat like an attack dog. Her eyes still would not focus. But there was nothing wrong with her sense of smell. What it told her was that there was a fire somewhere nearby. Smoke surrounded her. It was so hard to breathe! She reached outward for the steps. Still she could not see clearly. She forced herself to crawl up the stairs, afraid that someone would hit her again, and tripped on the last step.

There was a back door by the kitchen, wasn't there? The smoke was choking her, entering into her lungs. *Please God, help me get out of here!* She was so dizzy, mind and body wouldn't function together. She forced herself to the task of opening the door, knowing that her life depended on it. There was air, cool, fresh air. Now she could finally breathe again. She felt a sense of relief. She had no wish to die. But the dizziness returned. Blackness descended again.

Someone was pushing her, and none too gently; she protested. All she wanted was to sleep. Why wouldn't they let her sleep? She could sleep forever if they'd just let her alone in peace. She needed to be left in peace. But something, someone, was dragging her, pushing, poking, prodding.

"You're alive," the person said with a sense of relief. "Why didn't you stay out of it?"

It was Mike Gardner. He would be the one to find her!

She felt his strong arms, lifting her protectively. She tried to form words, but no sound would emanate from her throat. Instead, she felt a burning; it hurt to breathe. There didn't seem to be any air in her lungs.

"Take it easy," he said. "There's an ambulance on the way."

He held her against his broad chest. She snuggled against him. Did he caress her cheek? She must have imagined it. It didn't matter. She felt safe now, comforted.

When Kim's mind focused again, her eyes were clouded and every breath was an effort for her lungs. She was in a bubble—no, an oxygen tent. She couldn't cough or speak. She wanted to struggle against it but felt too weak.

"You're all right," a soothing voice said. She knew the woman meant to calm her, but she wasn't succeeding. "This is only oxygen. You're in the hospital. Just breathe slowly and don't try to move around for now."

A few minutes later, Lieutenant Gardner was looking down at her, frowning, his brow wrinkled. "You gave me a good scare. A few more minutes in there and you'd have been a French fry. Why'd you go alone? Damn it, I warned you, didn't I? By the way, the house burned down. Those old places go up real fast. You can tell me all about it when you're talking again—or better still, write me a report. I could do with an explanation. Oh, and you're going to be here a couple of days. They say you're suffering from a mild concussion as well as smoke inhalation. Could've been worse. This is one time having a hard head's an asset. There's an address book in your handbag. Who should I phone for you?"

She shook her head.

"If you don't pick somebody, I'll stay here with you. I don't want you to be alone. So you decide."

Grudgingly, she nodded her head. He had a family, people who would worry if he didn't come home. It would be unfair to make him stay. But whom could she possibly bother? Ma would get too upset, and she'd already had more than her share of misery. No, she didn't want Ma to know. Gardner was flipping pages and reading off names; as he read each one, he looked to her for a response. She finally nodded when he said, "Don Bernard," although why she should agree to bother him was beyond her. She wasn't even certain she could trust him. But there was no one else. And she had helped Don when his mother died. Still, it was terrible to think in those terms.

She hated to ask help from anyone. It was one thing to help other people, quite another to ask favors. Never had she done that before. Still, Lieutenant Gardner wasn't giving her any choice in the matter. She was hurting too much to think anymore; mercifully, she slipped out of consciousness again.

"Thank God! Good researchers are hard to find." Don Bernard was squeezing her hand. "Don't talk. I can do enough of that for both of us. That policeman tells me you're going to be fine, but he wants someone with you. I'll stay as long as they let me and then come back tomorrow. What did you think you were doing? You're a bit old to play Nancy Drew."

She tried to reply and found that all she could do was croak.

"No, don't try to speak, not for now anyway. The only reason you're alive is because you managed to get out in time, and the detective got you away quickly. The house burned down. There's very little left of it."

"Forbes?" she managed to choke out.

He lowered his eyes. "He's dead, I'm afraid. I don't know all the details."

She stared at him in shock and amazement. Forbes dead?

That made no sense at all!

Don Bernard stayed with her. She hated to admit how much it comforted her to have him there. He held her hand until she fell asleep again.

Mike Gardner returned the following morning. He understood her when she tried to ask about Forbes.

"When I got to the house, it was on fire. I found you, but I never got to Forbes. I was there before the firemen arrived. They did their best, but it wasn't enough. It's going to take a few days to sift through everything. The word so far is that it looks like arson. You got any idea who might have torched the place?"

He gave her a notepad and pen.

Her hand was shaky but she managed to write: *I think someone else was there but I didn't see anybody.*

"Okay, get some rest and we'll talk again when you're feeling better."

She tried to raise herself but her head began to throb with a dull ache. He seemed to understand; his silver eyes were soft as mist. He put his arms around her and held her supportively.

"Doc says they'll keep you another day. You're doing great. Just keep going along with what they tell you. Don't look so miserable. It could have been a whole lot worse." He gave her hand a squeeze as if she were a small child. "Stick to library work instead of Sam Spade stuff. Okay? You wouldn't want to put me out of a job, would you? I got two girls to support. The cell phone bills alone are enough to bankrupt me." His complaint was lighthearted; it was obvious he felt genuine affection for his children. She liked him the better for that.

In her remaining time in the hospital, Kim was poked, prodded and treated like the victim of a vampire. She never fell asleep before midnight and was awakened by the nurses each morning before six. In short, she left the hospital feeling pretty much as though she needed to check into one.

Gardner must have been keeping track of her, because on the morning she was to be released from the hospital, he showed up.

"I'm driving you home," he said. "Your friend the professor has a class to teach. Besides, I think we need to have a little talk, now that you seem to be feeling better."

"Lecture?" she asked.

"Me? Never!" He gave her a broad grin.

"I guess you got the message I left for you." She hated the croaking sound of her voice.

"You're lucky I got there in time."

"I am at that."

"I had a hunch something was very wrong. When I got near the house, I could smell the smoke. And you ended up at the professor's house why?"

He listened attentively as she told him in as few words as possible about the doll, the phone call to Forbes, her arrival at his house, followed by his strange disappearance.

"You thought he was up to something?"

"Yes, something diabolical." She told him briefly about the discovery in the basement. "It was fixed up like a medieval chapel, only for devil worship. Forbes told me as much." Her breathing was a little ragged and she paused for a moment. Her voice was still hoarse, barely more than a whisper.

Gardner didn't say anything, but waited for her to continue.

"I went to the professor's house because I believed that he was the link to the death of Lorette and Sandy. I still believe that."

"The city police are in on this with us. Their forensics people are better than ours, and their facilities are larger. They've examined the remains of the good professor and found that his skull was bashed in before the fire. He was brain dead before the flames ever touched him."

"Then he was killed like Sandy."

"And like you almost were." He gave her a significant look. "I want you to think about this. Why do you believe that someone else was in the house? Did you see or hear anyone?"

"Not exactly. I didn't see anyone. But before I was hit, I heard someone."

"Probably the killer figured that you were going to die in the fire along with Forbes so it wasn't necessary to finish you off."

"There wasn't any need, because I really didn't find out much of anything."

"I don't agree. You found out that Forbes was presiding over a group of devil worshippers. That would have gotten him axed, right? And anyone connected with him would have been in trouble as well."

"The university doesn't want that kind of negative publicity," she agreed. "But Dr. Forbes did have a reputation for being an eccentric. You can pretty much do as you please when you're as famous a literary critic as he was."

"Maybe he wouldn't have to worry, but those connected with him would. I doubt the administration would be all that tolerant or liberal-minded."

Gardner was probably right, she decided.

"The fire was meant to cover up murder and destroy evidence in the cellar. There's going to be a thorough investigation. I want you out of it from now on. Whoever is murdering university people is really determined and probably demented. He or she has already taken one crack at you. There's no need for another."

"You have my word, Lieutenant."

"Girl Scout's Honor?"

"I never was one."

"Have to have the final word, don't you? Well, rest your voice for a while."

He lifted her into his arms, took her keys and opened the door, carrying her into the apartment. Kim's pulse raced. Being held by this strong, sexy man thrilled her. They were so close. His eyes lowered and fixed on her lips. For one weird moment, Kim was certain he was going to kiss her, and she realized she wanted him to do exactly that more than anything in this world. Her heart was pounding and she could scarcely catch her breath. *What am I thinking? The man has a family. There can't be anything between us.* She stiffened.

"I can walk," she protested.

"Maybe. I'm not taking any chances."

Once she was settled on the couch, he went to her refrigerator, rummaged around and brought her a bottle of water.

Then he sat down beside her.

"You don't have to stay," she told him.

"Think I'll hang around for a while. Just consider it part of the service."

"You think someone's going to try to kill me again?"

"Could be. Drink up." He tipped the water bottle to her lips.

"I'm used to taking care of myself."

"Yeah, well, we can both see where that got you." His tone was grim.

She simultaneously wanted to punch him in the nose and run her hand through his thick, dark hair. She did neither.

"Lieutenant, you're a very perplexing man. You really infuriate me."

"Yeah, my wife used to say stuff like that."

"And you apologized?"

"Sometimes. Actually, she divorced me five years ago."

Kim lowered her eyes. "I'm sorry." *Liar!*

"Me too. Mostly I'm sorry for the girls. She left them as well."

Kim couldn't imagine a mother doing that. "It's hard to understand," was all she could manage to say in her croaky voice.

He shrugged. "She said she had to find herself. It turned out she had this boyfriend, a younger guy who didn't have much use for children."

Kim placed her hand on his in a gesture of comfort.

"Not much of a detective, am I? Didn't even know my own wife was screwing around. She said I was too involved with my work. I guess she was right. These days, I try to spend as much time as possible with my girls."

"Lieutenant, I have the feeling you're a very good father."

His eyes met hers squarely. "Call me Mike. And I'd like to spend some time with you that wasn't professional."

"You would?"

As if to answer her question, he leaned over and kissed her. He covered her mouth with his. She felt the blood in her veins begin to heat. She found herself kissing him back with all the passion that was in her. He deepened the contact between them. It was a mind-blowing kiss and it excited her. Maybe she'd been kissed before, but it never felt anything like this! His hands roamed over her body. She pulled back, gasping for breath. If she didn't put some distance between them, she would completely lose control. It was confusing and disturbing.

"Sorry, I didn't mean to take advantage of you."

She shook her head. "You didn't."

"I did. I understand you better than you think. You and I, we share something unique, special."

Her mind was still clouded by emotion when he left her.

Don Bernard arrived an hour later, surprising her.

"I thought you had a class to teach," she said.

"I decided to cancel it." His eyes were fixed on hers as if to say that he considered her more important.

She looked away in embarrassment. "You shouldn't have done that."

"Ridiculous! Don't you think you carry this self-reliance thing a bit far? We're friends, remember?"

"Friends," she agreed.

He gave her one of his charming smiles, which lit up his face and made him seem boyish. "Glad to hear it. I brought soup for your lunch."

Kim wondered how she could have suspected him of killing Lorette. She felt guilty and ashamed. Don Bernard was a good, decent man. Just because he might have been involved with Lorette at one time didn't mean he would ever harm her.

"Do you think Lionel Forbes killed Lorette?" Don asked as he worked in her tiny kitchen.

"I don't know. He didn't admit it to me. I can't really believe that he's dead."

"Yes, he was quite a formidable, charismatic individual. He rather tended to dominate those around him. It hardly seems possible that such individuals are mortal like the rest of us."

"I think someone in his circle killed him as well as Lorette and Sandy. I just can't understand why."

"Loss of career? Devil worship is not politically correct, the last I heard."

She gave him a quick look. "How did you know about that?"

He frowned. "The detective mentioned it. Actually, he asked me some questions. He seemed to think I might be involved in some way. I set him straight. Forbes and I might have been colleagues, but we were never friends, nor did we share any common interests outside of the obvious literary ones. I'm too squeamish to even watch a horror movie."

"I really ought to talk to Nick Margrove again. He's the only one who can help me discover the identity of the rest of that crowd."

Don frowned at her. "Let it go. You were nearly killed. The murderer targeted you as well as dear old Lionel. Hasn't it occurred to you yet that you're in danger? And certainly if you continue poking your pretty nose where it most decidedly does not belong, someone will finish what he started the other night."

His words sent a chill down her spine. "I felt connected to Lorette. We bonded. She deserved better." Kim was finding it difficult to express her feelings. Rarely did she think or talk about how she felt. She managed to neatly tuck her emotions away in a closed, dark compartment in her heart, never to be taken out and looked at in the light of day. Now she was being forced to reexamine those feelings. If she wasn't careful, the old pain would start again. She had to escape that at all cost. But maybe suffering was just another requirement of existence. Could any human being exist without it? Still, she had known enough anguish to last a lifetime.

"Don't you see how ridiculous it is for you to pursue this?" Don glanced over at her disapprovingly.

"Intellectually, I do. However, the taking of a human life should not go unnoticed, unmourned or unpunished."

"Commendably idealistic," he said with sarcasm.

"Don't mock me. I believe Lorette mattered. We all matter! It seems to me that life is held too cheaply these days."

"Other people's lives perhaps. Most of us value our own."

"I'm no different."

"But you've determined to make yourself a human sacrifice as a protest?"

He struck a nerve. Wasn't he describing what Carl had done? But she was not like him. She had no intention of hurting others, only helping them.

"I can assure you I don't have a martyr complex."

"Your sleuthing will only get you into trouble. I urge you to stop."

She stood up, but was unsteady on her feet. Don insisted that she take his arm for support. Her legs still felt rubbery so she didn't argue with him. He helped her sit down at the table and served her the soup.

"Would you like to share?" she asked.

He indicated that he wouldn't.

"I don't think I have anything else to offer you."

"Actually, you've got quite a bit to offer," he said, flashing a dazzling smile. His mood seemed to have inexplicably shifted.

"I was thinking along the lines of refreshments."

"Oh, that! Well, I had a sandwich on the way over. Can I do anything else for you?"

"No, it's not necessary. Thanks again for the soup. I'm going to have it and then lie down for a while."

"Then perhaps I should go. You look tired. And if I stay, I'll have you croaking some more and that can't be good for your throat." Still he stood there looking at her, frozen to the spot, or so it seemed.

"You are a good friend."

"I'd like to be a lot more."

"You have a way about you," she said awkwardly.

"Really? I thought that of you. I'll let you rest as I promised. But if you should need me, just call, night or day. For you, I'm always available."

"All I have to do is whistle?" she said, trying to keep her tone light. "Too bad I never got the knack of it."

"I consider you my friend and confidante. To prove it, you are the only human being on this earth outside of my family, whom I would trust to know my full first name," Don said.

"Which is?"

He hesitated. "It's Donalbain."

Kim raised her eyebrows questioningly.

"My dear departed mother, an amateur thespian, fancied *Macbeth*. I suppose it could have been worse. She might have named me Banquo—or perish the thought, Fleance." He gave her a wry smile that made her laugh. He brushed a stray lock of hair back from his forehead. "Glad I could amuse you. You need to laugh more."

"I won't tell anyone your name. I'm very good at keeping secrets. I've had my share of practice."

"When you're ready, you can share some of yours with me."

Her sense of awareness told her to be very careful what she shared with him. Probably, she was just too cautious, but she trusted the warning vibration of her seventh sense.

It was several days before she felt able to go back to work. Wendell did not seem overly concerned when she phoned to say that she was still under the weather. In fact, she thought she detected a note of relief in his voice. She valued her recuperation time. No more nurses dueling and poking at her with plastic-covered thermometers. She could sleep as much or as little as she chose.

Jim Davis phoned the second day she was at home. "How's it going?" he asked with what appeared to be real concern.

She told him that she was getting along very well.

"Take care of yourself. Everyone at school is talking about what happened." He paused momentarily. "There's all kinds of speculation. What exactly did happen?"

"I'm not certain myself." She realized that she was being intentionally evasive.

"Well, glad you're okay," he said good-naturedly, "but it's a damned shame about Dr. Forbes."

"Yes, a shame. Jim, about Dr. Forbes, you had him for a

class. Did he ever talk about satanism or devil worship?"

"What?" The question seemed to throw him. "Not that I can remember. Of course, he used to say the most powerful force in the universe is evil."

"Referring to the Puritan belief that man is born in sin?"

"So you know then."

"Not exactly."

"No one ever took him seriously. It was just the way the man talked. Kind of a weird old bird."

"Some people took him seriously," she said. "Were you ever invited to his house?"

"Me? No, I never was. Wasn't intellectual enough for him I guess." The voice was nervous. He was too quick with his denial. Was he lying? If so, why?

"But Dr. Forbes did like you?" That seemed a safe assumption.

"It was hard to tell who he liked and didn't like. One time in class, this gal was absent that he always seemed to favor. He looked around checking for absentees, saw she wasn't there and then said, 'Lovely, that loud-mouth bitch isn't here today.' See what I mean? He was really hard to figure. You never knew quite where he was coming from. He kept us all off balance and it was probably deliberate. Maybe he liked me, maybe not. I wasn't one of his chosen, though. And that was plenty much all right with me."

"Who were his chosen? Can you remember some names?"

He didn't answer right away. She had the distinct impression he was holding back.

"I'm not certain."

"Was Lorette very involved?"

"He wanted her. She went to his house only that one time."

"Did she tell you what went on at the house?"

"Well," the Western voice twanged slowly, "Lorette was secre-

169

tive about it, but I could see it had upset her. She was nervous and in a bad mood the next day."

"She didn't say anything?"

"Nope. Locked me out in the barn, so to speak."

After the conversation ended, Kim rested her head against the pillow on the sofa. The whole thing became more puzzling and sinister all the time. What had happened to Lorette the night she visited Forbes' house? What had so upset her? Drug use? That was something of a certainty. Lorette would have no part of that. Kim was sure of it. But would it upset her that badly? Not unless he'd tried forcing the drugs on her.

What of the Satan worship? Lorette was a sophisticated woman. Wouldn't it simply strike her as absurd? But Kim had seen with her own eyes that Dr. Forbes had been a practitioner of the Black Mass. He'd shown her his power. Still, it could have been some sort of trick that he rigged. Magicians did that all the time, didn't they? Maybe he had supernatural power and maybe he didn't. But her awareness told her that the man truly had channeled demonic power.

Before he was killed, she would have believed that he murdered Lorette and Sandy. But he was dead now too, and all three murders appeared to have been committed by the same individual—someone who wanted to see her dead as well. Another practitioner of the black arts? Or a psychotic, perhaps? Then again, what murderer could be considered sane? Kim trembled, thinking about it. Who might know the truth?

It came back to Nick Margrove. He had to know who the murderer was, or at least have some suspicion. Maybe he was the one who had murdered Lorette, Sandy and Forbes. But then that left a question of motive, didn't it? Why did people kill? For money, out of greed, for love, out of passion, for hate, or out of madness. Why had Lorette, Sandy and Dr. Forbes been killed? Out of fear? Her head began to throb again. She took some of the medicine the doctor had given her, closed her eyes and tried to rest.

Later, she began thinking again. Was she obsessive? Yet she couldn't stop her troubled thoughts. Mike Gardner had warned her to stay out of the investigation. She tried to put it out of her mind. *Time to get a life.*

It was then that she remembered the small diary sitting on the counter in her kitchen. Unable to rest, she walked over and picked it up. There were other mysteries to solve, more personal ones and just as painful.

CHAPTER FIFTEEN

It was while Kim was reading Jen's diary that Mike Gardner stopped by the apartment. She was surprised by his visit, and yet in some respects not surprised at all. He looked as formidable as ever, even wearing an off-the-rack suit, plain white shirt and unfashionable tie loosened at the neck. She didn't invite him in, wasn't up to being alone with him again.

"I just dropped by to see how you're doing," he responded to her raised brow.

"As you can tell, I'm not up to doing much of anything."

"Maybe that's for the best."

"I could think of better uses for my sick days."

He stood there looking at her thoughtfully, as if her well-being really mattered to him.

She regretted behaving ungraciously, broke down and invited him in. "So what is it?" She settled back on the couch while he took a straight-back chair.

"Same old. I need to talk to you about the university murders."

"Is that what you're calling them now?"

He gave her a wry grin. "That's what the newspapers are calling them. Haven't you been reading the papers?"

"No, I've been avoiding them."

"I can't afford that luxury. And shame on you, an information specialist who doesn't read the newspapers."

"Please, I feel rotten enough," she said.

"I talked to your pal Nick Margrove. I know you spoke to the kid too."

"He's definitely not my pal, although I really think he's the key to this."

"What makes you say that?" He leaned toward her, acting as if he valued her input.

"Nick was at Forbes' house the night that Lorette was there. He brought Sandy with him too. Sandy told me he was one of Dr. Forbes' chosen. We have no idea who they are except for Nick, so it stands to reason that he has some answers. Whoever killed Dr. Forbes most likely is someone protecting his own reputation."

"What did Margrove tell you?"

"Not a thing," she conceded. "But that proves nothing. I've never been sufficiently intimidating. It was my great failing as a high school teacher."

"Am I intimidating?"

She appraised him thoughtfully, her head tilted to one side. "I don't know, since you don't need to frighten me. But you do have a way of getting people to open up to you. My gut feeling is that you can be ruthless when it's necessary."

"Whatever works," he said with a shrug.

"You're a pragmatist, like Ben Franklin. Pragmatists always find a way to get things done."

He took her assessment in stride. "Is it your opinion that the Margrove kid did all three of them?"

Did them? Odd how even the police preferred euphemisms. "It's possible, but I don't know why. I believe it's kind of complicated."

Gardner nodded his head approvingly. "You're not a bad detective for a civilian."

"I'm a reference librarian. We deal with mystery-solving every single day. Someone needs information, I have to figure out where to find it. It takes searching."

"Like hunting for evidence?"

"A lot like that, yes. People give us clues and we go do the searching."

"Okay, I can respect that. I'll bring Margrove in and give him a full interrogation. That meet with your approval?"

She indicated that it did.

"There's something else I wanted you to know. Because this case isn't limited to the township, you're probably going to be questioned by other cops besides me. I'll try to see to it that you're not bothered much, but brace yourself. We're getting publicity now, and that means heat, pressure to get the case solved."

Absently, she had picked up the diary, clasping it tightly to her breast.

"Did I interrupt your reading?"

She shook her head. "I was trying to get something straight in my head. I've looked at this diary before, but I never was certain I really understood it. There are things I want to find out."

"Whose diary? Your friend Lorette? If it is, maybe I ought to have a look."

"No, it's personal. If it had been Lorette's, I would have given it to you. Honor bright."

His eyes were on hers, viewing her with interest and concern. Strange how she felt able to talk to him about things that she and Ma were totally unable to discuss. Maybe it was because he was an outsider, a disinterested party. No, she corrected. He wasn't those things anymore. He had somehow made their relationship personal. She would never forget that kiss.

"I just want to be sure you're not holding out on me," he said with a steady gaze.

"My mother had a younger sister who died in her teens. When

Ma talked about Jen, she'd get this funny look in her eye. I never understood. When I got older, I wondered more about Jen, but I never asked because the mention of Jen's name always made Ma sad. Jen was locked away in Ma's past life, her few remaining things in an old attic trunk. Every once in a while, I'd say or do something that seemed to remind her of Jen, and then she'd start to cry. I wanted to ask Carl about her, but he and I didn't communicate. He was mostly cold and distant with me."

"Why are you reading your aunt's diary?"

"I found it up in the attic when I was a teenager. What she wrote in it, I could connect with because she was a teenager when she wrote it. I felt very close to her. But when Ma found me reading it, she got upset and took it away from me. I didn't want her miserable, so I just accepted things as they were and left it alone."

"And now you can't?"

"I don't know. Ma's going away. I feel Jen was part of a past that I never got to know, that I should know."

"But if it makes your mother so unhappy . . ."

"Oh, it does. But things haven't been right between us for a long time. Ma thinks I've turned my back on family. When I changed my name, she and I had a terrible quarrel. I wonder if it will ever be right between us again. She hates the way I feel about Carl. I don't think of him as my father. I know that man never loved me." She could hear the bitterness and resentment in her voice. She lowered her eyes. "I believe that I was adopted."

"Why would you think that?"

"It was something Carl once said. He could be a cruel bastard, but he never lied about things." She would not, could not, tell him about that. The pain was too deep. The feelings still too confused. She had not even discussed it with Ma those many years ago. But she had never forgiven Carl. He died unmourned by her, something Ma never understood.

"I'm not condoning anything Carl Reyner did, but your mother was right when she said that war changes people. A lot of men came back from foreign places physical or emotional cripples, and in some cases, both."

"Were you in the military?" she asked, curious about him.

"Yeah, but not like your old man. It wasn't so bad for me. The Marine Corps was a positive influence in my life."

"Have you had to kill many people?" She shouldn't have asked him that question, but it was too late to retract it now.

He stood up, removed his jacket and showed her the police special that was holstered on his shoulder. "I don't use this much. I've been involved in some shooting incidents, but not many. I'm not a violent man. Still, I do what needs to be done." There was a grim, determined set to his jaw. "I try to help people who need help. That's what my job is really about, same as yours. Society needs both of us, me to protect it, you to inform it."

She felt connected to him at that moment, something she felt for very few people. She wanted to touch him, to place her hand on his. She reached toward him. Then suddenly, she withdrew, awkward with those feelings and wanting to retreat from them. He seemed to sense that because he changed the subject.

"Anyhow, I wouldn't bet my next paycheck that I can find out more from Margrove than you have. Of course, I might suggest that he's under suspicion for murder and see if he sweats a little. But from what I've observed so far, that kid hands out lies faster and smoother than a croupier deals cards. Then again, everybody lies to cops. It's an unwritten law."

"That sounds cynical."

"Just honest."

"Can you tell when people are lying to you?"

He nodded. "For the most part. Some of the guys in the department call me the psychologist, because I can generally figure what people are thinking."

"You're perceptive."

He met her gaze. "It kind of goes beyond that. You understand, don't you?"

She didn't answer him.

Mike liked Kim Reynolds—liked her a lot—and he didn't allow himself to feel that way about many of the people he met on duty; he was too much of a professional. He thought she had good instincts, even if she did have some problems in the form of emotional hang-ups. Probably she ought to be seeing a shrink. But she hadn't asked for his advice, and he wasn't about to offer it unless she did. He knew from hard experience that it wouldn't be appreciated.

He saw how she locked her hands together as if to keep herself in tight control. He also saw a frightened, lonely woman, naturally shy, who was fighting her private demons, but who'd summoned the courage to do what she thought was right. He wanted to take her in his arms again and kiss away her fears and doubts. Actually, he wanted a lot more. But he was a professional and he knew better than to push it. Still, when they had kissed he'd been aroused, and he knew damn well that she'd wanted him just as much as he'd wanted her. Their time would come.

Just as he'd told her, he was going to put some pressure on Nick Margrove and see where it led. He'd already gotten Margrove's schedule from the graduate school office and knew exactly where the kid was. He drove out to the campus to the language building where Margrove was teaching a composition course for freshmen. He balked only when he had to walk over a swaying footbridge that dangled high above a steep ravine. Nevertheless, when he saw with what little regard the students traversed the narrow walkway, he was damned if he'd give it any concern. One girl even whizzed across on a bicycle as he strode along. He shook his head and wondered if he was getting old, losing his edge.

Margrove was still working with his class when Gardner arrived. He remained in the hall for another fifteen minutes, waiting until the students were finally released. During that time, he badly craved a cold beer, but refused to let his mind dwell on it. That would have to wait until he was off duty. When the last of the students departed, he walked briskly into the classroom before Margrove could finish folding up his materials.

"Not you again. Look, I'm working now. I can't be bothered." Margrove quickly gathered up his books and notes.

"Fine, I can always take you in for questioning."

"On what grounds? I haven't done anything wrong."

"I'm not arresting you—yet. But police headquarters might be a better place for you to give me a statement. You know, something formal."

"I have another class in exactly twenty minutes," the youth said in what Gardner considered an annoyingly affected, nasal voice.

"How long have you been a coke user?"

Margrove swiped at his swollen nose with a tissue. "What are you talking about?" he said defensively.

Gardner grabbed him by the collar of his preppie shirt and shoved him hard against the wall.

"Hey, what the hell do you think you're doing?" Margrove was more frightened than angry.

"I want some straight answers from you."

"I'll have you charged with assault and harassment!"

"I don't see any witnesses, do you?" He let go of Margrove,

who was shaking. "How long you been treating your body so rotten?"

"It's just a cold."

"Yeah? I've seen colds like yours before. Ugly habit. Who's your supplier? Was it Forbes? Did he buy or sell or both?"

"I don't know what you're talking about."

"Sure you do." He hated snotty kids who put on superior airs.

"Why don't you go out and arrest real criminals?" the young man said indignantly. His pockmarked face seemed mottled in the darkened room.

"Know what I think? Maybe you killed all three of those people." He brought his index finger against the younger man's chest in a menacing gesture. "We can place you at Forbes' house with both of the dead girls. And we know you were one of his regulars at satanic rituals. You're in a lot of trouble, kid."

"Bullshit! You have no witnesses. There's no evidence that I killed anybody, and you won't find any. I'm not telling you anything, and you can't make me."

"You're going to headquarters," Gardner told him in a quiet but intense voice.

"Like hell I am!" Margrove turned, spat right in his face and pushed him as hard as he was able. Then he rushed toward the door.

There was no hesitation on his part; Gardner subdued his suspect with a swift blow to the gut. Margrove immediately doubled over, groaning loudly. Gardner took his arm.

"That's it, kid. We can make it tough or easy, but you're coming with me. Do I need handcuffs? If I have to, I'll put you under arrest."

Margrove shook his head sullenly and didn't speak again.

Gardner interrogated Margrove at headquarters, but didn't get the answers he'd hoped for. Margrove kept saying he was innocent. Then he demanded a lawyer. Gardner knew he'd have to let the kid go. There was no real evidence on which to base an arrest.

Afterwards, he was approached by Captain Rainey, a man ten years older than himself with a beer belly and white hair that was so slicked back it could have passed for a toboggan run.

"How's it going with your investigation into those university homicides?"

"Nowhere. I had to cut the kid loose I brought in. He's been hanging real tough."

"Think he's the perp?"

"Don't know, Cap, but he sure knows a hell of a lot more than he's telling us."

Rainey struggled to raise his belt over his protruding gut, found it a losing battle, and finally gave up. "We got people asking questions about this case. Three people get whacked, it starts looking like a serial killer's out there. It's getting media attention and you know what that means. So keep the pressure up."

Gardner let out a deep sigh; this case wasn't going down easy.

CHAPTER SIXTEEN

Kim woke up the following morning feeling much better physically than she had for some time. She phoned Wendell Firbin and told him that she would be back on the job the following day. He sounded less than pleased, but said that he would schedule her for evening hours.

She missed being at work. If she had to watch one more afternoon of soap operas, she vowed to start sobbing louder than any of the characters on the shows. A definite good sign was that she was hungry for the first time since the fire.

She boiled herself an egg, fixed toast, coffee and orange juice, and then did a light cleaning of the apartment. Afterwards, she took a hot shower and washed her hair. It was wonderful feeling clean and healthy again, feeling in charge of her life.

The telephone rang at ten o'clock in the morning. She was more than a little surprised when the speaker identified himself as Nick Margrove.

"Why are you calling me?"

"I have something to tell you, Ms. Reynolds." His speech sounded a trifle slurred, as if he hadn't gotten much sleep. "Put the pig back in the pen."

"What?"

"You understand me," he continued in a surly voice. "Get that cop off my back. I know it was you who told him about me in the first place."

"You're involved in the murders of three people. Naturally,

Lieutenant Gardner would want to question you further. Was he somewhat overzealous in his interrogation?"

Margrove let out an unpleasant, hollow-sounding laugh at the other end of the wire. "You could put it that way. The man was ready to cut me up in pieces and skewer until well done. I'm going to talk to a lawyer about him. He violated my civil rights. He can't treat me that way! I'm brilliant and everyone knows it. I could have gone to any college in this country. Imagine manhandling someone like me as though I were some common criminal! That cop is a cretin."

Hardly an apt description of Lieutenant Gardner, but she refrained from making the observation. "You did bring Sandy to Dr. Forbes' house, didn't you? She told me that."

"The dead don't talk. You might be wise to keep that in mind." With that, he hung up.

She wasn't certain whether he had threatened her or not. Should she tell Mike Gardner about the conversation? No, why bother him? It probably didn't mean anything except that Nick was frightened, just as he ought to be.

The phone rang again and she hesitated, thinking it might be Nick Margrove calling back. Instead, with some relief, she heard Don Bernard's mellifluous, cultivated voice at the other end.

"Are you feeling up to going out to lunch today?"

"That would be nice."

"I'll even let you pick the place."

"I'm not fussy, just so long as I don't have to graze. I haven't been eating very substantially of late."

"Then I know just the restaurant."

Don picked her up at noon and took her to a pub right near the campus. She knew it to be a favorite with the male faculty, although she had never eaten there. It wasn't the sort of place a woman usually went to by herself, unless she was looking to pick up a man at the bar.

"Grady's has the best beef in the city. They char a steak to perfection," Don said. He studied her thoughtfully. "We'll make yours rare."

"I'd prefer it not mooing at me."

His brows rose in a gesture of concern. "You're looking a little anemic."

"Is that a polite way of saying that I look terrible?"

"You? Never! Just a tad pale as if you spent an evening with a vampire."

"I feel as though I did, except there aren't any puncture wounds on my neck. They treated me like a pin cushion in the hospital."

The hostess led them to the bar to wait for a table. Don ordered a tall Collins; Kim settled for a cranberry juice with a twist of lime. Kim looked around appreciatively. It was a nice, old-fashioned place with a dark, polished mahogany bar and paneled walls. She felt very comfortable here with Don. They chatted easily and his witticisms made her laugh. He didn't take himself or life in general too seriously; she wished she were more like him.

"What sort of man do you find attractive?" he asked, taking her hand. His tone was light, yet somehow intimate.

"I prefer a man with a sense of humor—like you." But Mike Gardner had a sense of humor too.

Don leaned over and kissed her cheek. "You are completely ingenuous. It's one of many things I adore about you."

She was glad when the maitre d' told Don that their table was ready, since she was feeling completely out of her depth. Don went ahead and ordered salads and steaks for both of them. She asked for hers to be well done.

"Are you sure?"

"I'm not one for a lot of blood. Actually, my mother would tend to overcook everything, so I got used to burned or dried-out meat along with vegetables that fell apart."

"Not much nutrition left after all that. Was there some reason for it?"

"I think she once read an article on the dangers of under-cooking and it just stayed with her."

"Don't feel badly. My mother never attempted to cook at all. We always had a housekeeper who prepared the meals. Mother had no idea where the kitchen was, nor did she care. When our cook had a day off, we were forced to eat out." He took her hand again. "Anyway, as a bachelor, I've learned to put together a few interesting dishes. Perhaps you'll let me impress you with my culinary skills one day soon."

She understood what he was offering and wasn't certain how to respond. A part of her wanted to say yes to Don, but the old wariness was there, preying upon her heart and mind, and so she changed the subject.

"Lieutenant Gardner told me the newspapers are very interested in the campus murders," she said.

"Like Thoreau, I am not as interested in what is new as in what is never old."

"So you aren't following what's being written?" She spoke haltingly, regretting this subject, well aware that it was a sensitive topic.

Don's eyes met her own. "I believe it was James Fenimore Cooper who said the press, like fire, is an excellent servant, but a terrible master."

"You have an amazing memory."

He smiled at the compliment. "All part of the job. At some point, I thought it wise to swallow a book of quotations. It convinces others that I am truly wise and erudite. Just one of the ways I impress my students. Have I managed to impress you? That was the idea." He patted her hand.

Their salads arrived and they began to eat in silence. As she observed her surroundings, Kim was surprised to see Dr. Barnes and Dr. Packingham lunching together at a nearby table. They appeared to be engaged in serious conversation, looking very much like Cassius and Brutus. Were they conspirators? If so, what were they plotting?

"Sure you won't join me in a libation?" Packingham asked Barnes.

"No, I'm not accustomed to spirits, at least not those of a physical nature."

Packingham laughed in a way that indicated he was slightly inebriated.

"I don't think we'll be brought into it, do you? Filthy business," Barnes commented. "I must avoid scandal at all costs."

"Kim?" Don looked at her questioningly. "You seem far away."

"Only two tables away. Don, I'll be back in a few minutes."

He seemed surprised. She ignored his look of displeasure and walked over to the other table.

At the sight of her, Packingham frowned and Barnes started slightly. Obviously, they were not pleased to see her.

"I couldn't help overhearing you discussing the murders."

"Murders?" Barnes questioned in a tone of outraged sensibility. He was a big man, and his deep voice resonated. Several patrons turned curious glances in their direction.

"Perhaps I should say homicides, as the police do. You do think they were killed, don't you?" She looked from one man to the other.

Neither one of the professors responded.

"You both knew Lorette. I thought you were discussing what happened."

"Miss Campbell was a promising scholar," Barnes remarked, his voice booming in the quiet dining room. "Her early demise is tragic."

"Yes, she was a lovely girl, very bright, fine writing ability. Who would ever have thought she'd be involved with drugs?" Packingham commented, quickly downing the whiskey he was hunched over.

"She wasn't involved with drugs. That was what her killer wanted people to think," Kim said.

"Precisely what I thought," Barnes agreed. "All gossip. Gossip can ruin people. She wasn't the sort to get involved in such sordid stuff."

"What do you think?" she asked Packingham.

A slight tick appeared in the corner of his left eye. "I rather agree that she must have been murdered by parties unknown." His clipped British accent gave his words particular crispness.

Barnes' spine stiffened. "Surely, Miss Campbell's death was some sort of accident." Barnes signaled the waiter that he too wanted a whiskey.

"The police thought that at first. They even considered suicide." She watched both professors, carefully looking for some sort of a reaction.

"She was never despondent," Packingham said. His face was a mask, impossible to interpret.

"You knew Sandy as well. There's no question that she was murdered."

"I'm afraid I didn't know that young lady," Barnes said. His eyes were following the movement of the waiter who was approaching.

"She wasn't worth knowing," Packingham said, raising his superior nose.

"I disagree," Kim said.

He frowned at her. "She was a frivolous creature, bloody shallow, actually."

"Did you know Lionel Forbes?" she asked, looking from Packingham to Barnes.

"Only by reputation," Packingham said.

"That's odd. Sandy mentioned seeing you at Dr. Forbes's house."

"She was mistaken," Packingham said through tight lips.

"Lionel was the king of the mountain around here," Barnes said. "Naturally, I knew him. He was, however, rather arrogant and conceited. Actually had the outrageous effrontery to mock religion in my presence. The powers that be, however, were willing to overlook a great deal because of his exalted reputation."

The waiter arrived with Dr. Barnes' drink and he lunged for it. After taking a quick gulp, he relaxed a bit.

"What did they have to overlook?" she asked.

"The man was peculiar. He said and did bizarre things. I suppose it was part of his charm for the students. He shone like Lucifer. Students appeared to worship him—only the troubled, lost and foolish ones, of course."

"He had a student following," she agreed. "You wouldn't happen to know who some of those students might be?"

"I have no idea who they were," Barnes responded quickly. "Of course, from time to time one does hear things."

"Such as?"

He leaned over as if confiding some confidential information. "Homosexuals, perverts, and drug abusers. Forbes was morally corrupt, a total decadent. It is no surprise at all that someone killed him and chose fire as the means of his destruction. Symbolic act, if you ask me. If what has been bandied about is correct, the man was an abomination. Surely, this is the Lord's judgment upon him. In fact, perhaps the assassin deserves the Medal of Honor." Barnes sat back in his chair and smiled smugly as if well satisfied with his hyperbole. "The only thing Forbes and I agreed upon was the doctrine of original sin."

Packingham finished his own drink and said nothing at first, turning his glass in his hand with grave concentration. "God judges in different ways," he said finally.

Kim did not know how to interpret his comment, but it seemed merely to encourage Dr. Barnes.

"Proverbs tells us how to live through aphorism. It is not good to respect the person of the wicked, so as to turn aside the righteous in judgment. The Bible makes clear to us that we must beware of the wicked and follow the paths of righteousness. Perhaps Ms. Campbell and the other student who was killed were turned toward sin by Dr. Forbes."

"Do you believe in Satan?" she asked Dr. Barnes.

"Had you read the Old Testament carefully, you would have learned more." His voice was vibrating with scorn. "The name Satan comes from the Hebrew word meaning adversary. In the older books of the Hebrew Bible, those written before the Babylonian exile, *Satan* meant merely an opponent. David, for example, was not accepted by the Philistines because they feared he would turn against them in battle and become their *Satan*. In *Zechariah,* the prophet presents Joshua standing before God Almighty to be judged, and Satan standing at Joshua's right hand to argue the case against him. In *Job,* Satan has become the accuser of men with a sharpened tongue. It is Satan who kills Job's children, servants and cattle."

"But surely he doesn't act on God's command."

Barnes gave her a superior look, one black brow rising in an air of condescension. "Perhaps, but it is from this notion of an angel who both accuses and punishes men that the devil grows. Later Hebrew writers separate good from evil and see Jehovah as totally good. Evil is a powerful force in the universe, though perhaps not a single being or entity."

"Not to be worshiped?" She watched him intently.

His eyes bulged. "Sacrilege! Those who worship Satan pervert nature. They are sinners in the truest form and cannot be condoned. In the transgression of an evil man there is a snare:

But the righteous doth sing and rejoice."

Dr. Packingham signaled the waiter for the check. He seemed very uneasy with the conversation. Meanwhile, she had the feeling that the dialogue had gotten away from her. Dr. Barnes had refined to an art speaking without actually saying anything, a rhetorician never at a loss for words. Her eyes caught the plain gold band on the third finger of Dr. Barnes' left hand as he twisted it. She remembered the way he had ogled the legs of the pretty girls in his classroom. He must have looked at Lorette that way too. She turned now to Packingham, hoping that the busy waiter would ignore them for just a few more minutes.

"Lorette spoke to me about you, Dr. Packingham. You were sexually harassing her, and she wasn't certain what to do about it. Did she tell you that she would go to the dean or the president if you persisted?"

"I don't know what you're talking about." He glowered at her. "That's absurd!"

"Is it?"

"Really, you have no right to talk that way to him," Dr. Barnes rejoined indignantly. "This man is a guest in our country. Your rudeness and lack of good manners are unforgivable."

She dug her nails into the upholstered chair seat and continued. "I'm sorry if I offended your sensibilities. However, Dr. Packingham wanted to go to bed with Lorette, and so did you, I believe. It therefore seems fitting that the two of you have become friendly since you share something in common. You both take advantage of your position to seduce vulnerable young women."

"Flirtation is not seduction." Dr. Barnes' eyes shot lightning bolts in her direction.

Dr. Packingham glared at her furiously. The waiter left the bill and walked quickly away from the table.

"My treat," Barnes told his companion as he hurriedly pulled bills from his wallet.

"Did Lorette threaten you with exposure? She was furious that someone had blackened her reputation. Did you know that she was asked to leave the university? Only a faculty member—someone like you—could arrange that." She spoke in a quiet but determined voice.

"I was very fond of Lorette. You are ridiculous. Kindly never speak to me again." Barnes' face was redder than a rare roast beef.

"Did Lorette threaten to tell your wife? Even if you weren't responsible for defaming her, Lorette might have thought you were."

"I had nothing whatever to do with any threat of dismissal. Perhaps I lost my pulpit and my first wife due to an indiscretion, but that will never happen again. I avoid scandal assiduously." He squared his shoulders with dignity and walked hurriedly toward the exit, followed by Packingham.

When Kim returned to her table, she found Don staring at her, a deep frown on his face. "I hope you never become my adversary. Poor windbag Barnes, you really went for his jugular."

She felt the heat rising to her face but could do nothing to stop it. "I just want to find out what happened, for Lorette's sake. Should her murder be just another unsolved crime?"

He shrugged. "I wasn't planning to discuss her with you, but I suppose I'll have to clear the air in that regard. I did not pursue Lorette Campbell. She seduced me. You can believe that or not. And when she felt she had gotten whatever benefit from me that could be obtained, namely an A in my course, she simply moved on. I'm not proud of the way I behaved. I should have displayed a higher level of character and integrity, but the fact remains, I didn't. Barnes may be a different story. He has something of a reputation for chasing young women. Granted, he's hypocritical. And Packingham may be a womanizer as well.

However, that does not change the fact that Lorette was a sexual opportunist."

"She was not a whore, if that's what you're implying." Kim could feel the heat rising to her face again.

He raised his hand in a sign of peace. "I'm sorry. You seem to be taking what happened to her quite personally. You are sensitive and feel things deeply. Nonetheless, she and you were nothing alike. You are quite naive about her."

She looked away from him. When the waiter returned and asked if they wanted dessert, they both refused. Don drove Kim back to her car so that she could bring it home. The sight of the burned-out shell that had been Dr. Forbes' home horrified her. Forbes had died in that fire; she might very well have died with him. It sobered her immensely. She and Don had not spoken for a long time. Now she turned to him.

"I don't want to quarrel with you. You're my friend. I know that."

"Even friends can't agree about everything," he said, his voice softening. "I'll phone you soon." He gently brushed her lips with his own and then she left his car.

That night, she slept badly, dreaming that she returned to Lionel Forbes' house. She had come dressed in a hooded cloak drawn around her head and body. She walked down the stairs to the cellar. She could hear chanting voices. Forbes was at the front of the group, standing at the altar. He pointed his finger at her. The room circled about her, an eerie montage of red and black colors blurring.

"I am the devil," he announced, his cobalt eyes riveted to hers. "If you fail to worship me, I will destroy you!"

Suddenly, hooded figures were laying hands on her. She saw their faces, but they did not look at her with any form of recognition. Lorette peered down at her; then she saw Sandy, and Nick Margrove. There was one other whose face remained unrevealed. They led her to the altar, forced her to lie down upon it. Dr. Forbes produced a sharp knife, a large, machete-like instrument with peculiar carvings on the silver hilt. "Now you become one with us." The knife came down toward her heart as the others held her struggling body. The eyes of the magician absorbed all other light from the room until their brilliance blinded her. And as the knife came down, she let out a scream of terror.

Kim awoke, sweating, trembling, feeling ill. Her headache was back in force. She looked at the kitchen clock. It was three in the morning. She got out of bed and washed down two aspirin with a drink of spring water. But it was several hours before she could relax enough to sleep again. Strange, she thought, *the one place that the dead still live is in the mind.*

CHAPTER SEVENTEEN

Kim phoned Jim Davis the following morning. She asked to meet him and he agreed. The problem was she wasn't certain what she wanted to discuss with him. But some nagging doubts remained in her mind regarding his relationship with Lorette. Her sensitivity was sending out signals.

For Jim's convenience, they planned to meet at the graduate student lounge at Kinley Hall. Kim was early and decided to drop by and have a word with Pat Norris. The secretary wasn't her usual efficient self today; she seemed frazzled.

"I hardly have time to say hello to anyone this week. We're so incredibly busy. Everyone in the English department seems to need work all at once. I hate it when it's this hectic. And then there's all this mess."

"Mess?"

"Didn't you notice how sloppy the rooms are? Frank's been out. Didn't even bother to phone and let us know he wouldn't be in. We're going to have to replace him if we don't hear from him in another day or so. The cleaning crew is complaining about being short-handed."

"Where is Frank?"

"Wish I knew! I'm furious with him. He was always dedicated and did a good job. I've never seen the corridors so littered before."

"Have you talked to any of the other custodians? Maybe they know why he hasn't shown up."

Pat removed her eyeglasses and rubbed her eyes tiredly. "No, I've asked. No one knows."

Kim went to the graduate student lounge to wait, wondering about Frank. Could there be any connection between Frank's disappearance and Dr. Forbes? When had he cleaned for Dr. Forbes last? An odd thought gnawed at the back of her mind. Jim came shortly after she returned to the lounge and they had a cup of coffee together. The tension between them was palpable.

"So you formally dropped Packingham's course?" she asked, feeling awkward.

"Yep, it's official. Didn't need the damn credits anyhow."

An attractive blonde walked into the lounge, her eyes lighting up when she saw Jim. She lost no time in moving in like an eagle swooping down on prey.

"Hi," she said to him, placing her hand on his arm. "I was hoping to see you here. Are you free at lunchtime today?"

"Busy," he said with a dismissive shrug.

She gave Kim a dirty look, as if she were to blame and stalked away.

"Seems like if you don't make yourself available, the gals hit on you instead of vice versa."

"Time you joined the living," she said sympathetically. "In fact, I thought you already had."

"What if the dead won't stay buried?" Jim spoke as if he felt guilty about something and she had to wonder.

He sighed deeply, walked over to the window and looked out. Kim was aware there was nothing to see out there but the parking lot. He looked preoccupied.

"What's bothering you?"

"Just thinking about Lorette. Wondering if we could have made a go of it together if she hadn't died. Can't get her out of my mind. Still don't believe she's dead."

"I know." Kim put a comforting hand on his broad shoulder.

"Any time you feel like talking about it, just give me a call."

He nodded his head absently. "Thanks, Kim, you're okay. It just doesn't make any sense, does it?"

"No, not to me either."

Looking for sanity in an insane world, maybe that was the ridiculous thing, she decided. If life was absurd as Sartre declared, then why was she so determined to find logical explanations? Murder was insane, an act of lunacy.

She and Jim parted on friendly terms. She probably should have asked him hard questions, such as had he and Lorette quarreled before her death and if so, why? Was he the jealous type? After all, it was not uncommon for spurned men to murder their wives or former sweethearts. But she liked Jim too much to believe that he would do something like that. She couldn't push him on the subject of Lorette's death. Yet she sensed there was something more that he might have told her, something that he was holding back for personal reasons. Lieutenant Gardner would have said that was the difference between a professional and an amateur. He would have known what to ask and just how to ask it. Perhaps she really did not have the instincts needed to dig for serious answers. She felt very weary, and the day had barely begun.

There were footsteps behind her as she walked down the deserted corridor. Suddenly, someone lunged at her, shoving her none too gently into an empty classroom. Her heart pumping rapidly like a Thoroughbred racing toward the finish, she turned to see who had grabbed her.

"You!" Her eyes opened wide.

"That's right. I saw you where you shouldn't be, nosing around again, causing trouble." His hand rose as if to strike her.

It was then she saw that he held a knife. For a brief moment she was paralyzed with fear. Her nightmare of the previous evening returned to haunt her. Then she remembered something she'd been taught in her self-defense course. Kim brought up her right knee and pushed it forcefully into her assailant's groin. She kicked the knife out of his hand. Only then was she able to breathe again.

"What'd you do that for?" Sprawled out on the floor, Nick Margrove looked as harmless as a pimply-faced adolescent who'd fallen over his own feet. She had to remind herself that he might have done her real harm if she hadn't acted decisively.

"It would have been more to your liking if I let you assault me?"

He groaned loudly, continuing to lie on the wooden floor. "You really hurt me, you know that!"

"People must defend themselves when they're threatened. Are you a killer, Mr. Margrove? Did someone else put you up to this?"

"Screw you! I didn't kill anybody." His face was red with rage.

"For an English major, you show a decidedly poor vocabulary. I've always believed profanity was the mode of expression of mental midgets. Did Dr. Forbes put you up to murdering Lorette and Sandy? Did you have a falling out and then kill him?"

"I'd never have hurt Dr. Forbes. He was a great man and an outstanding teacher. He taught everything that matters. He helped me experiment with life."

"You participated in his satanic worship rituals, didn't you?"

He shrugged in a noncommittal manner.

"Did you know about an inferno collection? I am right in assuming that?"

"I never saw it. I hadn't proven myself worthy." He got gingerly to his feet.

"But you knew about it? Who else knew? Who was involved in the group?"

Suddenly, he moved, pushing her off balance. Before she

could think of what to say or do, Nick Margrove hurried out
the door. She was relieved to see that she hadn't injured him
after all, but was disappointed that she hadn't succeeded in getting him to tell her anything relevant. She stood staring at his
knife and wondered what he would have done to her if she
hadn't stopped him. Was he merely trying to frighten her? She
had no idea. She slipped the discarded weapon into her handbag.

Should she call Lieutenant Gardner and report the assault?
She decided against it for two reasons: one, he would be very
displeased that she was still looking into Lorette's murder, and
second, he had already questioned Nick Margrove and found
out nothing. She was convinced it was a mistake to inform him
of what had occurred.

However, the thought that she was being remiss in her
responsibilities nagged at her mind, growing in intensity. Still,
she could manage to forget about it while she was at work
because the job kept her so busy. But the following morning,
there was no such distraction. It also occurred to her that Margrove had attacked her on the parking deck and could well have
been her assailant at Dr. Forbes' house. If that were true, he
was very likely a murderer despite his claims to the contrary.

She phoned Gardner around ten o'clock. He was already at
headquarters. She told him about her run-in with Nick Margrove the previous day. As expected, he was annoyed with her
for not informing him sooner. She could hear it in the tone of
his voice, although he didn't outright lecture her.

"I'm having the kid picked up. You're going to press assault
charges, and that's how we'll nail him."

She didn't argue with the policeman. Gardner was right, of
course; even if Nick were not the murderer, he probably had a
pretty fair idea who might be.

The rest of the morning was spent rereading the last part of Jen's diary. Ma's younger sister had been a sensitive, gentle girl of fifteen. In the last section of the diary, she told of her love for a boy near her own age, how deep their feelings for each other ran. She romanticized about the commitment they made to each other. Some months later, she expressed her sorrow that this special boy had moved away to another state with his family. In the final pages, she agonized over keeping a secret from her family:

No one must find out. I'll hide it from them as long as I can. Mother has had enough grief. I could talk to Sis but she's having all this trouble with Carl. He has to have another operation. He's in so much pain. I can't bother them with my troubles; it wouldn't be right. No one has to know, at least not right away. If only he were still here! But what could he do anyway?

Kim found herself unable to read any more and set the diary aside. Before Ma left, they would have to talk, to clear away the cobwebs and let their relationship see the light of day. That could only happen if Ma were honest about what had happened to her sister.

Again consigned to working the late shift, Kim made the best of things and worked cheerfully with Rita who was grumbling about having to work too many evenings.

"I'm not going to answer phones tonight. Tell the grad student that's her job."

There were so many requests for help that before Kim knew it, the dinner hour had rolled around. And suddenly with no surprise, Lieutenant Gardner walked up to the reference desk. Just the sight of him made her blood heat. It was like being hit by lightning.

"Can I help you?" she asked as if he were just an ordinary patron.

"Yeah, you get a dinner break around now?"

"Want me to take it immediately?"

It was obvious that he did. She told Rita, who grimaced at her. "Well, what if I want to go first? After all, I do have seniority."

"Whatever you like," she said pleasantly, ignoring Rita's petulance.

"No, I have to talk to her now." Gardner flashed his badge at Rita Mosler and she recoiled anxiously.

"Well, take your time then."

"Thanks for being so understanding," Gardner said. Rita appeared to miss his irony.

"You work with her a lot?" Gardner remarked as they passed through security.

"Very often," she acknowledged.

He shook his head. "So where do people eat around here?"

"The Commons has a place, but it's more for lunch than dinner. I usually brown bag it in the evening. There's lots of places out near the bookstore, even a McDonald's."

"Just the closest place." His tone was grim. She decided then that the best place would be the Student Center. It was large, impersonal and there was a variety of things to buy.

It was a crisp autumn evening and the walk was pleasant, but Mike Gardner's expression remained dour. They both purchased sandwiches and coffee and Gardner picked an isolated spot to sit.

She studied his craggy features as he carefully spread a packet of mustard on his bologna sandwich. His fingers were long and artistic.

"So you like bologna, Lieutenant?"

"Only in my sandwiches," he said.

She took a sip of coffee and found it bitter.

"My wife used to make me bologna or turkey sandwiches for lunch. But she put so much mustard on them, it ruined the sandwiches for me. I think it was her way of punishing me for not having more meals with her at home. I should have paid attention."

They ate together in relative silence. He seemed to want her to finish eating before he told her whatever it was he'd come to say. But she found it difficult to swallow her food, wondering what his news could be.

"So you had a good day?" she prodded, finishing off her BLT.

"Up to a point. I see a lot of dead people in my line of work, but I never really get used to it."

"What dead people are you talking about?"

His eyes darkened like clouds before a gathering storm. His mouth was taut. "You might as well know. Nick Margrove turned up dead today. When we couldn't locate him, I put out an all points. Too late. He seems to be the most recent victim of our killer. Some kids spotted him floating face down in the river. I don't have the autopsy results yet, but preliminary findings indicate that death was not due to natural causes."

"I don't think the details are important for me to know. Thank you for waiting until after I ate to tell me about it."

"There's something else." His eyes met hers directly. "There's already been one attempt on your life. I want you to be very careful. I've got this bad feeling."

She thought over what he said. "You really think I'm in danger?"

"You may have been the last person to see Margrove before he disappeared. The killer might think he told you something, something that implicated him. You don't know anything, do you? Because if you do, you've got to tell me. You're smart enough to see that." His eyes had the intensity of searchlights.

"He didn't tell me any more than he told you. Honor bright, Lieutenant."

He accepted that with a grave nod of his head. "Okay, but you have to promise to phone me day or night if anything comes up." He removed a black notebook from his jacket pocket, took out a ballpoint pen, and neatly wrote out his home phone number. Then he ripped the paper out of the small loose-leaf binder and handed it to her. "Day or night. I mean that. I'm going to really be pissed off if you don't."

"Okay, but I don't expect any further problems."

"You do have a long nose."

"Lieutenant, I don't like my appearance insulted."

"You know what I mean. You have a habit of poking around where you don't belong. This killer is obsessive. Could be he's not finished."

"If anything occurs to me or anything happens, I promise to call."

"The thing is, all our leads have dried up now that Margrove is dead. He was the only connection we had to the others. I figured if we kept after him with enough persistence, he'd either lead us to the killer or make some kind of a confession. Now that he's dead, I think the case is dead too."

"You're not going to just forget about it?" she asked in an alarmed voice.

"No, but there are other pressing cases I have to investigate. Believe it or not, we actually do have other crimes that need solving."

She told him that she understood, even if she really didn't. They parted company then and Kim took a brief walk on campus lost in thought before returning to the library. If this case went unsolved, it wouldn't mean much to a professional policeman like Gardner. After all, just as he said, there were plenty of other cases that demanded his time. But it was different for her. She was personally involved. The killer might not forget about her, but she wasn't going to forget about her friend's murder either.

CHAPTER EIGHTEEN

Don Bernard phoned her early the following morning. "I'm doing a lecture today on Shakespeare's villains. Want to come by? Afterwards, perhaps we could have lunch together again."

"Only if it's Dutch treat. I don't want to bankrupt you."

"I can't think of a nicer way to become poor." His voice was as rich as finely textured velvet.

"After an invitation like that, how can I refuse?"

She hung up the receiver, thinking that Don was a very charming man. What, if anything, might come of their relationship, she did not know. Don was in his late thirties and had never married. She doubted he had ever been seriously committed to any woman.

Although the room was already neat, she looked around to see if anything needed straightening. Realizing the obsessive nature of her action, she quietly stopped, sat down and took stock of herself. What she saw did not entirely please her. At one time, she felt too much, had been hurt too easily by others. She'd learned to hold people at a distance, to exercise control and restraint in human relationships, but now all she had was an empty, lonely life, a void where there should have been real feelings. Lorette had been no different. They'd both been afraid. She did not want to eventually die realizing that she'd never lived. Maybe one had to accept pain, to understand that it was inescapable and part of the human condition.

★ ★ ★ ★ ★

Kim arrived on campus at ten. She meant to come at the beginning of Don's lecture, but she hadn't slept well again, and it caused her to get a late start. Lurid, intense dreams had plagued her once more. Kinley Hall looked anything but tidy. Candy and gum wrappers were strewn in the corridor. In the graduate student lounge, coffee cups lay around and the trash barrel overflowed.

She stopped by Pat Norris's desk. "So I take it Frank still isn't back?"

"You take it correctly," the secretary responded peevishly. "I've asked for a replacement."

"Does anyone know what's happened to him?"

Pat shook her head, and the frosted curls of her newly restyled hairdo undulated like waves.

"I was under the impression that he was very reliable."

"So was I. He never missed a day of work, even when he was under the weather." Pat's voice lowered. "He was known to imbibe a little. But it didn't seem to interfere with his performance."

"Have you called his home?"

Pat gave her an exasperated look. "Of course."

Kim's mind speculated. "Does he have any family?"

"None that I know about. And I don't know of any friends either. Most people didn't take to him that easily."

She thought of the custodian's leering smile and agreed silently.

"Why all this interest in Frank?" Pat asked her.

"Just curiosity. We talked a few times."

Walking down the corridor, Kim fished into her pocketbook and drew out Lieutenant Gardner's number. Should she call him? If she told him what she suspected, he'd probably laugh at her. And he'd be right. She had no solid facts, only suspicions that were likely wrong. She shook her head and put the piece of paper away. She wasn't eager to make a fool of herself.

She walked quickly up the stairs to the second floor and quietly entered Don's classroom. Professor Bernard was in excellent form, full of vitality and excitement. Every student in the room seemed rapt in his lecture. He was discussing Richard III and he smiled in her direction, noting her presence. She smiled back and tried hard to pay attention, but good as he was, her mind kept wandering back to the janitor's disappearance.

Lunch with Don was pleasant. He was still on a high.

"You inherited your mother's talent for performing."

"Think so? I'm not an actor by any means, but I do think teaching compares to some degree. It's important to enthrall a class, to give a dynamic performance."

They were in a local Chinese restaurant, and she was biting thoughtfully into a shrimp roll. "Was Lionel Forbes like that? Did he captivate his students?"

"Most assuredly. The man had the gift to mesmerize. I heard him speak on several occasions. Strong visceral appeal. The Adolf Hitler of the intellectual set."

She shuddered. "Suppose he wasn't really dead?" There, she had said it. Now she waited for some response.

Don stared at her in surprise. "Oh, I believe Hitler's definitely dead. They've only been sighting Elvis lately." Don was treating her question with levity and it bothered her.

"You know I'm referring to Dr. Forbes."

"And you know better than anyone that Lionel burned to death in that fire, since you nearly died in it yourself."

"The police assumed it was Dr. Forbes who died in the fire because that was what they expected. But what if it was another man, someone just about Dr. Forbes' size and build?"

Don shook his head. "I don't think there's anything to this, but you ought to talk to the police if you're convinced."

"I'm almost ready to do that," she told him. She nibbled on a sparerib distractedly.

Don took her hand. Then he kissed each of her fingers in turn. "Tasty sauce."

"I think you better let me wipe my hands."

"You're not an easy woman to romance. I want to get to know you better. What are you doing tonight?"

"Don't you think we're rushing it a bit?" The old uneasiness returned.

"Not at all. I ask myself why I haven't done this before. So what about tonight?"

She made up her mind with uncharacteristic speed and decisiveness. "Why don't you come by my apartment for dinner?"

"Sounds perfect."

"Only it has to be tomorrow. I'm working the evening shift again. But I believe I can get someone to change with me for tomorrow."

"Better idea. There's an English Colloquium tomorrow. Stop by at the dinner hour and we'll spend some time together. I don't want you to have a problem with your supervisor."

"Fine. I'll meet you, and my invitation is good for the evening after. I have a day off then."

"I like the fact that you're including me in your future," he said, exuding warmth.

After Don took her back to Kinley to pick up her car, she drove over to the library. Early for her shift, she sat at her desk and checked out her mail. Nothing threatening this time. She breathed a sigh of relief.

But the thought nagged her that she ought to find out conclusively about Frank's disappearance if that were at all possible. She put in a call to Personnel. There was no time to apply for the information she wanted in person. She'd also discovered that very often just as much can be accomplished over the telephone.

She made an effort to speak in an authoritative manner, going through two secretaries before she was connected to the right administrative assistant. But the woman wasn't going to make it easy for her.

"Why did you say you needed the information?" The voice was dubious and not easily convinced.

"I am a secretary to Dr. Chesington, the English Chairperson, and I have been delegated to discover why Mr. Swallinsky is not at his job. Do you have any idea why our custodian has not been in recently? It would seem that your office should be informed. Dr. Chesington is quite distraught." She put the woman on the defensive.

"I assure you we will be looking into it."

"Actually," Kim said, "I intend to look into the matter myself. Could you give me Mr. Swallinsky's address and telephone number right now?"

"That is somewhat irregular."

"Hurry up, please; Dr. Chesington is not a patient man. Believe me, you don't want him angry at you."

That seemed to clinch it. Kim was asked to hold on while the assistant checked. She felt uneasy during what seemed an interminable amount of time, but finally the lady returned to the phone. She had never done anything so disreputable in her entire life and wondered fleetingly if she could be arrested for telephone fraud. But she held resolutely to her purpose.

Both the address and phone number turned out to be local. As soon as she'd hung up with the personnel assistant, Kim phoned Frank's apartment, but just as Pat Norris had told her, there was no answer. She let the phone ring at least nine times.

She decided to drive over to his apartment and see for herself if there was any sign of him.

She was working with a very agreeable person today, and there was no problem with her taking the dinner hour and break together. That gave her a full hour and a half, plenty of time to check out Frank Swallinsky's place, which was in the city.

His building turned out to be an old brick apartment house. It looked sturdier than the worn wooden frame houses in the neighborhood. But the area had seen better days. She saw no adults around, just some small children playing in front of the building.

There were five floors to the apartment house besides the basement level. Frank's name appeared on a small plate next to a bell along with the other tenants. There was not a plate for each bell so it seemed that the building wasn't fully occupied. She glanced around before ringing. Garbage overflowed cans at the sidewalk and graffiti was sprayed across the bricks.

She rang Frank's bell, not getting a response. A woman carrying groceries came along and opened the door with a key. Kim slipped in behind her. She took the stairs quickly, got up to the third floor and hurried down the sinister, darkly lit corridor. It wasn't difficult to find 3C, Frank's apartment. But when she rang and knocked, no one answered. Finally, she tried the door just in case it was open—no such luck.

She ran down the stairs again and out into the fresh air. The building had made her feel claustrophobic. No, it was more than that; she had a bad feeling, an instinct, that all was not well with the diminutive custodian. She walked around by the basement and found the superintendent's apartment. Fortunately, he was working inside.

The super was a wiry Hispanic of medium height with a swarthy complexion and thick black mustache and brows. He wore a sooty T-shirt, faded jeans and a checkered flannel jacket that had frayed edges.

"What you want?" He was less than cordial, eyeing her with suspicion.

"Are you the superintendent for this building?"

The dark, bright gaze of the man darted out at her shrewdly from under his bushy brows. "Why you want to know?"

"I'm looking for a tenant, Frank Swallinsky. Do you know him?"

"I know all the tenants here." He looked her up and down as if sizing her up.

"Have you seen him lately?"

"Why you want to know?" He seemed to be verbally flexing the muscles of his *machismo*.

She was careful to keep her tone calm and neutral. "The people at his job are worried. No one's heard from him for about a week."

"Me, I mind my own business."

"Something bad could have happened to him. Have you seen him at all?"

"You think he's in some kind of trouble?"

She was growing impatient. Why would he only answer a question with a question?

"We don't know," she said striving to sound benign.

"Well, I haven't seen him for a while."

"How long?"

"A week maybe. I don't know for sure. If I see him, you want me to tell him you was here?"

"What I really would like is access to his apartment."

The super eyed her coldly. "You a cop? You got a warrant?"

"No, not exactly, but I am very concerned about Mr. Swallinsky's well-being. He might very well be lying in his apartment hurt—or even dead."

"You get a warrant, lady. Don't bother me till then. I don't want no trouble here." With that, he turned around, walked into his apartment and slammed the door in her face.

As she drove back to work, Kim knew that it was time to call Lieutenant Gardner again. Right or wrong, he had to be told of her suspicions. Back at her desk, she checked to make certain no one was nearby to overhear her conversation.

She caught Gardner at home. She could tell from the lieutenant's voice that he had not expected her call. Then she told him where she'd been and he was even more surprised.

"You went into a high-crime neighborhood with a real potential for danger and didn't bother to tell anyone where you were going? Now why doesn't that surprise me? No offense, but you need a keeper! You got no street smarts whatsoever."

"There's no need to be so sarcastic, Lieutenant. I just didn't want to give you incorrect information." She then explained to him how both Dr. Forbes and the custodian were about the same size. "Frank often cleaned Dr. Forbes' house for him. They were on good terms. He could have been at the house that evening. No one's seen him in at least a week." She took a deep breath, inhaling deeply, then talked in a rapid clip, afraid he would stop her if she wasn't quick about it.

"I think it may have been Frank who died in the fire. Dr. Forbes was a diabolical man. I don't believe he's dead at all."

"Have I got this right? You think Forbes is still alive?"

"It's a real possibility," she affirmed.

"What if I were to tell you that Forbes' dental records compare identically with the skeletal remains of the corpse?"

"Was it just bridgework? Couldn't that be placed in a corpse's mouth to fool your people?"

He sighed patiently, "Yeah, maybe. But it's not likely. Still, I'll check it out."

"I'm sorry to bother you, but it could mean something."

"This guy, Frank, did he have any family?"

"None that I know of. But he seemed to like his job. The thing is, I don't believe he would leave for no good reason."

"Happens all the time. He could have a reason you don't know about. Who's to say?"

She felt awful disturbing the policeman when he was off-duty. Still, if she was right, it was necessary. She heard him sigh.

"All right, I'll check out this Swallinsky. You might as well know, I think it's a waste of time but I'm willing to examine every lead."

"Good, and if I'm totally wrong, I won't bother you again. I apologize for interrupting your evening."

"Just give me your word, no more dangerous situations."

"Of course not. I'm just a quiet, ordinary librarian."

"Yeah, right. I'll be in touch with you soon. And you can bother me anytime." The way he said that last comment made her smile.

Kim finished work that evening feeling a good deal more relaxed. Still, she remembered she had Nick Margrove's knife in her handbag, which she clutched to her breast as she walked toward the deserted parking deck. Strange, but she felt again as if someone were following her, watching and waiting to pounce and attack her. Last night, she'd felt the same way, as if evil was ready to prey on her in some hideous form—like a child thinking there was a monster hidden in her closet. Nothing happened, and she'd felt foolish for being fearful. She could well be suffering from an overactive imagination.

She'd been planning to stop at one of the large supermarkets along the highway. Deciding against it, she kept heading straight for home. Food was the last thing on her mind. She found herself shivering, although the night was not cold. Why did she feel a sense of foreboding, as if something were very wrong?

Her awareness was definitely in overdrive. She was as tense and alert as if she was jazzed on caffeine. Something was very wrong.

A few minutes later, she made a discovery that convinced her it was not a mistake to trust her special instincts after all.

CHAPTER NINETEEN

The traffic filtered out as she drove south. The night was peaceful and scenery flashed past in quick frames like a silent movie. In the rearview mirror, she saw another car's headlights beaming brightly and wondered if she was being followed. There was no reason for anyone to tailgate her since the road was clear. Speeding up, she looked in the mirror only to find the other car still with her following uncomfortably close. She tried to make out the driver but couldn't. The car had tinted glass windows that allowed those within to see out, but no one could see inside very well, especially at night.

The car continued to follow her, increasing her nervousness. All she could observe was that it was big and dark, but she could not tell its make or model. Also, she noted with alarm, something was obscuring the license plate numbers. The car was definitely tailgating her now, flashing high beams. Her heart began to palpitate. She switched from the middle lane to the right, hoping that the other vehicle would pass, but it didn't. Instead, it swung in right behind her.

Kim brought her foot down heavily on the accelerator and gunned the engine. The Corolla took off like a gazelle, but the big, black car followed like a panther hungry for prey. Suddenly, it pulled into position next to her vehicle. She felt the impact before understanding intellectually what was happening. Pushing the engine for all it was worth, she lurched forward. She wasn't far from home; soon she'd leave the highway behind. But her pursuer would not relent.

She was driving too fast, she realized. Maybe a policeman would be monitoring the road. At this point, a ticket would be welcome. *Gardner, where are you when I need you?* The other car kept right up with her all the way.

With horror, Kim saw the traffic light ahead turn red. She pulled over to the shoulder to ride down it, hoping to bypass the other cars, but in doing so, she had to slow down. The black automobile was again on her tail. It rammed the back of her Toyota not once but twice before she could speed up and get away by making a right turn. The country road she was now on was totally devoid of traffic and very dark. Her adrenaline kicked in. She began zigzagging back and forth across the road, refusing to give the other car a chance to position itself again. She knew this road and was sure her attacker did not. That might be her salvation.

Soon there would be a bridge. She had to make her move quickly. If he caught her on the bridge, she was dead. At the next intersection, she cut off without warning, skidding across. He was still with her, but she continued making sharp turns and moving with suddenness until he was finally out of sight and she'd lost him.

It was only then that she allowed herself the luxury of really breathing again. Her body was soaked with perspiration. Her hands ached from clutching the steering wheel so tightly. Inside, she was quaking.

She was about to go home when she realized that anyone so committed to frightening or harming her could easily be waiting outside her apartment at this moment. Her address and phone number were listed in the directory. Where should she go?

There was only one possible answer, although she didn't want to accept it. She had to go to Ma where she would be safe. The Toyota seemed to return to the highway of its own accord, magically drive itself east, toward Ma, toward the Atlantic Ocean, toward peace and safety.

There were lights on in the parlor. She pulled up in front of the house and got out. Neither her hands nor her legs were too steady, and her mouth was completely dry and gritty, as though she'd been lost in a Sahara sandstorm.

Ma welcomed her. Although surprised, she didn't ask why her daughter had come.

"I've got a little problem," Kim said by way of explanation, keeping her voice as calm as she could manage. "I want to stay the night if that's all right."

"Of course, would you like something to eat or drink?"

"No, but I need to use the phone."

"You should get one of those cell phones. Everyone has them these days, Even children carry them. I'm getting one for my trip down to Florida. Good to have for emergencies."

"You're right, Ma. I'll do that. Right now, though, I really need to make a phone call."

Ma tactfully avoided asking questions, although Kim was certain that she had many. After Ma courteously left the room, she went directly to the phone that was on a little table in the foyer between the parlor and the kitchen. Her phone call was to Lieutenant Gardner. She told him what had happened, pouring it out like pancake batter, the words sticking to each other. God, she sounded out of control! She was ashamed of herself, but could not seem to help it.

He asked for her address and phone number. "Stay where you are," he ordered. "I'm sending a man to keep an eye on you."

"It's not necessary. Whoever this awful person is, he doesn't know that I'm at my mother's place. But I'll have to return to my apartment in the morning. All my things are there."

"How early?"

"Around ten o'clock."

"All right. I'll post surveillance to start at nine-thirty a.m. and no arguments accepted."

She had no intention of arguing. What she felt was a great sense of relief.

"Thank you. I'm very grateful."

"I told you before, it's my job to help people. But you're special." She wanted to say that he was very special, yet held back. "I'll see you soon."

She had a disturbing thought. "Wait! This person will try again, won't he?"

"If I had to guess, I'd say so. He or she obviously thinks you know more than you do. Guilt and fear form a volatile compound."

She was certain Gardner was right. Her marrow dropped to zero degrees.

"Look, it'll be okay. Just keep alert. I'll be in touch soon." With that, he clicked off. She sat staring at the phone for quite a while.

"What now?" she asked herself aloud. Being frightened wasn't going to help. Everything was going to be all right, she reassured herself, hugging her arms tightly around her body the way she had done when frightened as a child.

"There are still some of your old things in the bureau upstairs. I saved that peach-colored robe you liked, and there are several nightgowns."

She hadn't even heard Ma approaching.

"I know it's late, but I think I'd rather just sit here for a while. I'm not sleepy."

"Do you want to talk about your problem? I'm a good listener."

She remembered very well how Ma had always listened

sympathetically to her problems when she was a little girl.

"It's worse than a bruised knee this time."

She saw Ma's face sadden.

"I didn't mean to hurt your feelings. I just don't think I'm ready to discuss the matter yet is all."

"Are you in some kind of trouble?"

How was she supposed to answer that question? There was no point in worrying Ma if she could help it.

"No, not really."

"I could always tell when you lied. You're not very good at it. Maybe because you don't lie often." Ma turned a warm smile on her.

"I don't mean to keep you up. If you're tired, please go to bed."

"Now, how often do I get to see you? Of course, I want to stay with you as long as you'll let me."

Kim felt the lump forming in her throat again. She wanted to say, *Ma, I love you,* but she could not bring forth the words. Instead, she said, "I could do with a cup of tea."

Ma was immediately on the move again. It always pleased her to be doing things for other people. A few minutes later, Ma was pouring her a cup of hot tea in the kitchen.

"Are you upset over some man?" she asked, pouring herself a cup of the amber liquid as well.

"I don't get involved."

Ma gave her a worried look. "How come? You should think about getting married."

Kim shook her head. "I doubt that I will."

"Why is that, honey?"

"It's not something I like to talk about or even think about."

"Did it have anything to do with—us?"

She knew by *us* Ma meant her and Carl.

"I guess there's no point in dredging up the past. It's dead

217

and buried." Just like Carl was.

Ma sipped her tea reflectively. "I always wanted to protect you, but could be I only hurt you."

"I know you meant well. I just don't see marriage as important in the scheme of things, at least not for me."

Through her mind flashed unbidden the image of a night long ago. She and Johnny Dunbar in the throes of their first love, sitting in his car kissing, hugging, petting.

"We ought to go in now," she told him, noting that the windows had begun to steam from the breath of their enthusiasm.

"Not yet, Karen, not yet." Then he'd kissed her deeply again.

"What the hell do you think you're doing?"

They'd jumped apart guiltily. Carl was staring into the car. He looked like an avenging ghost through the fogged glass. Johnny immediately stepped out of the car, came around and helped her out.

"We were just saying goodnight, sir."

"Don't come around here anymore! I know your kind of trash." He seized Karen by the hand and dragged her up the porch stairs and into the house. She was mortified and protested angrily. But his anger was greater than hers.

"No more backtalk, you hear me, you little slut!" He pulled her toward him by the hair.

Tears formed in her eyes from the pain. She could smell alcohol on his breath and knew that he'd been drinking again. She also knew enough not to answer him; he was mean when he drank. Ma was always making excuses for him, but Carl Reyner was a bitter man with a temper that turned ugly when alcohol broke down his inhibitions.

"Let me tell you something, little girl. You're going to come to a bad end if you don't watch out. I'll be lucky if you don't have a bastard. It's genetics."

"Dad, please, we didn't do anything." She couldn't stop crying.

"Don't let me ever see you with a boy like that again! I know what they want. And I'm not your father, so don't call me Dad anymore."

He let go of her and she ran from him, ran from the pain of his words, the shame and humiliation he'd made her feel. She'd never told Ma what he said to her that night. And he never referred to it. Perhaps he'd been too drunk to remember. It didn't matter. She knew as surely as she breathed that his words were true.

"Karen?"

"What?"

Ma patted her shoulder. "You looked far away."

"I was for a moment. Ma, I know there are things you don't want to talk about, but I think maybe we should talk anyway. It's time, and then some. Carl told me when I was fifteen that he wasn't my real father."

Ma looked at her, obviously surprised. "He told you that? He said he never would."

"It's all right. It's better that I knew."

She was going to talk about Jen and what was in the diary, but Ma looked so upset at her disclosure that she felt this was not the right time.

"Know what? I think I am tired after all. It's been a long day."

"Sure, dear, we can talk more whenever you like."

"I have a free day after tomorrow. Maybe we can get together then. It's time you and I had lunch out together. My treat. Just to celebrate the start of your new life in Florida."

The following morning, she drove back to her apartment. There was, in fact, a man sitting in a dark sedan on the opposite side of the street from her place. He looked very much like a policeman and she breathed a deep sigh of relief. Gardner had promised to protect her, and he was making good on his word.

She locked her door behind her and went directly to the bathroom to take a shower. The soap and hot water both cleansed and baptized her and relaxed the knot of fear in her stomach. At noon, she lunched on cottage cheese and banana, about all she could manage to get down, then dressed for the day. Since she was meeting Don for the graduate symposium, she wanted to look attractive. She took extra pains with her appearance, using some blush and eyeliner and setting her hair with an electric brush into a softer, wavy style. She selected a short navy-blue skirt and matching blazer, choosing a red blouse to go with it. The lacy texture of the blouse added a feminine charm to the outfit without detracting from its professional aura. She'd bought the blouse on a whim but never worn it. She looked in the mirror and was well satisfied with her efforts. Whatever happened today, she was not going to act the part of a frightened mouse anymore.

It was time to go to work. She left the apartment, double-checking the lock. The day was gloomy; dark clouds lowered in the sky, and the chill of late autumn was in the air. The policeman was still there and followed her as she drove the pale blue Toyota into traffic. Still, try as she might, she could not forget about last night, and a queasy feeling settled into the pit of her stomach unbidden. Someone who had killed before wanted her dead. Was she driving to her ultimate fate—a destiny of death?

CHAPTER TWENTY

She played the radio on the drive to the university, tried to listen to an inane talk show, found she could not concentrate and turned to classical music instead. The car seemed to be finding its own way to campus. She parked on the deck just as she ordinarily would. Her police escort parked nearby and followed her into the library. He remained unobtrusive, but knowing that he was around made her feel more confident.

The first few hours of her shift were unremarkable, except that she was much more self-conscious. She was on with Rita tonight, which reminded her again about the inferno collection. After the dinner hour, she would try to get in to look at the collection one more time. In it somewhere could be a clue as to the murderer, or so she hoped. The police would need a search warrant to examine the cabinet. She, on the other hand, could take an informal, cursory look and see if there was anything of significance in the collection.

"You're dressed fancy today," Rita noted. In her mouth the words sounded more like an accusation than a compliment.

"I was invited to the English symposium this evening."

"Free food?"

She nodded.

Rita sniffed at her. "Well, bring something back for me."

"I'll try." She didn't think the wine and cheese that was usually served at such events would carry out well, but it was best to stay on Rita's good side since she would be asking to borrow her keys again.

When time came for her dinner break, another policeman had replaced the first one. She noticed how much emptier the streets were at this hour. But soon enough the evening students would be here replacing the day students, and the streets and parking lots would no longer appear deserted, but would bustle for University College. It would be just as crowded as in the daytime with the adults cruising around, trying to find parking anywhere they could.

It was totally dark now, no stars to be seen; even the moon was obstructed by thick clouds. Kim recalled when she was little and would imagine seeing a woman's face in the moon. It was a benign face like that of her ma, always smiling at her. God, how she wished she could see that face tonight! She had this awful, intuitive feeling that all was not quite right despite her police escort.

Once inside the graduate student center, she felt more at ease. The building was one of the newer structures on campus, bright, cheerful and modern. She realized she knew very few of the students and only several of the professors. Wine and soft drinks were being served. She helped herself to a cola. Around her, students and professors stood chatting in small groups in the large main room, which was set up with many rows of chairs facing a stage. Some chairs were of the comfortable variety that usually lounged about the room, but most were folding chairs that had been brought in for the evening's program. There were also tables set up at either side of the room with a variety of different foods.

"Well, you look hungry to me."

She turned and found Don smiling at her. "I didn't see you."

" 'Course not, you were looking hungrily at those tables groaning with goodies. Let's go sample some."

"I didn't think I was that obvious," she said, trying not to smile.

"Only to me. I was watching you closely. Besides, why else would any sane person come to one of these?"

"To be with you, of course." This time, she did smile, and he smiled back.

"I'm touched and flattered. Let's pig out!"

And that was what they did. She wondered if this was her last supper, the condemned woman eating a hearty final meal. Well, she had to shake such grim notions. She was hardly a prisoner on death row.

"I personally made the quiche, so you'll have to try it and pretend you like it even if you hate spinach."

"So you cook too. That's very interesting."

"I believe I did mention it to you, but perhaps you thought I was jesting? Haven't put you off? Real men don't eat quiche, let alone bake it, do they?"

"That depends," she responded diplomatically. She took a generous helping of his quiche along with salad. There were large apples and she placed one in her handbag.

"For later?" he asked.

"For Rita Mosler whom I work with, or she'll never forgive me."

"Just tell her to come over here. No one will mind. There's going to be plenty left, even after these starving grad students wolf down all they can hold."

"It is a lovely buffet table," she said.

"But, alas, it would be nothing without my quiche."

Don seemed to know everyone and exchanged greetings with quite a few people, making certain to introduce her. She noticed Jim Davis and Dr. Packingham exchanging words. Jim's face was flushed, and although he towered over the smaller, thinner man, it was obvious that he was much more upset than the professor.

"I don't like your attitude," Jim was saying. "Maybe you don't think much of the paper I'm presenting at this colloquium, but other people have faith in my abilities." He brought his index finger up and poked it directly at Packingham's concave chest. "Don't cause me any grief tonight, or you'll be the one who's sorry."

She'd never heard Jim sound so menacing and his tone surprised her.

"Come now, Davis, your jealous-boyfriend role will take you just so far."

"You hit on women like Lorette, try to force your attentions on them. That makes you lower than gully dirt in my book."

"Bloody absurd! Ms. Campbell was more than willing to spend time in my company and told me as much privately. The only reason she appeared to demur was because of her fear of you, Mr. Davis. You intimidated her, bullied her. She was afraid of physical violence from you." Packingham sneered through thin lips. "She considered you a barbarian. No one knows who killed her, do they? I have my own theory on that subject."

"You're lying about Lorette, and you had more reason to kill her than anyone because she rejected you." Jim raised his fist in a threatening manner.

Don moved adroitly between the two men with Kim following closely behind him. Ian Simpson-Watkins arrived on the scene simultaneously. He glared at Jim and then turned to Packingham.

"Professor, I've been neglecting you. As a visitor to our country, it would be my pleasure to take you under my wing, so to speak, and introduce you to those of our faculty and students you may not be familiar with yet." He guided the Englishman away from Jim.

"I guess I kind of lost it there for a minute. The man makes me so damn mad!"

"Better off staying away from him," Don said.

"You're right," Jim agreed, stuffing his fists into his jean pockets. "Sometimes my temper just gets out of control."

"Why don't you get something to eat and join us?" Kim said.

He shook his head. "Not right now. I'm still too angry. I'd probably just choke on the chow." He walked briskly away.

They watched him stalk out the door of the lounge. From across the room, Packingham's small eyes narrowed into slits as he watched keenly. A malevolent smile crossed his lips.

"A volatile young man," Don said.

"More so than I realized," she agreed.

She noticed Dr. Barnes walking over to Packingham. The two engaged in polite conversation, but it quickly became apparent to her that whatever they were discussing was a matter of serious concern. She could tell by the frown on Dr. Barnes' face and the grave expression of Dr. Packingham. Once or twice they looked in her direction, then quickly away. Were they talking about her? Plotting against her? My God, when had she become so paranoid?

While Don was talking with several of his students, she strolled over to the hot beverage table and poured herself a cup of coffee. As she turned to go, Kim literally bumped into Dr. Barnes. He looked less than pleased since she managed to splash coffee on his well-polished black shoes.

"It would be you, wouldn't it?" he said testily. He summoned himself up to his full stature, chest out, preening like a peacock. "See here, you've been making a general nuisance of yourself of late. My colleagues and I would rather you amuse yourself at someone else's expense, otherwise we'll be forced to take unpleasant action against you."

"Such as trying to kill me?" Her own anger was just barely

under control.

His eyes blinked rapidly. "How dare you make such an accusation? Get out of my way!" The dark brows knitted in outrage, and the large eyes were bulging in bullfrog fashion.

She could touch his fear; it was that palpable. He would not want it known that he pursued students. If Lorette had threatened to expose him publicly, there was no doubt in Kim's mind that he was capable of murder.

Dr. Barbara Neilson sauntered up to the podium situated on the raised stage to continue with the agenda. She picked up a felt-covered microphone and called the group to order. Kim remembered vaguely that Dr. Neilson was a well-published feminist, greatly admired by the younger women in the program because of her militancy.

"I will be introducing our first speaker of the evening since she is one of my students. Before I do, I would like to say that we are in for a rare treat this evening. Three exceptional graduate students have been chosen to read their papers to us. These three presentations were selected from a great many entries, and each represents outstanding scholarship and originality." Dr. Neilson's smile looked somewhat out of place on her stern countenance. She was austerely thin, her spine straight as a broom handle. She was dressed in a dark, man-tailored suit. Her short gray hair added to the no-nonsense, stern aura of her person. Her eyes held no spark. She seemed dried out, lifeless.

Kim suddenly had a dark premonition. *If I'm not careful, I'll end up looking like that in twenty years.* The thought sobered her. She did not want to bury herself in a library to the exclusion of all else.

"Without further ado, I would like to explain the selection process and then present each of our student participants."

The program promised to be long. She wouldn't be able to stay for all of it, and perhaps that was just as well. Don moved in beside her, smiling warmly. They sat together and listened to Dr. Neilson as she continued to speak in a dry, unemotional voice. "Quite a few of you are aware that we've lost several of our best students of late, and also that Dr. Lionel Forbes has tragically passed away. Their loss diminishes each of us. Let us offer a moment of silence in memory of their departed souls." Dr. Neilson lowered her head gravely. The silent room took on a funereal aspect.

The minute ended and the program continued. Kim noticed that Jim Davis had returned just as the first student took the podium. The first presenter was a pale young woman. Her paper was an exploration of whether or not the Master letters of Emily Dickinson proved that she was really a closet lesbian involved in an incestuous relationship with her sister. It was hard not to notice how delighted Dr. Neilson was with her student's premise. Her face fairly beamed with a sudden animation that Kim would not have thought possible. The student was a poised doctoral candidate, who read her paper with just the right amount of emphasis to hold the interest of the audience.

The second paper was not as well presented. It was read in a boring monotone by a young man whose speech pattern imitated the annoying affectation of many of the English professors. The pretentious piece was a new interpretation of *Othello,* and the young man took every opportunity to read long sections of the play in his deadly monotone. An elderly professor sitting across the aisle from her was sound asleep and snoring noticeably, head titled back in his chair, by the time the fellow finally finished reading.

The third presenter was Jim Davis. At first, he seemed ill at ease as he lumbered up to the stage. But as soon as he launched into his paper on Mark Twain's importance in the local color movement, Jim became animated and lost his stage fright. He read expressively, his ideas offered in a clear and lucid manner.

Kim glanced over at Professor Packingham and saw that his eyes were burning holes into Jim. When Jim finished reading, Packingham was the first to attack, under the guise of offering constructive literary criticism. Jim was forced to stand there and take it politely. The good thing was that American Literature was not Packingham's area of expertise and there wasn't all that much he could criticize.

Kim glanced at her watch and realized it was getting late. She whispered to Don that she had to go back, and he promised to phone her the following day.

As she walked quickly outside, someone hurried through the doors and came around blocking her path.

"What do you want?"

"A word with you," Packingham said in a cool, controlled voice.

"About what?"

"You think I'm some sort of villain."

"Aren't you?" Their gazes locked. "What you did to Jim in there was rather cruel."

"He's a violent individual and doesn't belong among civilized human beings. Lorette was afraid of him. She told me she couldn't trust him."

"Did she give a reason?"

"I didn't care to ask."

"Excuse me, I have to leave." She walked brusquely by him, relieved to see that her police escort was out there, sitting and waiting in his car. Fresh air felt good on her face after being in that stuffy room for more than an hour.

Rita was waiting impatiently for her when she returned to the reference desk. "About time!"

"Sorry, I got caught up in the colloquium. It's still going on at the Graduate Student Center. There's plenty of food. Don Bernard said you should drop over."

That seemed to placate her. "All right, but I might be a little more than an hour, just the way you were."

"I understand completely. There is just one thing." She hesitated but then asked. "Could I borrow your keys for a moment?"

"Oh, for heaven's sake! You forgot yours again?" Rita did not bother to mask her annoyance.

"It's the last time I'll ask you, I promise."

Rita tossed her the keys with a glower. "It better be! You have to be more responsible if you're going to keep your position here."

The graduate assistant working with them tonight was busy helping another student. Kim waited to make certain the student could handle the reference question, then she hurried back to the offices. As before, Wendell's office was dark and locked. She turned the key quickly so that she would not change her mind. She could easily be fired for what she was doing. Nevertheless, she was determined to go through with her search. Unfortunately, now was not a good time for her to examine the inferno collection. It would have to wait until the library emptied out a little. She hurried back to the desk and began helping patrons.

A little after nine o'clock, Jim Davis approached her at the desk.

"Can I help you?" she asked him in a professional manner.

Jim looked over at Rita's countenance and understood that personal conversations would not be a good idea. "Yes, could you show me how to use the MLA Bibliography?"

They walked toward the computers, but Jim stopped her where no one was near enough to overhear them. "I need to talk to you for a minute."

"Sure, what is it?"

"How did you think my presentation went? The buzzards

really picked me clean."

"You did a wonderful job."

He gave her a wide, boyish grin. "Really think so?"

"Absolutely. Just ask Don Bernard. He'll give you a fair-minded evaluation."

"Not like that bastard Packingham, I hope." He pushed up the sleeves on the suit jacket he wore over his denim jeans. "I figure to get anywhere in life, you got to take chances, but I didn't figure on being used for target practice."

"Criticism is their game."

"Lorette was supposed to present a paper tonight," he said suddenly, his eyes darkening. "I wish she were here."

"I never understood why Lorette broke up with you."

He seemed to lose his composure. "We didn't exactly break up. She was angry about something. Guess I made an error in judgment. Then she said she couldn't trust me anymore. She shouldn't have been so upset."

"Upset about what?"

He ran his hands through his sandy hair. "I'd rather not talk about it."

She tried to keep her exasperation out of her voice. "But you have to talk about it. Don't you see, it could be important."

"Look, it had to do with Dr. Forbes. I don't want you thinking less of me."

"What I think doesn't matter all that much. You weren't truthful with me, were you? Dr. Forbes did invite you to his house. Was it you who suggested including Lorette?"

"No, that was his idea. But I guess I did encourage her to go. He was real interesting, unusual. I thought it was just the kind of experience she'd enjoy, you know, 'cause she had this thing for the supernatural."

"And did you have a thing for the supernatural?"

"Look, I wasn't one of them. Forbes, he just had this way

about him, you know? But it's not my kind of lifestyle."

"You knew about Lorette's past, didn't you? Did you tell Forbes?"

"Yeah, I guess I did at that. He had this way of probing into people. It was scary. He asked me questions about Lorette and I was dumb enough to tell him what he wanted to know. That's what made her so angry with me."

"Who else was in his chosen group?"

"Damned if I know! I was only invited once myself and didn't go."

"Before Lorette was invited?"

"That's right."

She wondered if he was lying again. Then Rita came up to them, and there was no chance for further private discussion.

"Really, Kim, you're taking much too long with this young man. Have you seen the line waiting at the desk? I will finish with him. I'm quicker than you are it would seem. Now hurry back to the desk!"

She went back to the information desk. Nor did she get to talk to Jim again as she'd hoped. He had disappeared from the library by the time she could look around for him.

She decided the best thing to do was to let Gardner know about Jim's connection to Forbes. Finally, she'd found another link. Even if he wasn't a member of Forbes' select group, he might know more than he'd told her. As soon as Rita left for the night, Kim excused herself, left the graduate assistant, Judy Bryant, a young Irish exchange student, on the floor alone, and went back to her own office. She phoned Gardner's home again, sure that he would not be at the police station now. This time she got one of his daughters, who sounded young and sweet; the girl explained that her dad was watching his favorite police show on television.

"Sorry to interrupt," Kim said when he finally got on the

phone, "but I wanted to tell you two things. First, Jim Davis had more involvement with Dr. Forbes than he admitted. I thought you might want to question him."

"I won't even ask how you found out. We'll get on him. Next?"

She cleared her throat. "Lorette asked me about an inferno collection at the library. I believe that collection is here locked up in my supervisor's office. I'm going to look through it tonight. I think it's a definite lead, a crucial one."

"Get out of there! We'll get a search warrant."

"By then, it could be gone. I have an intuition about this. No, it's tonight or never."

"Listen to me, I don't like it, and there's something else you should know . . ."

"Got to go, Lieutenant."

She cut him off and hung up the telephone. Wasting time arguing just wasn't smart. She probably should have waited to tell him about the inferno collection until she'd actually examined it like she originally intended. The devil was in the details, wasn't it? If there was something here that she should know about, it was time to take a close look. Lorette had considered it important. Time to find out. She took a deep breath and let it out shakily. She had promises to keep.

CHAPTER TWENTY-ONE

The key to the inferno collection was just where she'd found it before. Wendell Firbin was too fastidious for anything else. She unlocked the mirrored cabinet and quickly looked inside. The manuscripts were very old and fragile, delicate to the touch. She had noted that previously, but this time she would be able to examine them. She felt a sense of mounting excitement.

Kim moved Wendell's desk chair over so that she could sit and read. A set of bound papers caught her eye and she lifted them to her with infinite care. *Incunabulum.* The manuscript was printed before 1501 and had to be priceless. She examined the black leather-bound sheets gently but more thoroughly. It was a Latin Bible, but not like any she had ever seen before. She continued to study it, fascinated by the peculiar book. Her Latin was not the best, but she understood enough. Without a doubt, it was an inverted Bible, the kind witches would use to celebrate a Black Mass. She would have supposed that such a thing would have been burned long ago, denounced along with the heretics who valued it.

She laid it aside and selected yet another manuscript for close perusal. This was not quite so old; she placed it as seventeenth or eighteenth century.

It was a diary, she saw at once. The handwriting was small and spiky. The name inside was Abigail Williams—the girl who started the Salem witchcraft trials. Kim tried to remember: had Abigail been accused of witchcraft or had she accused others?

Perhaps she'd done both.

Suddenly, she heard footsteps behind her and her heart began to beat rapidly. She turned around.

"What are you doing in here?"

Her mouth seemed unable to form words, her saliva thickening to the consistency of sour cream. Wendell Firbin was staring at her wrathfully. For a moment, she had a sense of déjà vu. For a brief second, it was Carl she was looking at.

"I was about to glance at these old documents."

"Ah, but you've already seen enough, haven't you?"

"Enough for what?"

"Don't play childish games with me. I won't have it." He was practically snarling at her.

"I realize you're going to fire me," she responded, swallowing hard.

"Stop your babbling. What are you doing here?"

She was trying to do something that mattered, to find out who murdered Lorette and the others. However, that was not the thing to tell Wendell; she knew that instinctively.

"The cabinet has an interesting look. I thought to examine it more closely."

"Of course, you did. You're a very curious individual, aren't you, just like a cat? And you know what happened to the cat, don't you?"

"The cat?" she repeated.

"Why yes, curiosity killed it." He gave her a smile that flashed pearly teeth she associated with a hungry tiger. He seemed to take great satisfaction in unnerving her.

Her mouth opened wide as the realization hit her. Of course, how could she have been so stupid not to see it in the first place? The inferno collection was in Wendell's office, entrusted to him for safety. It could only be because he was a member of Lionel Forbes' chosen group. And that comment about a cat jarred something in her memory; hadn't Dr. Forbes said something about sacrificing a cat? That act had appalled Lorette.

"I have to leave now," she said, trying to get out of the chair, but Wendell's hand pushed back on her shoulder forcefully. "Really, I must go. Judy needs me out there to close up for the night."

"I took care of that myself. She's gone, as you will soon be."

"Well then, I might as well be on my way."

"You and I will leave together. We'll take your car." He smiled again, an eerie distortion of his facial muscles.

"Sorry, I have other plans."

"How unfortunate. Lionel thought so well of you. I, of course, knew better. He never was a good judge of character or the lack of it. Too full of himself, thought he knew everything."

"Where is Dr. Forbes?"

"You'll see him soon enough."

"He wanted me to join the chosen. Perhaps I should consider it."

"I believe it's been decided that the coven has no need of new members."

"But you are a member or two short."

"Let's not play mind games. Time to be on our way." His eyes were as icy as a winter lake.

She found herself shivering, knowing what he was about. "I have no intention of going anywhere with you."

"That remains to be seen." Wendell removed a revolver from his jacket pocket and aimed it at her chest.

She realized that she was trembling uncontrollably. "They'll know."

"No, they won't. And no one will care. Shall I tell you how you're going to die? Very peacefully, as it would happen. I have cocaine in my pocket. Did you know it mixes with liquid quite nicely in its powder form? You will have a nice little drink, a nightcap. I'll wash the glass clean, put it back in your hand after you're dead, and no one will be the wiser. It will look as if you died of natural causes, a heart attack. The cocaine will deactivate the vagus nerve that helps regulate heart rate. Once cocaine hits the brain, it triggers a jolt of adrenaline. At the same time, it blocks the body's ability to reabsorb the adrenaline. The rush overworks the heart and disrupts the signals being sent from the brain to the heart resulting in cardiac arrest. Fascinating drug, cocaine, so many uses. I've made a study of it."

"You used it to kill Lorette." She accused him with unblinking eyes.

"Quite true. Your little friend Sandy was very high when I took care of her as well. Nick was even simpler. I merely gave him an overdose and then disposed of the body."

"And Dr. Forbes? Is he the evil genius behind this?"

Wendell pressed his fingers to the sides of his long, narrow nose as if in pain. "In a manner of speaking. This entire fiasco is his fault. Lionel thought he could do whatever he wished. When he told me how he invited you to the house, I knew that he had become dangerous to himself as well as others. I was in the house at the time, waiting upstairs for the right moment to dispose of both of you. I am sorry I ever became involved with that egomaniacal fool! At first, he was my mentor and I his disciple, like Emerson was to Thoreau. But I had to protect myself and my career. Your friend Lorette threatened Lionel with telling all about his activities to the president of the university. She overheard Lionel discussing the inferno collection with me the one night she came to our worship. I was certain she would implicate me."

"You were the one who tried to ruin her reputation."

"It was necessary. But she blamed Lionel because he knew about her past history. She didn't know that Lionel discussed his choices with me and told me about each candidate's background."

"All that killing. It's total insanity! Why murder Sandy and Nick as well?"

"Lionel spoke to me about the inferno collection in their presence, and your friend was with them. Very careless of Lionel. Until that night, no one but Lionel ever saw me directly or knew of the collection. I remained an anonymous hooded, cloaked figure at the ceremonies. The morning you were late coming to work, your friend came looking for you, and I saw my opportunity. She'd recognized me. I told her that Lionel had destroyed her reputation and that I would tell the university administration all about his rituals and his use of the inferno collection. I offered to meet her at noon by her automobile and follow her home to hand her proof."

"So that was why Lorette didn't meet me."

"You have my assurance the killing will end tonight, with you."

"What if I don't choose to leave here with you?"

"If you make any sort of scene, I will instantly inject you with this syringe. You may die just as your friend did." He removed a hypodermic needle from his jacket pocket and displayed it inches from her face.

Kim forced herself to think clearly, rationally. "You'll have to lock up the collection," she said.

He gave her that awful smile again. "You're so easy to read. You lock it up. I won't be turning my back on you for an instant."

She did as he told her, then he took the key and put it back where it belonged, never removing his eyes from her. Although the gun went back into his pocket, an iron hand descended painfully on her arm.

"Don't think of trying to fight me or my response will be immediate."

As she moved through the library, a sense of unreality came over her. This was not happening; she was not held in the grip of a killer. She had to force herself to think, not give in to fear or panic. Outside, with any luck, there was a policeman waiting for her. He would intervene. It would be all right.

"Where are we going?" She noticed with alarm that he was pulling her toward the side exit.

"No one will observe us leaving this way."

"You want me to drive my car, don't you? My car in on the deck. We have to go out the front entrance."

"All right," he conceded grudgingly, "but if you try to make a single move to alert anyone, you're dead instantly."

She made no answer or protest. Arguing with Wendell only enraged him; she'd finally caught on to that. The man was anal retentive, a total control freak. She must not speak. The night enveloped them in damp, cold and fog. She saw no sign of the police car now and wondered at it. Had they given up on her? After her call to Gardner, did he call his people off?

"What's wrong with you? Keep moving."

Wendell squeezed her arm until she cried out. She forced her legs to continue relentlessly to her car. The deck was deserted, as it often was at that time of the evening. There was no one to turn to for help. She would have to think of something.

Her hand shook so badly that her car keys fell to the ground before she was able to open the car door.

"Clumsy cow!" he insinuated in her ear.

Don't answer, she reminded herself. She managed the lock this time.

"Drive," he commanded.

She turned the engine over. All she could think of was that she wanted to go home, to be with Ma again, to feel safe. But she hadn't been safe there either, had she? There had been Carl until just before she graduated high school, until he had done that terrible thing and killed those people for no sane reason. He'd been sick, just like Wendell was sick.

"What are you waiting for? Get out of here!"

"If you're going to kill me anyway, why should I do what you say?"

She had infuriated him now; she could see that in the wildly angry look he was throwing at her, but his voice remained quiet, insidiously smooth.

"You want me to kill you right here and now? It makes no difference to me."

She wasn't volunteering to be his next victim. She pulled out of the parking deck and into the street, signaling carefully. *Keep calm! Signal every move. They're out there looking to help. Don't give up!*

Even if the police couldn't help her, she wouldn't give in to fear. She could hear Ma's voice in her head: *God helps those who help themselves.* It was Ma's favorite saying. She felt comforted. Nick's knife was still in her handbag. If she could find a way to reach inside, she might have a chance against Wendell. She would wait for the right moment and seize her opportunity.

"You know I'm your intellectual superior, don't you?" he said suddenly.

"As long as you hold that gun against me, I won't argue the point."

"Drive faster, but not too fast. Don't even think of attracting the attention of the police."

They were out on the highway when she noticed the car tailing them. No, it was not her imagination. So the police hadn't given up on her.

Gardner, I need you. Help me!

"What are you watching?" He looked around and caught sight of the unmarked car. "Switch lanes," he ordered.

She said nothing, following his orders. The other car stayed with them.

"Lose him!"

"How do you expect me to do that?"

"The same way you got rid of me the other night. Do anything less and you'll regret it." His voice hissed menacingly into her ear.

He began giving her directions, telling her what to do and where to go. They wouldn't be heading to her apartment after all, now that he understood the police were following.

"Why don't I just drop you off somewhere?"

"You have a bizarre notion of humor."

"It comes from too many years of teaching adolescents," she said. "Look, you have to realize that the police are on to you."

He laughed out loud. "Delightful, really! You would actually expect me to believe that?"

"Why not? I figured it out, didn't I?"

"Did you? Well, perhaps you did. But you're certainly the only one. The police are idiots."

It occurred to her that Wendell was nothing more than a bully who got off on intimidating people he considered weak, women in particular. But like most bullies, he was really a coward at heart. Cowering was pointless; it would just encourage his insanity.

"They will find you," she said. She could have told him that the police already knew about the inferno collection in his office. But if he did manage to kill her, and the odds didn't seem to be in her favor at the moment, then she didn't want Wendell forewarned. He might dispose of the collection.

"You'll be found dead in your automobile in an isolated location."

"I described your car to the police. They're bound to locate you."

He gave a mirthless laugh. "That was Lionel's car. I simply borrowed it. He had no further use for it, and it was perfect for my purposes. However, you did prove temporarily elusive. I must remember to thank Mary Parkins for mentioning to me that she'd seen you in my office. I realized you had to have borrowed the keys from Rita. She's the only other person I've trusted with a complete set. I scheduled the two of you to work together again tonight because I thought I'd catch you looking through the inferno collection. And then I watched and waited and then pounced. So you see, I've been on to you for some time. You wanted to destroy me. Well, it is I who will destroy you, squash you like an insect."

The trembling had begun again. She had to gain control of herself. She no longer saw the police car in the mirror. Her efforts to lose the police had been halfhearted at best, but apparently they'd succeeded. Wendell's awareness of the situation was obvious. He looked smug and pleased with himself, the nostrils of his narrow nose flaring.

"Straight ahead for now. I'll let you know when and where to turn."

In the self-defense course it now seemed she'd taken too briefly, the instructor told the class how important it was to keep the mind tranquil in moments of extreme stress or danger. In a pond without a ripple, there were no distortions, only reality. She focused on keeping her mind a calm pool. The Twenty-third Psalm ran through her brain: "Yea, though I walk through the valley of the shadow of death, I will fear no evil." Then she recalled that the psalm was always recited at funerals and shuddered. No, that was not reassuring. She must keep focused, even if her mind felt as if it were numbed with Novocain.

"Why are you slowing down?"

"Was I?"

"Take a right now," he ordered, indicating the turn coming up.

It was unexpected and she skidded while turning the sharp curve. She realized they were heading into a secluded wooded area. She was only safe as long as she was still driving. Slowing the speed imperceptibly, she glanced over at Wendell.

"I can't believe that educated people could go in for devil worship."

"Lionel was right when he said evil is the most potent force in the universe. Should we not worship the greatest power? Lionel actually succeeded in channeling the power of Satan into himself during his ceremonies. He became empowered with demonic strength. I intend to do the same, to become the high priest. I, too, will become a demon with preternatural abilities. *Better to reign in hell than serve in heaven.*"

"Your mind is twisted, demented."

The nostrils flared again. "You are a naive fool. Speak no more!"

There was no one in the area. She was alone with a crazed murderer. She took a deep, shaky breath and exhaled slowly.

"Pull over there," he said, indicating a turn into the black woods.

She ignored him and kept driving.

"Did you hear me?" His voice was shrill, incredulous.

"I'm driving," she told him with as much force as she could manage. Her special sense of awareness warned her that continuing to be in control of the car was her only hope of survival.

Wendell removed the syringe from his pocket and lunged toward her. So he had not actually changed his original plan that much. Using the gun was really window dressing for intimidation purposes, too messy, not his actual weapon of choice. Kim braced herself as best she was able and hit the brakes for all they were worth. She was wearing her safety belt and was not harmed. Wendell had strapped himself in as well. It was not in his nature to ignore any detail. But the forward thrust threw him off balance and gave Kim just long enough time to reach into her handbag to grasp Nick's knife.

She slashed him in a fast, smooth movement, taking her slight advantage without hesitation. She thought that Nick would have been pleased to know that his knife was used against his killer. Justice could be ironic.

She stabbed Wendell in the hand that held the syringe. With a yowl, he dropped his weapon to the floor of the car. Unfortunately, his unimpaired hand seized on her wrist, and he wrestled the knife from her grasp, eyes glittering with a look of hatred. She elbowed him in the chest causing his grasp on her to loosen.

As Kim jumped out of the car and began running down the road, looking desperately to wave down another vehicle, she heard a car coming at high speed from behind her. Wendell was using her own car to try and run her down! As he bore down on her, for a moment her eyes were glazed like a doe caught in headlights, but her paralysis was over quickly and she reacted by racing into the woods as the car narrowly missed her.

A branch cut across her cheek and her ankle twisted, but she was okay; she was alive. Kim realized that the car had stopped. He was coming after her. She tried to quiet the sound of her breathing; it wasn't easy. Her heart pounded like an anvil.

She couldn't see him, yet she could hear him looking for her, moving through the trees. As stealthily as possible, she slipped back toward the road, knowing it was her only hope. Maybe she could make it to the car and then drive away.

She had the Toyota in her sights now and was just about to climb into it when a hand grabbed at her from behind. She screamed, and as she did, another car pulled up, shining headlights on both of them.

She somehow managed to kick Wendell, and then she was running again, this time toward the other automobile, ignoring the agonizing pain in her ankle. A man got out and held his arms out to her and she collapsed into them.

"It's okay," he said. Gardner turned to the man standing beside him. "Stay with her. I'm going to get him now." He removed a bullhorn from the rear of the police car.

Gardner walked on while the thin figure of Wendell Firbin began running in the opposite direction. "We know who you are and what you've done. There isn't any escape. There are cars coming here from all directions. There is no getting away. If you don't surrender immediately, you'll be shot."

As if on cue, two more police cars pulled in behind her car from the other direction. One was university police, the other had city markings. Wendell Firbin surrendered meekly to Lieutenant Gardner, complaining bitterly about barbaric police-men and their brutality. In actuality, no one touched him, except to search him, remove the gun, and cuff him as his rights were read. She wanted to spit in his face.

"Quite a killing spree," Gardner said. "You murdered a number of innocent people."

"No one was innocent," Wendell said.

"You've got a decided lack of conscience."

"Pity was invented by the weak." He truly would reign in hell.

Firbin was placed into the back of a police car and driven away. Gardner returned to Kim.

She told him about the syringe in the car. "By the way, where was your man? I thought he was going to keep following me."

"He did. We knew where you were. We placed a device on your car that let out a signal. That's why he could afford to pull back. You see, we were afraid that if we were spotted, Firbin might try to kill you immediately."

"He did see the car."

"That was what we figured when he had you pull off the road out here. It's the reason our guy let you out of sight for the moment. You'll notice we all came after you just as soon as you stopped the car."

"No offense, but it's a good thing I didn't depend on the police for help."

He gave her a wry smile. "We do our best. No one claims we're perfect. Oh, there is one other thing. You were right about the janitor. We found him dead in his apartment. Same method of death. Apparent heart failure. He'd been drinking heavily."

"But you found cocaine had been mixed into the drink?"

"Girl's a genius." His teeth shined like white porcelain in the darkness.

"No, Wendell was planning a similar death for me."

"I should have shot him."

Gardner helped her into his Ford. She was trembling, and he held her tightly in his arms, stroking her hair, until she stopped shaking.

"You're quite a woman." He kissed her forehead with gentle concern. "I'll drive you home. Someone will bring your car back to you in the morning."

"Why did he kill Frank too?"

"He'll tell us soon enough," Gardner responded as he put the car in gear. "My guess is that the janitor knew him, maybe could identify him as being at the house. You did say he cleaned for Forbes."

She suddenly felt drained, exhausted. Like Dorothy, she wanted to click her heels together and say, "There's no place like home." A shame she didn't own a pair of ruby shoes.

"You feeling okay?" he eyed her critically.

"I've been better."

"Just don't make this kind of thing a habit," he said.

"I'll try not to."

CHAPTER TWENTY-TWO

The police returned her Toyota the following day just as Gardner had promised, but minus the syringe, for which she was grateful. She needed no reminders of what had happened the previous evening. She'd slept late that morning, and every joint in her body ached. The ankle had swollen slightly and she needed to ice it. But the important thing was that she'd survived the ordeal. It was great to be alive.

She managed the drive to visit Ma, bringing Jen's diary along with her. Ma viewed her with concern when she first arrived.

"What happened to your face?"

"I walked into a tree branch. It's nothing."

"And the ankle? I see you're limping."

"I'll get it taped."

Ma sniffed at her. "I guess you don't want to tell me what happened to you?"

She shrugged. "To tell the truth, it was just a small accident and everything's fine."

"I notice that people who want others to tell the truth don't always do it themselves. But I won't ask questions you don't want to answer." Ma led her to the most comfortable chair in the living room and pushed the ottoman over by her bad foot.

"I guess I ought to reciprocate and not ask questions you don't want to answer."

Ma eyed her warily. "Why don't we trade? What was it that you wanted to know?"

Kim pushed the diary toward her. "I read Jen's diary again, and this time I was thorough. I have the same feeling about what I read now as I did when I was fifteen. Ma, tell me the truth about Jen."

"It was so sad; I just didn't think you needed to know. I thought to spare you any misery I could. Since you didn't know her, what was the point of telling you?"

"I suppose I do understand. I wasn't going to give you the details of what happened to me, but since you care, you have a right to know." She went ahead and told Ma all about Wendell Firbin, how he murdered Lorette and the others then tried to kill her as well.

Ma listened attentively, alternating shock with sympathy. "I'm so thankful that you're all right!" Ma said finally and hugged her tightly. "Who would have guessed a librarian would behave that way? I'll say a special prayer of thanks tonight that you were spared."

Kim realized that Ma's intentions were good and always had been.

"Ma, I love you," she said. "I will always love you. But I want to know who my real parents were. I have a right to know, and I'm hardly a child anymore."

"Your real father was decent and caring, but he couldn't be a father to you."

"Yes, I understand that."

"Do you?" Her face was tense now, worry lines forming between her brows.

"He was just a young boy, wasn't he? Was Jen my real mother?"

The look of surprise was genuine. "What makes you think that?"

"I read her diary, remember? She wrote about a boy she loved, one who moved away and how it broke her heart. Then she wrote about a secret that she couldn't share with any of you because it would cause you too much pain. She said that she'd delay your knowing about it as long as she could. Then she stopped writing in her book."

"Yes, I see how you might think she was writing about having a baby."

"And then . . ." She hesitated, knowing it would pain Ma to hear what Carl had said concerning her sister, but now was a time for truth. She continued doggedly. "Carl was drunk and angry the night he told me that he wasn't my father. He also said I had bad genetics."

"He told you that?"

She saw the pain register on Ma's face and felt terrible for causing it. Ma stood up and began pacing the room. "Karen, honey, my sister Jen was not your mother. The secret she was keeping from me and your grandma for as long as she could was that she was sick. It turned out she had a blood disease like leukemia. In those days, they didn't have the cures they do now. She wasn't even sixteen when she passed away." Tears welled up in Ma's eyes.

Kim rose and went to her mother, throwing her arms around her. "Ma, I'm sorry. I really had no idea."

"I should have told you. It was just so hurtful. And you do remind me a lot of her. She was my little sister. A kinder, sweeter girl never lived." The tears streamed down her mother's face, and then she choked back a sob. "Your grandma was never the same after that. It was hard on her losing your grandpa two years before, but the worst thing in the world is losing a child you love."

"I didn't mean to stir up bad memories."

"You have a right to know everything. I just didn't tell you because I told myself I was protecting you. Maybe I just was protecting myself. I didn't want you to think less of me."

Kim stared at her mother in dismay. "Ma! What are you talking about?"

Her mother lowered her eyes, fixing them on the worn carpet. "When they sent Carl home, he was more dead than alive. The doctors saved him, but there were parts of him that just couldn't be fixed. Carl Reyner couldn't father a child." She sighed deeply.

"Carl was in the hospital for a very long time after he came back. I was very lonely and unhappy. I very badly wanted a child of my own. There was a man I knew, a very kind, caring person who was unhappy in his marriage too. We just sort of comforted each other. After I got pregnant, I told Carl that he could have a divorce if he wanted it. He was angry at first, but then he said he loved me and would be a father to any child that was mine. Poor man. I guess it was just more than he could manage. I'm sorry. Please don't blame him; he did the best he could. I blame myself for your suffering."

"I'm fine," Kim said reassuringly. "No one ever had a better mother, and whether I'd been adopted or born to you, it wouldn't matter because I couldn't love you more. I just felt hurt that you wouldn't trust me with the truth. As for Carl, well, maybe it's past time I forgave him. I've come to realize just how precious life is. I don't want to waste any more of mine holding grudges. I shouldn't be blaming Carl for mistakes I've made. As to the people he killed, he's had to answer to a higher authority."

Ma kissed her and started to cry. Kim hugged her mother tightly; her own eyes misted.

"So what would you think if I came down to Florida this year when I get my vacation?"

"I'll be looking forward to it."

"Great, because as you know, I've never been to Florida. Maybe we can do some sightseeing together."

Ma gave her a warm smile, tears still glistening in her eyes.

"I'd love that."

When she left the house, taking a final look around, Kim felt differently about many things. Most of all, she felt better about herself. She had finally managed to bury the dead.

The phone was ringing as she stepped into her apartment. She scooped up the receiver before it stopped and answered in a breathless voice.

"How are you?"

The velvet voice at the other end brought a smile to her lips. "Better than I expected," she told Don.

"I had a very interesting call from a concerned party earlier."

"And who would that be?"

"Police Lieutenant Gardner. He seems to care a great deal about you. But he's tied up. Wanted me to phone and see if you needed anything."

"Yes, I like him too, even if he was a little slow on the uptake last night."

"Maybe you ought to apply for his job."

"Maybe I should. But he needn't start to worry quite yet. I ache all over today. I think I prefer a quiet, peaceful job."

"Odd, I thought that was what you had."

"Me too, but it didn't turn out that way."

"Gardner told me about Wendell. Who would ever have thought it? The man was the embodiment of rectitude."

"Well, he turned out to be a punctilious murderer."

"By the way, I'm coming over and cooking you dinner tonight. Expect me around five. My special pasta sauce takes at least two hours."

"Don, you don't have to go to any trouble for me."

" 'Course I do! Gardner would never forgive me if I didn't. Do you want a policeman coming after me with a drawn revolver?"

She enjoyed his good-natured teasing. "I rest much easier knowing that I've won the friendship of two good men."

"Frankly, Kim, my feelings run deeper. And I get the impression your police detective has stronger feelings as well."

Kim realized she was going to have to give that matter some serious thought.

EPILOGUE

He came to her the following afternoon. Kim hadn't realized how much she'd been longing for him. It was as if she'd been holding her breath just waiting in suspended animation and nothing else really mattered.

They stood staring at each other.

"How are you feeling?"

Better, now that you're here.

"I'm all right."

"You look beautiful." He gave her an appreciative smile.

"You're the only person who thinks that."

"Not true. What about the professor?"

"Don?"

He gave a nod of acknowledgement. "Yeah, my competition. I know he's been to see you."

"We had dinner together last night. We're just good friends."

"I don't think he sees it that way."

She shrugged. "You can never have too many friends."

He drew closer. "I don't want to be your friend."

"What do you want?"

"That's a loaded question. I was fascinated by you from the moment we met."

"I'm not exactly a fascinating woman."

"Really? Who says? Because I find you very desirable. The only thing that stopped me from telling you before was professional ethics. Now I don't have to hold back anymore. You don't either."

He pulled her into his arms with a bold movement and held her tightly against him. His mouth descended on hers, ravaging. She craved his heat. She couldn't seem to get close enough. His lips were moist, soft and firm all at once. Soon their tongues were mating in a drugging, wildly erotic kiss. Kim felt as if her very bones were dissolving. She was shaken by the potency of the passion. Finally, they came apart, breathless, gasping for breath.

"You and I have a telepathic connection," he said.

"Prove it." That sultry voice hardly seemed to belong to her.

"I will," he said. "Just so you know, I'm off duty. We're going out for dinner—a double date—you, me and the girls. I told them about you and they're eager to meet you."

"You sound awfully sure of yourself."

"I'm sure of us."

He proved himself a man of action, drawing her to the couch and sitting her on his lap. She felt his probing erection press hard against her soft core. They kissed again and then his mouth began to roam, tasting her ear, her throat, her neck, following a plundering path, as his hands caressed her breasts. She allowed him free access to her body. His thrilling touch caused her blood to erupt in her veins like a volcano. His fingers circled her nipples and they tightened in anticipation.

"God, you feel so good," he whispered.

Her own hands began moving, running down his hard chest. He pulled off her sweater and she wished she was wearing some sexy, silky bra instead of her serviceable white cotton underwear. But he didn't seem to notice or care. In fact, the bra quickly found its way to the floor, followed by her slacks and panties.

"You are beautiful, just like I said. You drive me crazy." And then his mouth was on her breast, sucking, licking. She ran her hand through his thick, dark hair, as she moaned in pleasure.

Very soon they were both naked, lying tangled in each other's arms. As his tongue circled her nipple, his fingers probed the sensitive flesh between her legs. Hopelessly lost to lust and desire, she was wonderfully wet and more than ready for him when he entered her. Although he was a big man and fully aroused, they seemed to fit together perfectly. They fell into a rhythm as old as time, and when he began thrusting into her, she opened herself fully to him. In that final, climactic moment, their psychic connection was as total and complete as their physical connection. She shattered into myriad glittering shards of pleasure. The euphoria Kim felt was followed by a realization, an epiphany. She knew without any shred of doubt that she and Mike were truly meant to be together.

She was moved to the bravest act of her life. "I love you," she told him.

"Sweetheart, I love you too."

Mike loved her and she loved him. That was what really mattered. Kim wished Lorette could have known this kind of happiness. But somewhere, Kim decided, her friend's restless spirit was finally at peace.

ABOUT THE AUTHOR

Jacqueline Seewald, who has taught writing courses, including Creative Writing, at the high school, middle school and college level, has also worked as an academic librarian and educational media specialist.

Six of her books of fiction have previously been published. Her numerous short stories, poems, essays, reviews and articles have appeared in such publications as: *Affaire de Coeur, Sasee, Library Journal, Publishers Weekly, The Christian Science Monitor, Pedestal, Surreal, After Dark, Lost Treasure, Romance Rag, The Dana Literary Society Journal, Vermont Ink* and *Palace of Reason.*